The Fifth Stone

Books by Raegan Teller
Enid Blackwell Series

Murder in Madden

The Last Sale

Secrets Never Told

The Fifth Stone

The Fifth Stone

Raegan Teller

Pondhawk Press LLC

Columbia, South Carolina

Pondhawk Press LLC
PO Box 290033
Columbia, SC 29229
www.PondhawkPress.com

Publisher's Note: This book is a work of fiction. Names, characters, places, and incidents are a product of the author's imagination. Locales and public names are sometimes used for atmospheric purposes. Any resemblance to actual people, living or dead, or to businesses, companies, events, institutions, or locales is completely coincidental.

ISBN 978-0-9979205-6-7

Dedicated to the people who inspired this story.
You know who you are.

"We are never so vulnerable than when
we trust someone. But paradoxically, if
we cannot trust, neither can we find love or joy."

– Walter Anderson, Playwright

CHAPTER 1

Catherine Murray wasn't prepared to die today. Even though she had already lived a full life, some years good and some bad, she wasn't ready for it to end. Not today.

Her thoughts flashed through all the things she had wanted to accomplish as the town historian at the Madden Historical Society. She mentally checked off the list of old acquaintances she had intended to contact but never did. Why had she put these things off? She had not said any goodbyes, as she had no hint that her life would all come down to this fateful moment.

And what about her great-niece? She would never get to apologize for the awful thing she had done to her.

Her captor gripped her arm tightly. "If you scream or try to run, you're dead. Got that?"

Catherine nodded her head. "But why . . . I don't understand . . ." She couldn't form words for the thoughts racing through her mind.

Her captor pointed to a blank headstone. "You see that stone there, the one with no name on it?"

Catherine looked where the captor pointed and nodded again.

Her captor increased the grip on Catherine's arm. "Pretty soon, that's where you will spend eternity."

Catherine fought back the tears. Crying would do no good and might even make her captor angry. Overcome with helplessness, Catherine tried to imagine what eternity would be like in this small, unkempt cemetery. Would anyone know she was here? Would anyone put flowers on her grave? She slumped slightly under the weight of the situation. If this was to be her final resting place, then so be it.

Something sharp and metallic was now touching her neck. Any hope that she had for survival faded when she realized it was a needle pressing against her neck. She froze, careful not to move the wrong way. If her captor applied any more pressure, whatever was in that needle would enter her bloodstream.

CHAPTER 2

Karla woke from the dream with a start, sitting up in bed, drenched in sweat. For the past month, she had been trying to get in touch with her friend Catherine Murray at the Madden Historical Society. Catherine knew everything eventful that had happened in the small South Carolina town. But Catherine had not returned her calls.

Karla rarely thought of her empath abilities as a gift, mostly because she only dreamed about bad things that might happen. As Karla's gift had developed, her empathy increased to the point that she took on others' energy, feelings, and emotions, which left her exhausted at times. It wasn't something she could turn off and on. The biggest benefit to Karla's being an empath was that she could read people quickly and accurately.

Tonight was the fourth time she had dreamed about Catherine. Each was progressively disconcerting. Yet, Karla had to admit that neither she, nor any other empath, was totally accurate. Some bad dreams were just that. And most dreams were symbolic, which left a lot of room for interpretation. Tonight, she dreamed Catherine was sitting before a king on a throne, and she was wearing a dunce hat. Despite the humiliating circumstances, Catherine was laughing along with those who made fun of her. But then she turned, as if to look directly at Karla, and begged for help. Karla awoke terrified.

After making herself a cup of chamomile tea, Karla returned to bed with a resolution to go to Madden to see the one person whom she trusted enough to hear her concerns.

CHAPTER 3

The *Tri-County Gazette*, like all weekly, small-town newspapers, covers everything: local news, awards, petty crimes and vandalism, high-school football and other sports, debate team winners, and social soirees hosted by the town's prominent citizens.

Enid Blackwell, a senior reporter at the newspaper, was at her desk finishing an obituary about a local, prize-winning gardener, whose roses almost always won a prize in a local garden club contest, when Jack Johnson, the owner and senior editor of the newspaper, walked in. "Have you seen my glasses?" he asked.

Without looking up, Enid reached across her desk and handed them to him.

Jack wiped the glass lenses with his shirttail and put them on. "Don't forget you're on obit duty this week."

"When are you going to hire someone to do that? It's been months since our obit writer left. There's an art to doing them, you know."

"I know you don't like writing obits, and I'm interviewing someone today. But, I think you do a great job profiling dead people." He pointed to the overflowing trashcan beside her desk. "Lots of do-overs, I see."

Enid's fingers stopped moving across the keyboard as she looked up at Jack. "That's what happens when you get interrupted a lot."

Jack held up his hands in surrender. "Okay, I'm outta here." As he turned to leave, he almost ran into Ginger, the newspaper's office manager.

"Someone's on the phone for you, Enid," Ginger said. "It's important."

"I rest my case," Enid said to Jack. "Who is it?" she asked Ginger.

"You won't believe it," Ginger said.

Jack and Enid exchanged glances, mostly because Ginger was behaving in a very un-Ginger-like way. Typically, she was sullen and argumentative, not bubbly and excited. "Okay," Enid said. "Which line is he on?"

Ginger pointed to the new phone system on Enid's desk, recently installed. "Well, duh. He's on line one, the only one blinking." That was more like her.

"Thanks," Enid said. She waited for Jack and Ginger to leave her office, as she customarily did for privacy, but neither budged. What was wrong with everyone this morning? She tapped line one on the phone and answered. "Hello. This is Enid Blackwell. How may I help you?"

This time it was Jack and Ginger who exchanged glances.

Enid listened to the caller and replied, "Thank you for letting me know. I'm honored." Before she even put the receiver back on the phone, Ginger grabbed Enid by the shoulders and screamed. "You've won a journalism award from the SC Press Association for investigative reporting. Wow! That's way cool." She looked at Jack. "Now that the paper will be famous, can I get a raise?"

Jack laughed. "Whoa. Let's not get ahead of ourselves." He leaned over and hugged Enid. "Congratulations. Well deserved. The investigative work you did on those two cold cases was exemplary." Enid and the newspaper had received praise from around the state, as well as some national recognition. A couple of her articles were picked up by the Associated Press, thanks to her ex-husband Cade Blackwell, an AP investigative reporter.

Enid stood up so she could embrace Jack. His warm hands on her shoulders were like a comforting blanket. "Thanks."

"I'm going to get some of those yummy cinnamon buns from Sarah's Tea Shoppe to celebrate," Ginger said. "I'll be back in a few." She turned with a flourish and vanished out the door.

Jack held Enid by the shoulders. "I'm so proud of you."

"Like Ginger said, it's great for the paper, too."

"Yes, but you earned it. The paper is just lucky to have you."

Enid's legs felt like rubber, so she sat down in her chair. "Did you know about this?"

Jack rubbed his chin. "I might have gotten a whiff of it."

"I guess that means Cade knows, too." He and Jack had worked together years ago and still maintained a friendship.

"He might. But I'm sure he'd love to hear it from you. I'll leave you alone to call him." He turned to leave Enid's office.

"Wait, Jack." Enid paused. "I don't even know how to thank you for all you've done to support me. When I showed up here a few years ago, I was an emotional wreck and a rusty reporter. You believed in me, and I'll never forget that."

"You're easy to believe in." Jack smiled. "Now get back to work. Oh, and empty the trash, would you? Looks unbecoming in here for an award-winning reporter."

Despite the fact that Enid and Cade had divorced more than three years ago, she kept his number in her VIP contacts on her iPhone. They had settled into a comfortable relationship and occasionally worked together on special projects. He had been instrumental in her being recognized for her investigative reporting, and he had even talked his boss into hiring her back at the AP where her journalism career began more than ten years ago. She had never really turned down the AP offer but didn't accept it either. Her life in Madden was mostly uneventful, and that's how she liked it. On some days, she even admitted to herself that she had a nearly perfect life.

She tapped on Cade's number in the list of contacts. He answered almost immediately. "I was hoping you'd call," he said. "Congratulations."

"You're not even going to pretend to be surprised, are you?" Enid said.

"No, I'm not. I just wish I could be there to celebrate with you. We can do that later."

Enid admired the way Cade took a simplistic view of their relationship. He came in and out of her life effortlessly, with no entanglements. She was more of an all-in or all-out kind of person, and it was hard for her to push aside their years together, including the emotional roller coaster ride before their divorce. "That would be nice."

"You sound like you're still in shock."

"Actually, I am. Small-town newspaper reporters don't win awards very often. They usually go to big names like you."

Cade laughed. "I'll add 'big name' to the list of things you've called me. The quality of your work speaks for itself.

Besides, small-town papers provide an important service in communities, digging deep into local news and reporting on events that don't make the dailies."

"You make my job sound like a noble profession."

"It is. And, much to my surprise, the job suits you well."

"Thank you for all your support," Enid said, glancing down at the phone blinking on her desk. "Can we talk later? I need to take a call."

"Of course. I've got to run, too. Congratulations again, babe. You are one hot reporter." Cade hung up before Enid could think of a suitable comeback. She punched the blinking phone light.

"Enid Blackwell here. How may I help you?"

A breathless voice replied. "Miss Enid, can you come over here right away? I need to talk to you."

"Roscoe, is that you?" Roscoe Pratt began working an internship at the Madden Historical Society last year while he was finishing his master's thesis on preserving small town history. He worked for Miss Murray, the historian matriarch of Madden.

"Yes, ma'am. It's me." Roscoe had a youthful, almost feminine laugh that always made Enid smile. "Can you? It's really important."

Enid glanced at the stack of papers on her desk and the unopened emails on her laptop. "Of course. I'll be over in a few minutes."

CHAPTER 4

The Madden Historical Society was housed in the Blackwell Center, an old brick building renovated with funds from Enid's former mother-in-law, Fern Blackwell. The building was just a block from the newspaper office on Main Street, but after walking briskly in the hot and humid weather, Enid's blouse was sticking to her back by the time she arrived.

A small sign under the doorbell requested that visitors ring for assistance, but before she could, Roscoe opened the door. He wore a bright-colored bow tie and a white shirt every day. Despite being one of the few young black men in Madden, he had assimilated to the town's culture quickly, winning the respect of its citizens with his knowledge of and respect for small towns. "Come in, please, Miss Enid. Thank you for coming right over." He gestured toward the sitting room. "Please have a seat in here. I'll bring some iced tea. Or would you prefer lemonade?"

Enid was ready to reply, but before she could, a female voice sounded down the hallway. "She drinks unsweetened iced tea."

Enid turned toward the familiar voice. When the woman walked down the hallway, Enid gasped. "Karla, is that you?"

The tall, dark-haired woman put a tray of glasses on the table in front of the velvet settee and then held her arms open. "Yes, Enid, it's me. So good to see you."

The two women held each other for a moment while Roscoe stood to the side. They had a history together, but a brief one. Karla had been instrumental in helping Enid identify the bones found at Glitter Lake Inn a little more than a year ago.

"When did you come back to the area?" Enid asked her.

"Yesterday. I'm staying with friends in Ridgeway. Such a lovely little town."

Roscoe gestured toward the sofa. "Can we all sit?"

"Of course," Enid said. "Karla and I can catch up later." She sat on the sofa beside Roscoe, and Karla sat in the big red velvet chair to their left.

"I'll go ahead and start," Roscoe said, turning to Enid. "As you know, Miss Murray left suddenly, right after I got my master's degree."

"Yes, congratulations on your achievement," Enid said. "But what do you mean about her leaving?"

"She left abruptly without giving me many details. I didn't press her, because, at the time, I didn't think it was any of my business. She knew I would be leaving but asked if I could stay another couple of weeks. I had planned to begin my job search, but I agreed to stay. After all, she has been so good to me." Roscoe clasped his hands together.

"So that was in May, right?" Enid asked.

"Yes, ma'am."

"But this is the end of July, more than two months later," Enid said. "Did you agree to stay that long?"

Roscoe stiffened and sat up straight. It was easy to slump into the soft antique sofa. "No, ma'am. I would never have agreed to that. Now, don't get me wrong. Madden is a nice little town, and I'd do most anything for Miss Murray, but there's no work here for me."

"Are you getting paid for your work now?" Karla asked.

"Mayor Carter agreed to pay me a stipend if I'd stay. But I've got to tell her this week that I'm leaving."

Enid rubbed her temples. "Wait, I'm confused. What did Miss Murray say to you about all this?"

"See, that's the thing, she hasn't. I got a couple of text messages from her saying she was fine and had decided to extend her stay. When I asked her when she planned to return, she never replied. I got a total of four texts, but then they stopped."

"Catherine has never sent a text in her life," Karla said.

Enid had never called Miss Murray by her first name and was uncomfortable referring to the dignified historian by it. "Does she even own a cell phone?"

"I've never seen her with one," Roscoe said.

"Neither have I," Karla said.

"When I called the mobile number where the text originated, it was one of those mechanical voices asking me to leave a message," he said.

"That's odd," Enid said. "I honestly had not realized Miss Murray, Catherine, had been gone that long. As close as the newspaper office is, I don't have a reason to come here very often. And we don't run in the same circle of people." Enid turned to Roscoe. "Are you worried about her?"

He squared his shoulders. "I was more irritated with her than worried. Until this morning."

"That's when I showed up," Karla said. "As you know, I have dreams sometimes. Of course, we all have them, but mine can be particularly revealing at times. Last month, I began dreaming about Catherine, but in the one last night, she was crying out to me for help."

Enid's hand flew to her mouth. "Oh, my. Could you tell where she was or what was happening to her?" Even though Enid wasn't totally convinced that dream empaths had special abilities, she didn't discount them either, given the help Karla had provided last year.

Karla shook her head slowly. "I don't know. That's the maddening thing about my dreams. I can't command more information. They come to me as the universe sees fit to reveal them. And I must admit, I'm a reluctant empath, so I haven't tried to hone my insights."

Enid reached into her leather tote and pulled out a notepad and pen. "I'd like to take a few notes and get that phone number you got the texts from."

Karla stared at the notepad as though it were a foreign object, appearing to be in deep thought. Roscoe chimed in. "I want you to help us find out if Miss Murray is alright. I'm worried now." He glanced at Karla. "We're both worried about her."

Enid scribbled some key information from their conversation. "Do either of you have ideas or any theories about where she went?"

Roscoe raised his hand, as though he were in a classroom. "Yes, she said she was going to visit family." He lowered his hand. "But I don't know who or where." He sighed. "That's not very helpful, is it?"

Karla turned to Roscoe. "You had no reason to question her at the time. She doesn't have any local family, other than a great-niece in Charleston. And, as far as I know, they're not very close. This is just not like Catherine."

"Did she keep any personal information here at the historical society?" Enid asked.

Roscoe shook his head. "I didn't want to snoop, but I looked through her desk. I didn't see anything personal other than a few teabags."

Enid looked at Karla. "Do you have a key to her house?"

"No. At least not any longer. She gave me one a year ago and invited me to stay any time I was in town, but I had never used it. Later, she told me she had changed the locks after she had given a contractor a door key. She said she'd give me a new one, but I never got it."

Enid handed the pen and notepad to Karla. "Give me the address and I'll get Josh, Sheriff Hart, to have one of his deputies check out her house."

Karla wrote the address on Enid's notepad. "I'm afraid I have to leave," Karla said. "I have some work to do out of town. If I have any more dreams or learn anything new, I'll get in touch immediately. And please let me know if you hear from her." She put her hand on Roscoe's arm. "If you need to move on, I'm sure Catherine would understand. Don't feel obligated to stay and cover for her."

"Yes, ma'am. I will."

"She's right, Roscoe," Enid said. "Thanks for getting in touch with me. That's all you can do right now." She stood up. "I'll let you know if I can find out anything."

On the walk back to the newspaper office, a familiar, unsettling feeling enveloped Enid. Jack called it her "reporter's instinct," but now it just felt like fear.

CHAPTER 5

At one time, Enid had fantasized about having a life with Joshua Hart, the former police chief in Madden. Since she had first met him a couple years ago, he had been named the sheriff of Bowman County, South Carolina. The relationship between the handsome, single law officer and the attractive local reporter quickly became news fodder. While they still considered themselves a "thing," as some of the locals called it, they kept a low profile and were rarely seen out together to avoid the conflict of interest rumors that plagued their relationship.

Reaching Josh by phone was nearly impossible during the day, so she decided to drive to the sheriff's office, which was less than thirty minutes away. Besides, the drive would give her a chance to collect her thoughts about Catherine Murray's strange situation.

When she pulled into the parking lot of the law enforcement center, she saw Josh's car in his reserved spot. She parked a few spaces away and grabbed her tote containing her notepad, wallet, iPhone, a protein bar, and a bottle of water.

Inside the two-story brick building, she went through security and then took the elevator to the second floor where Josh's office was located. When the elevator doors opened, she was startled by Josh standing a few feet away, talking to one of the Bowman deputies. Enid often kidded Josh that if he ever got out of law enforcement, he could be a male model. His dark hair and skin came from his Native American ancestry. But his smile came from his soul. He was a gentle man doing work that was anything but gentle. He turned to look at her. "Ms. Blackwell, this is a surprise. What brings you here?" Before she could answer, he said to the deputy, "I'll catch up with you later."

The deputy nodded and, after surveying Enid from head to toe, he walked down the hallway toward the stairs.

"Hello, Sheriff Hart," she said. "May I have a moment of your time?"

Josh glanced around to see if anyone was nearby before he leaned in and whispered, "You can have me and anything I have." He straightened up and spoke in a normal voice. "Come on to my office so we can talk."

Just like Josh's office had been in Madden, his workspace revealed a man who was dedicated to law enforcement. His bookshelves were filled with tomes on investigating murders, profiling, police procedures, and other work-related topics. No personal photos or anything else revealed information about the man beneath the uniform.

"Have a seat," he said, motioning to one of the chairs in front of his desk.

Enid sat in the one nearest the door. "I'm sorry to show up without calling first."

"Don't be ridiculous. You can track me down any time. But something must be on your mind for you to drive all the way over here."

"It's Catherine Murray. She's gone missing. Well, actually, I'm not sure if she's missing or if something has happened to her. Or maybe she's fine, just visiting relatives somewhere. I'm not even sure this is a police matter, but I was wondering if you could have someone check her house."

"Give me her address and whatever information you have, and I'll have someone go over there. We do welfare checks all the time."

Enid pulled out her notes and gave Josh all the information she had. When she mentioned Karla, Josh looked up from his notes. "You mean Karla Burke is back? She has an odd way of showing up unannounced when strange things are happening."

"You know she has these dreams, and she feels Catherine is in danger."

"It's hard to argue with her insights, considering how much she's helped us in the past," Josh said. "But as I recall, she admits her dreams are not always accurate. I'll let you know what we find out. If Catherine is still out of town, there's not much we can do other than make sure no one has broken into her house. If you know who she may have gone to visit, I can have someone check on her there."

"Well, that's the thing. We have no idea where she is."

"Well, then we'll just check her house." Josh smiled and glanced at the time on his Fitbit watch. "Sorry, babe, but I've got a meeting I've got to run to. We'll do what we can, and I'll call you later."

Enid stood to leave. "Oh, I also wanted to tell you that I won a journalism award for my investigative reporting."

Josh jumped up from his chair. "What? Are you serious? That's great." He started to step from around his desk, then stopped. "We've got to celebrate." He formed a fist and tapped his heart gently.

CHAPTER 6

Near the end of his workday, Josh decided to check out Catherine Murray's house himself. Sometimes he needed to get away from his desk and the burdens of being a county sheriff. The work was satisfying enough, but it was confining and often too political. Josh was grateful to the governor for appointing him to fill this position when the previous sheriff died, but there were days when he longed for something else. With so many people making demands on his time, this work was a far cry from the solitary, undercover work he had done in New Mexico. Some days he even missed being the Madden police chief, where he had been in charge of everything, including making sure the toilets worked and the printer had paper. Now it seemed he had everyone looking over his shoulder.

He also needed to process the personal news Enid had dropped on him. While Josh rejoiced at her journalism award, he also knew it could pull them even further apart. He had long suspected she would go back to work for the Associated Press or move on to a larger newspaper. And the conflict of interest issues they were already dealing with would likely get much worse when word of her award got out.

Lost in thought, he almost forgot where he was going and passed the last turn to Miss Murray's house. She lived in an area that had once been a small farming community.

Older houses, mostly with white wooden siding, dominated the landscape. Many of the streets had been added years after the area had moved away from farming to textiles. As a result, some of the roads were built around the remaining barns and other outbuildings, many of which were now abandoned.

The road made a wide swing to the right to go around a two-story barn. Graffiti covered most of the building from the ground up to about six feet, about as high as a grown-up or tall teen could reach without a ladder. The tags could be the mischievous work of bored teenagers. However, this area was not immune to gangs, just as no place was these days, although most of them were local start-ups hoping to make a name for themselves doing petty crimes. Occasionally, the local gangs got into more serious trouble by committing aggravated assault on their rivals.

Josh pulled over to the side of the road for a closer look at one of the graphics sprayed in bold white paint: the number "14." It stood out from the rest of the graffiti, not just because of its size but because of what it represented: the tag often used by one of the most violent new groups in the state, the White Saviors. They went by WS14. At a recent workshop for law enforcement, Josh learned that 14 is the numerical shorthand for a white supremacist slogan known as the 14 Words: "We must secure the existence of our people and a future for white children." While the White Saviors had adopted the 14 tag, other hate groups also used the same symbolic numeral, so he couldn't be sure WS14 was behind it. He hoped it wasn't them, because they promoted extreme violence. Unlike many gangs populated by blacks and Hispanics, this group was an all-white collection of skinheads, neo-Nazis, and extreme nationalists. They were known to torture their victims, often rival gang members, and dabble in satanic worship. No one was sure where WS14 actually started, but they had been popping up around the state over the past couple of years. This tag on the old barn was the first time Josh had seen possible signs of them in Bowman County.

He took a picture of the hate-group tag with his phone. When he got back to the office, he would compare it to the images in their case files.

He glanced around before getting back into his car and then drove back to Miss Murray's address a few blocks away. After checking his notes to be sure he had the right location, he checked the yard, walking around to see if there were any broken windows. He tugged on the front and back doors to see if they were securely locked. The blinds were pulled down on the front windows, so he couldn't see inside, but nothing seemed to be out of order. The grass had been recently cut and emitted the pungent smell of wild onions.

After peeping inside the mailbox beside the front door, Josh found no envelopes or anything else. Someone was definitely taking care of the place. Enid hadn't mentioned any nearby relatives, but perhaps friends or neighbors were tending Miss Murray's house and yard.

The house across the street looked very similar to Miss Murray's. An older Impala sat in the driveway, so hopefully someone was at home. Josh walked across the street and knocked on the door, and a neatly dressed woman who looked to be in her sixties came to the door.

"Hello, ma'am." He pointed to his badge. "I'm Sheriff Joshua Hart. Sorry to bother you, but could I ask you a few questions?"

The woman studied the badge. "Have I done something wrong, officer?"

"Oh, no, ma'am." He gestured toward the metal porch glider. "Could we sit here a moment?"

The woman glanced at the badge again and then at Josh's face. "You're even more handsome than the paper showed. I read about the governor making you sheriff." She smiled for the first time. "Sit down there. Can I get you something to drink?"

"No, thanks." Josh settled into the glider, which swayed back and forth a few times before he could stop it. "Do you know Miss Murray across the street?"

The woman, sitting in a nearby wooden rocker, stiffened. "Of course. We've been neighbors for nearly forty years."

Josh scribbled in the small notepad he carried in his shirt pocket at all times. "May I get your name, please?"

"Sylvia."

"Last name?"

"Ryce. That's with a 'y' not an 'i.'"

"I was asked by a friend of Miss Murray to do a welfare check on her."

"I don't think Catherine is on welfare," Sylvia said. "And if she were, I'm sure she wasn't trying to cheat anyone."

Josh couldn't control a smile. "A welfare check is what we call it when we check on someone to be sure they are alright. In this case, it's more of just a property check since no one appears to be home."

"Oh, I see. I just wasn't familiar with that term." Sylvia ran her hand across her lap to straighten her dress. "I have no reason to think she's not alright. But I have to tell you, it did bother me a bit. In fact, if I'm honest, it hurt my feelings that she took off without telling me or saying goodbye." A frown covered Sylvia's face. "She's never done that, so I wondered what I had said or done that upset her."

Josh had been in the South long enough to understand, or at least recognize, some of the social mores. There were certain things you did and didn't do. One of the taboos was taking off without telling your friend and neighbor. "Does Miss Murray have relatives nearby? Looks like someone is taking care of her place."

Sylvia turned to look toward Miss Murray's house. "Most of the time my grandson Robert cuts her grass. He's been helping her for years with all kinds of odd jobs."

"Has he seen her recently or mentioned how he's being paid?"

"No, I guess he's just running a tab. He doesn't charge her much anyway."

Josh handed her his business card. "Well, as I said, I'm just doing a welfare check. I'm sure everything is fine, but if you see anything suspicious or if you talk to her, give me a call. Talk to one of the deputies if I'm not available."

As he was walking down the steps, he turned back to Sylvia, who was still rocking back and forth. "By the way, I noticed some graffiti on the barn down the street. Is that just kids, as far as you know?"

Sylvia stopped rocking. "That's disgraceful, isn't it? That was the old Thompson tobacco farm. The barn was where they cured the tobacco leaves. Why, Mr. Thompson would turn in his grave if he knew what the place looks like now. But he's been long gone, and the farm was abandoned. I heard the state might have taken it for back taxes, but that could be just gossip." She shook her head slowly. "A shame." She then seemed to remember Josh's question.

"Oh, you asked if it was kids doing all that stuff. I imagine so."

"Well, thanks again for your time. Like I said, just call if you notice anything out of the ordinary."

Sylvia nodded. "These days, I'm not sure what would be out of the ordinary. Things are sure changing in this world."

CHAPTER 7

Enid uploaded the last article for this week's *Tri-County Gazette.* When she first moved to Madden a few years ago, the big news was garden parties, graduations, and the occasional petty crime. But when the big-box-store distribution center moved to the outskirts of Madden, new faces showed up every day. Many of the managers had settled in Columbia, preferring to commute than to live in the small Southern town. Others embraced Madden's charm and moved in. The town was divided on whether their presence and the new growth was good or bad. Some argued that otherwise the town would have been doomed to abandonment and decay, like many of the surrounding areas. Others pointed to the increase in crime and traffic, along with higher property taxes, as evidence that their old way of life was gone forever.

Having lived in Charlotte several years ago, Enid wanted to assure the citizens of Madden that three cars at the traffic light near the distribution center was not a traffic jam. Or that local kids who vandalized were not enticed to do so by "outside" influences. But even though Enid and Jack laughed about it, she respected the Madden citizens' concerns and their determination to protect their way of life.

A loud crash outside of her office yanked Enid from her thoughts. She jumped up and ran down the hallway. Jack was kneeling down, picking up a glass pot sitting in a puddle of spilled coffee. The area smelled of scorched grounds.

Enid ran to the restroom to grab paper towels. "Here, let me help you."

"Where is Ginger?" Jack asked.

"She left to attend her friend's wedding. Remember? She asked for a few days off." She blotted up as much coffee as she could with the handful of paper towels. At least the stain matched the brown, flat-weave industrial carpet. "You said she drives you crazy, so I thought you'd enjoy her being gone."

"She does drive me crazy. The most disrespectful kid I've ever met."

"She's not a kid anymore. She's twenty-three. And she just has a different outlook on life. Besides, you have to admit she's a pretty efficient office manager." Enid laughed. "And you're starting to sound like an old fogey."

Jack sat down on the floor and leaned against the wall, laughing out loud. "Thanks, I needed to be put in my place. You go on and finish your work. I'll clean all this up."

Enid threw the wad of wet towels in the trash. "Come on, I'll help you. We're a team."

After they had restored order to the small break area, Jack looked at his watch. Unlike the paper's younger reporters, Jack still wore an analog watch, refusing to rely on his phone or a "fancy fitness gadget" to check the time. "Have you finished all your articles?"

"Yes. All done."

"I've got a couple more hours of work, and then I thought maybe I'd come over to your place and fix dinner. You know, to celebrate your award. I'd invite you to my place, but I've having the kitchen floor replaced. It's a bit of a mess over there now. I'm putting down that wide-plank flooring throughout the kitchen, dining room, and living room. You know, the one you helped me pick out."

"It's going to be beautiful. I can't wait to see it."

"Then we're on for dinner?"

Enid paused briefly. Jack was her best friend, as well as her editor. At times, he seemed something more. But always, he was her friend, so she was cautious not to step over the line and mess that up. "I appreciate it, but—"

"If you've already got plans tonight, we can do it some other time."

Pushing her hesitation aside, Enid replied, "No, tonight is good."

· · ·

Jack arrived at Enid's small but comfortable bungalow around six o'clock with several shopping bags full of food. "Hope you don't mind me coming a little early. I wanted to get started."

"No, of course not. Looks like you're cooking for an army, though."

"Leftovers are always good to have." He handed a bottle of champagne to Enid. "Put that in the fridge and then you can peel the shrimp."

"Does that that mean that you're cooking shrimp and grits?" Enid grinned.

"Yes. Your favorite."

For the next thirty minutes, they chatted away like the old friends they were, while handling their assigned cooking tasks. After stirring the grits for the last time, Jack pushed Enid out of the kitchen. "Go on now. I need to set the table.

I've got this. Go read a book or something for a few minutes."

Enid decided to sit on the small front porch. Although the ceiling fan mostly just pushed the hot, humid air around, she had become acclimated to the South Carolina Midlands summer heat. She checked a few emails on her phone and pulled up CNN news to see what was happening in the world. As she finished reading an article on Brexit, she heard a car on the gravel driveway leading from the road to her house. It was still daylight, and she recognized the driver. *Oh, crap.*

She ran into the kitchen where Jack was stirring the pot of coarse ground grits. "Cade is here."

"Cade? What do you mean, he's here?"

"I mean *here*. He just drove up."

"Did you invite him?"

Enid threw her hands up. "Are you serious?" She stormed out of the kitchen and went to the front door. Cade was standing there with a bouquet of flowers in his hand. She pushed the screen door open. "Cade, what a surprise."

Cade walked in and kissed her on the cheek. "And I'm happy to see you, too." He held out the flowers. "I stopped at a roadside stand just outside of Madden. She said she knew you, and that you liked this mix of daisies."

Enid motioned toward the sofa. "Thanks. Have a seat and I'll let Jack know you're here."

Cade sat on the sofa. "I saw his pickup in the driveway. Am I intruding on something?"

Enid picked a dead leaf off one of the flowers. "He's cooking dinner for me, to celebrate my award."

"Ah, I see. Well, don't let me—"

"Cade, a pleasure to see you," Jack said, walking from the kitchen wiping his hands on a dishtowel. "Enid didn't mention you were coming."

Enid glanced at Jack. "I wasn't aware of it myself."

"Well, doesn't matter," Jack said. "We've got plenty of food. Join us for dinner."

"I don't want to intrude," Cade said, looking toward Enid.

Enid wasn't sure which irritated her the most. The fact that her ex-husband showed up uninvited and unannounced, or that Jack just took it all in stride. Even though Jack and Cade had known each other long before she met Jack, their male bond was irritating at times, making her feel left out.

The blues tune that was Enid's ringtone penetrated the tension in the air. She pulled her cell from her pocket. *Oh, no. This can't be happening.* She answered the call. "Hi, Josh." Enid glanced at Jack and Cade, both of whom were staring at her. "Well, actually, I can't talk right now. I've got guests." Guests? Why did she say that? And why was she feeling so guilty? "Jack's here making dinner, and then Cade came in," she blurted out.

Jack and Cade were both looking down at their feet.

For more privacy, Enid walked out on the porch to continue her call. "I'm sorry, it's just that . . ." She listened as Josh politely told her not to worry about it. "I'll call you later," she said. "Love you."

The call ended without a reply from Josh.

CHAPTER 8

Josh straightened the papers on his desk at the Bowman County sheriff's office. He wasn't the neatest person in the world, and he surely didn't obsess over having things lined up. But this morning, he felt the need for order. Or perhaps he wanted to exert control over something, even if it was just the paper mountain on his desk.

He glanced at the large clock on the wall. Enid would be here in a few minutes to discuss his welfare check on Miss Murray. When they talked last night, he had almost told Enid he was too busy to see her today, but he knew that once he started lying or letting jealousy consume him, their relationship would begin sliding down a slippery slope.

Before he could be honest with Enid, he had to be honest with himself. He was disappointed that she had declined his offer to go to New Mexico months ago. He wanted to reconnect with his sister Heather, whom he had not seen since she was a teenager, and he also wanted Enid to see his home state. Thinking maybe the timing was just bad, he had postponed the trip twice. He now had to face the fact that she just didn't want to go with him. Did she think she would be in the way of his reunion? Or did she just not want to be with him? What else would prevent her from going? A tap on the door interrupted his thoughts.

Enid was standing at the door to his office. "Is this still a good time?"

Josh stood. "Yes, of course." He re-straightened one of the paper stacks, as Enid watched.

"That's as neat as I've ever seen your desk," she said.

"Look—" Josh and Enid began speaking at the same time. "You go first," he said.

"I'm really sorry about last night. If I had known you wanted to come over, you know I would have declined Jack's offer to cook dinner. And I had no idea Cade would show up."

Josh ran his hand through his hair. It was so black it was nearly blue. A few premature gray hairs in his sideburns framed his dark eyes. "You don't have to explain. I mean after all, I have no claims on you." He couldn't look at Enid's eyes. He knew she was struggling with how to make their relationship work as much as he was. "Let's talk about this later." He gave her his best smile. "I'm sure you want to know about my check on Miss Murray's house."

Enid cleared her throat. "I do. What did you find? Was everything okay there?"

Josh filled her in on his conversation with Sylvia, the neighbor. "As far as I could tell, there wasn't anything out of the ordinary. At least nothing related to Miss Murray."

"What exactly does that mean?"

Josh smiled. Enid was ever the reporter, digging for information. "What I meant was that it seems we've got some potential gang presence nearby. I need to make sure the deputies are keeping an eye on the situation before it gets out of hand."

"Which gang?"

"Am I going to regret mentioning this to you?"

This time it was Enid who smiled. "Probably. Which gang?"

"They're relatively new. Call themselves the WS14. I don't know much about them, other than they're a white nationalist group intent on keeping power in the hands of white people. They probably aren't too excited that the county sheriff is an American Indian."

Enid scribbled in her notebook. "I think I've heard of them. I'll do some research."

Josh held up his hand. "This probably has nothing to do with Miss Murray, and you need to be careful." Before Enid could reply, he added. "Never mind. I've said that so many times it's become meaningless."

"I will be careful. Thanks. I know you're busy, so I'll get out of here. If you learn anything about Miss Murray, you'll let me know?"

"Of course."

A female deputy walked into Josh's office. "The governor is on the phone for you. He said you didn't answer your cell phone."

Josh glanced down at the silent phone on his desk. "Guess I forgot it was turned off."

Enid stood to leave under the watchful eye of the deputy. "Thank you, Sheriff Hart, for checking on Miss Murray. I'll be in touch later."

Josh waited until Enid had left before taking the governor's call. "Hello, sir. How are you today?" He listened for a few minutes, scribbling some notes. "May I have some time to think about this? I mean, I've barely settled into this job, and I don't want to disrupt things around here any more than I have to. You have lots of good men who could fill the role." Josh stopped taking notes. There was no point.

"Yes, I'll call you tomorrow, sir, to finalize the details. Thanks for your support and confidence in me."

After the call, Josh looked at the neat stacks of paper. "So much for putting my life in order," he said aloud.

· · ·

Enid parked her small car in front of the barn Josh had described. After glancing around to be sure she was alone, she took some photos of the spray-painted gang tags. At some point, a cyclone fence had been added around the old barn, as though to create a perimeter and preserve its space in the encroaching neighborhood. But vandals had pulled a section of the fence down, so Enid stepped over the metal fencing to get closer to the barn.

The structure was about fifty feet from the fence. Looking around again, Enid walked toward the partially open barn door and peeped inside. In contrast to the glaring summer sun outside, the inside was dark and smelled musty. She tried to push the door open further, but the overhead track was rusted and wouldn't budge. She tried to slip through the narrow opening, but there wasn't enough room. Her shirt caught on a nail and ripped, so she backed away.

She walked around to the side of the barn, then to the rear, hoping there was another way inside. While the front of the barn faced the street, the back entrance was merely feet from a tall stand of pine trees, so dense that the sunlight didn't penetrate it. There was no door on the back entrance.

As soon as she stepped over the raised threshold of the door, she felt something move beside her foot. She jumped back, nearly falling to the ground. Recovering her balance, she turned on her cellphone light to illuminate the interior of the old barn. A black rat snake, about five feet long, slithered off toward the corner. She had learned many things from Josh, including how to recognize poisonous snakes. This one was harmless, although still scary. Josh had shown her a rat snake near his house and explained that they liked to eat rodents. He said they were somewhat shy, unless cornered or provoked. She didn't plan to do either. After shining her phone light inside again and seeing no sign of the rat snake, she stepped further inside.

The air in the barn was oppressive in the humid heat of mid-summer. As her eyes adjusted to the darkness, she saw a table or platform of some kind in the middle of the building. Sweeping the phone's light in front of her to check for the snake or anything else that might be lurking, she slowly stepped forward to examine it.

The object appeared to be about four feet high, about six feet long, and several feet wide. It was crudely constructed of weathered wood. She took a couple of flash photos. The stifling air was getting to her, and she had a sudden urge to get out of there.

As she turned to leave, she saw a figure pass by the doorway near the woods. In those seconds, she was unable to determine if it was a man or a woman. It didn't matter, since women were just as capable of inflicting harm as men.

Enid walked around the table she had just photographed and made her way to the front of the barn. She tucked her phone back in her pocket and pushed on the door with as much strength as she could muster. This time, with adrenaline coursing through her body, she was able to move the thick wooden door several inches—just enough to slip through and get out.

She ran to the downed section of fence and stepped over it. In the process, she cut her leg, and she could feel warm blood running down it. Since she had not locked her car, she quickly glanced in the back seat to be sure no one was hiding there before locking herself inside. Hands shaking, she threw the car in reverse and pulled back onto the road. As she was driving away, she looked in her rearview mirror. A young man was standing in front of the barn where she had just escaped. Despite the sultry weather, he had on a hoodie that covered much of his face.

CHAPTER 9

Enid sat on the edge of the clawfoot tub and dabbed alcohol on the gash in her leg. A pile of blood-stained tissues filled the small trashcan next to her. She walked across the cool tile floor of the small bathroom and pulled the first-aid kit from her linen closet, leaving a red trail behind her. She put a thick wad of gauze on the cut and applied pressure, but the bleeding continued.

Bracing herself for the onslaught of lectures Jack was sure to give her, she called him.

"I was wondering where you were," he answered. "If you told me, I forgot. Sorry."

Enid pressed on the wound again. "No, I didn't. I'm home."

"Home? I don't remember implementing a remote work policy." When she didn't reply with a tart comment he likely expected, he added. "Are you alright?"

"Are you in the middle of something? I hate to bother you, but I need to get to Urgent Care."

She heard Jack gasp. "What's wrong? I'm going to call 911."

"No, I'm not dying or anything. I've just cut my leg, and it won't stop bleeding."

"How did you . . . Never mind. I'll be right over."

. . .

Despite the numbing effect of a local anesthesia, Enid winced as the Urgent Care physician stitched her leg. He finished with a surgeon's knot and applied an antibacterial ointment. "That was a nasty cut," he said, wrapping a bandage around her leg. What did you say you cut it on?"

She glanced at Jack who was sitting in a metal chair in the corner of the room. "A wire fence," she said. "On a jagged piece that was sticking out. I didn't see it."

"When did you last have a tetanus shot?"

"Last year."

"She tends to get hurt on the job a lot," Jack said.

"I see," the doctor said. "Well, whatever you're doing, you need to be careful. I need to see you in two weeks to remove those stitches. But if you have any redness, swelling, or excessive pain, come back in right away."

"I will," she said. "Thanks."

Jack went over to the table to hold Enid's arm to steady her as she got off the examination table. "Don't kid yourself," he said to the doctor. "She won't listen to you either."

"Wives aren't supposed to listen to spouses, but they sometimes listen to their physicians."

"We're not married," Jack said. "But you're right. She does act like a wife sometimes." He held onto Enid's arm. "You steady on your feet?"

Enid nodded.

"Thanks, Doc. I'll get her home now."

Enid held Jack's arm as they walked to his pickup. "Please don't lecture me. Not right now. I feel a little woozy."

He helped her get into the front seat and fastened the seatbelt across her lap. "I won't lecture you. It won't do any good."

As Jack drove her back to her house, Enid leaned her head back and thought about the doctor's mistaking them for husband and wife. Part of her was amused, but it was also disconcerting. Not for the first time, she thought about life without Jack. If she moved on to a larger newspaper, what would her daily life be like without him? He had encouraged her to do so, but she wasn't sure if he really meant it. She had the same thoughts about Josh once, trying to imagine life without him, but their jobs had created conflicts of interest that had driven a wedge between them. Her leg was throbbing, and she just wanted to sleep, but she owed Jack an explanation.

She had nearly dozed off when she heard his voice. "I'm taking you to my house. No discussion."

One thing she had learned about Jack was "that" tone of voice really meant he had already made up his mind about something. Most of the time, she could soften his stance on an issue, but not when he used that voice. "Only for tonight," she said.

When they arrived at his house, he helped her to the guest room. "You nap. I'll go make sure your house is secured and then I'll be back. Keep your cell phone handy and call me if you need to. I'll get Ginger to . . . Dang, I forgot she's not there to close up the office. I'll have to run by there, too."

Enid laughed. "Admit it. You actually miss her."

"Don't get cheeky with me, or I'll call Cade to come sit with you. And, I might even call Josh and tell him Cade is here."

"Ouch, that was mean. Take your time. I'm fine. I just want to sleep now." Enid laid her head back and closed her eyes. Jack brushed a strand of copper hair from her forehead before he left.

C H A P T E R   1 0

Enid woke up with a dull headache. Where was she? Looking around the room, she saw the familiar shapes of Jack's guest room. It was almost dark out, so it had to be after eight pm. When she tried to swing her legs off the bed to get up, she let out an involuntary yelp. "Ouch, crap."

"You okay in there?" Jack called out from the hallway.

"Fine. Just give me a minute and I'll be up."

"Anything I can do to help?"

"No, thanks."

"Well, alright then. I've got a light dinner for us, if you feel up to it."

Enid didn't feel hungry, but she was ready to move around a bit. "Sounds good." She hobbled to the bathroom right outside her door in the hall. When she looked in the mirror, she almost didn't recognize herself. Her hair was matted from sweating earlier in the day, and her makeup was smeared from sleeping. She took a washcloth from the linen closet and made what repairs she could. She ran her hand through her hair and then saw her overnight bag in the corner. She peeped inside: makeup, comb, brush, shampoo. Even clean underwear and a change of clothes. Dear Jack. What a friend he was.

She put her blood-stained trousers in the trashcan and washed her leg, being careful not to wet the bandage. There wasn't much she could do for her hair, since she couldn't take a shower.

When she walked out of the bathroom, Jack was standing at the end of the hallway. "Need some help?"

"I'm fine. Thanks for bringing my bag of things over." She tried to tell herself that either Cade or Josh would have done the same thing, but she knew it wasn't true. Perhaps Jack's caring for his wife when she was dying of cancer had honed his caregiver skills.

"I'll help you wash your hair at the sink after we eat. Come on, dinner's ready."

Enid walked slowly toward the dining room, but Jack stopped her. "I thought we might sit on the screened porch. That is, if you feel like it. With the ceiling fan on, it's not bad at all."

"That would be nice." The aroma of something good cooking filled the air. "Smells delicious."

"I heated some chicken soup from the freezer and made a salad to go with it. They say chicken soup is good for the soul and anything that ails you."

"That sounds perfect."

Jack helped Enid to her chair. Several mason jars with battery-operated fairy lights filled the dark corners of the porch. A candle sat in the middle of the small table covered with a blue cloth. "This is all so nice of you," Enid said. "How can I repay you?"

"Just enjoy the meal and heal quickly."

As they ate, the wind kicked up a bit and a breeze swept through the porch. "That cool air feels good," she said.

Jack nodded, and they finished the meal mostly in silence. "I'll get the dishes later, after we talk. Would you like to go inside?"

"No, let's sit over there." She nodded toward two big wicker chairs with overstuffed cushions. "It feels too good out here to go inside."

With Jack holding onto her, Enid limped over to the chair, and he sat next to her. "If you'd rather wait until to-morrow, that's fine," he said.

"No, I owe you an explanation. And an apology."

She told Jack about her visit with Roscoe and Karla and how they were concerned about Miss Murray. She also told him about Josh's welfare check and his conversation with Sylvia, the neighbor. "I just thought local gang activity might be a good story, but I wanted to check it out before I pro-posed it to you."

Jack jumped up so quickly it startled Enid. He paced across the porch a few times. "What the hell were you think-ing? Did it ever occur to you that you could have at least told me what you were doing and where you'd be? Have I ever held you back?" He paused. "Okay, maybe I've tried to discourage you from pursuing a few things, but you ignored me anyway."

Enid patted the arm of the empty chair next to her. "Come back and sit down. I said I owed you an apology, and I meant it. What I did was foolish, but I didn't think it would be dangerous."

Jack settled back into his chair and leaned forward, rest-ing his elbows on his knees and putting his face in his hands. "What would I do if something happened to you?"

"On the bright side, I doubt Cade would hold you re-sponsible if anything happened to me on the job, and I really don't have any other family left." She took Jack's hand. "Except you. I don't mean to make light of all this. I know losing your wife has made you more vulnerable to losing someone you . . . someone you care about."

Jack sat up and turned to face Enid. "It scares me that I care so much, and I don't want to scare you by getting too close."

"Our friendship is very special. And sometimes it does scare me, but I'm not going to run away from it. And I'm not ready to discuss this any further tonight."

"Fair enough." Jack sat back in his chair. "You said you took some photos of the gang tags. Can I see them?"

She pulled her phone from her pocket and handed it to Jack. "Here, I haven't looked at them."

Jack zoomed the photos to get a better look. "I've seen these before."

"Where?"

Jack looked at the photos again. "Honestly, I can't remember, but it was somewhere in the tri-county area. I doubt I even made a note of it, but I'll check in the morning." He handed the phone back to Enid. "Are you thinking this has anything to do with Miss Murray's disappearance?"

"First of all, we don't know that Miss Murray, Catherine, is missing. It's odd that she abandoned Roscoe the way she did. She knew he was waiting for her to return so he could leave for another job. And it's just as odd that she didn't let Karla, her closest friend, know anything. I'm sure Catherine will turn up soon, apologizing for alarming everyone, but I still worry about her. In the meantime, should we check into the WS14 and other local gang activity and do an article?"

"Sure. Go ahead and check it out, and then we'll decide if it's worth alarming our readers. There's a fine line between keeping them informed and scaring them needlessly." Jack stood and began clearing the dishes. "You get some sleep. I'll get all this."

Enid stood on her toes and kissed Jack on the cheek. "You're too good to me. I don't deserve you."

Jack set the plates back on the table and gave her a hug. "I'm the one who doesn't deserve you." He pulled away. "Now go to bed so I can clean up."

CHAPTER 11

When Enid woke up in Jack's guest room the next morning, she again forgot where she was. Disorientation was something she had experienced in her previous job working for one of the big banks in Charlotte, North Carolina. The position required her to travel frequently, and sometimes she'd wake up not remembering which city and state she was in, or why she was even there. The only thing she missed about that job was her big paycheck. Luckily, the cost of living in Madden was significantly less, and she also lived a much simpler life now. But while she had friends here, she lived alone, and circumstances kept her and Josh from spending more time together.

The incident with Josh the other night still bothered her. She owed him more than just a lame explanation of why Jack and Cade were at her house. When she got back to her own place, she would invite Josh over for dinner tonight. She pulled on her jeans and shirt and packed the remaining items in her overnight bag.

She expected to find that Jack had already left for the office and that she would find a note on the kitchen table. But when she opened her bedroom door, the smell of bacon filled the air. "I hope that's turkey bacon," she said as she walked into the kitchen.

Jack stood at the stove and turned around to greet her. "Not on your life. None of that fancy-schmancy, fake-bacon stuff in my house."

Enid picked a piece from the paper towel-lined plate. "Umm. That's good. But you didn't have to cook for me. I could have gotten something at home."

"What? Granola and yogurt? That's hardly a meal, so just quit whining and sit down. After we eat, I've got to run some errands before going to the office. You sure you're okay to go home?"

"I'm fine. My leg is much better this morning. But if you don't mind, I'll work from home today. I've got some calls to make, and I want to do some research on the local gangs."

During the meal, they chatted about Ginger's return, which Jack admitted he was looking forward to, and about the changes in and around Madden because of the influx of newcomers. "I've seen more deer around my place since they leveled the land down the road for that new housing development," he said. "I guess the poor creatures don't have any choice but to eat my plants since they've been run out of their habitat. I've never been one to stand in the way of progress, but I really hated to see those woods disappear."

"I know what you mean." Enid pushed her plate away. "That was delicious, even if it does poison my body." She grinned at Jack. "Thanks again for taking care of me. You go on to do your errands, and I'll clean up the kitchen. I insist. It's the least I can do."

"Alright, but if your leg bothers you, just leave everything. It won't be the first or last time I've left dishes stacked in the sink."

"I'll be fine. You have a good day. I'll check in later." As Jack walked into the hallway, she called after him. "By the way, I'm inviting Josh over tonight. Just wanted to let you know."

"Don't worry. I won't show up unexpectedly." He turned and walked out the door before Enid could reply.

. . .

Less than ten minutes after Enid had left a message for Josh to call, her cell phone rang and his face filled the screen. "That was quick," she said.

"I need to talk to you, too, so I'm glad you called. But first, tell me what's up."

"I thought I'd cook dinner for us tonight, if you're free."

"What's the occasion?"

"Nothing. Just thought I'd treat you. I can roast a chicken. At least I've learned to do that."

Josh hesitated before answering. "It's just that I've got to go to Columbia this afternoon, and there's always the possibility I'll get pulled into dinner."

"We can do it some other time then." She tried not to let the disappointment show in her voice.

"You sure? It's not every day I get a special invitation like this, and I don't want to let you down."

"No, it's fine, really. What was it you needed to talk to me about?"

"I have some news you might like."

Something in Josh's tone prompted Enid to sit down. "Oh?"

"The governor has asked me to be his liaison on the state's gang task force, specifically to work on the white supremacy hate groups starting to pop up. I'll work closely with the South Carolina Gang Investigators Association but report directly to Governor Larkin."

Enid wasn't sure how to react. "You haven't been in the sheriff's role very long, and this assignment could be a disruption. How do you feel about it?"

"One of the senior deputies will cover for me. It's just a twelve-month assignment. Governor Larkin said he needs my experience working with drug gangs in New Mexico, and I don't mind helping for a year. Besides, it could make it easier on us. With me doing a special assignment, there's less likelihood of us crossing paths and having to deal with the appearance of a conflict of interest."

"You need to follow your instincts. If you think this is a good career move, then you should accept it."

"I thought you'd be more excited."

"I just want what's best for you. And don't worry about dinner. We'll do it another time."

After Enid hung up, she realized she had not told Josh about her visit to Urgent Care. Probably just as well. No need to worry him further. Yet, the omission bothered her. They used to share everything. No bit of news had been too small. But things were different now.

After making a few phone calls for upcoming articles, Enid did some online research about the White Saviors gang but couldn't find anything specific to this group. She did find that in 2018, a gang-monitoring group's study identified fourteen known hate groups operating in South Carolina. A news report stated that as many as nineteen groups were active in the state. Some were white nationalists, but others were black nationalist groups, like the Nation of Islam. Whatever their color or focus, the common denominator was hatred for anyone different from them.

Enid tried to take comfort in Josh's saying he wasn't sure whether the number 14 tag on the old barn was authentic or just a prank.

CHAPTER 12

It was still early enough for Enid to drive back to Miss Murray's neighborhood and talk to Sylvia, the neighbor Josh had interviewed. This time though, Enid was taking reinforcements. She tapped on Jack's cell number in her contacts. When he answered, she asked, "Have you got time to ride with me for an interview?"

"Wait. Did I hear right? You're asking for help?" He laughed.

"Not help, just back-up. I want to interview Miss Murray's neighbor."

"Alright, by the time you get here to pick me up, I'll be finished with this edit."

When Enid arrived at the *Tri-County Gazette* office, Jack was standing in the parking lot beside the old brick building. She pulled up beside him, and he got in the car. Before fastening his seatbelt, he pulled something from his shirt pocket. "I got you a present."

"What is it?"

"Hold out your hand." Jack put a small plastic object in her hand. It had a keychain ring on it and a fabric pull of some kind.

Enid touched the pull.

"No! Don't pull that. It's a personal security alarm." He pointed to a gray loop on the side of the object. "When you pull that thing there, a god-awful alarm goes off. It's ear-piercing."

Enid looked at Jack. "Are you serious? A personal alarm?"

"Just put it on your keychain or hang it on your purse. It might come in handy. You never know."

"But what if I accidentally pull that cord?"

"Guaranteed to get attention. Just stick the pin back in."

"Great. More attention. Just what I need." Enid put the alarm in her cup holder. "Thanks."

When they arrived at Sylvia's house and rang the doorbell, no one answered. "Oh well," Enid said. "I guess this was a wasted trip. Sorry I pulled you from work."

"That's okay, I needed a break."

"Let's go across the street and look at Miss Murray's house. Maybe we'll see something Josh missed."

Jack threw his head back and laughed loudly. "Oh, so now you're a better investigator than Sheriff Hart. Is that it?" He shook his head. "Or are you just being nosy?"

Instead of answering, Enid walked across the street, limping slightly from the throbbing pain in her leg. As Josh had reported, the grass was cut and nothing looked unusual. Enid walked around the side of the house to the backyard.

"Wait. Where are you going? Don't you know this is trespassing?" Jack called out to her.

Enid ignored him and looked around looking for anything unusual.

"What are you doing back here?" a woman's voice called out.

Enid spun around toward the woman, wincing as she put pressure on her leg "I'm Enid Blackwell, a friend of Miss

Murray. We were just checking on her, and we didn't see a car nearby or know anyone was here."

"I always park out of sight from where I'm going. Occupational hazard of being an investigator." She was thin with a short, blonde pixie haircut, probably in her early thirties.

"Are you conducting an investigation here?" Enid saw Jack come up behind the woman.

"I'm an insurance investigator, but I'm not here on business. My name is Ruby-Grace Murray. Catherine is my great-aunt. She's the only person who uses my full name. Almost everyone else calls me Roo."

"Roo?"

"My parents couldn't decide on Ruby or Grace, both family names, so they hyphenated my first name. It's actually a pain to explain to people. That's one reason people call me Roo. It's easier, and I kinda like that Roo was a *Winnie the Pooh* character."

"I remember that. He was a kangaroo." Enid pointed toward Jack. "The man behind you is Jack Johnson. He's the editor of the *Tri-County Gazette* and my boss. I'm a reporter. I don't believe I've seen you around Madden."

"Aunt Cat, that's what I call her, she mentioned you. I've read your articles. Good work!"

"Thanks," Enid said. "Do you live nearby?"

"No, I live in Charleston."

"South Carolina?" Jack asked.

Roo smiled. "Yes. I forget there are twenty-two other cities across the country named Charleston." She shrugged. "During an investigation, I had a reason to look it up is the only reason I know. Anyway, I don't mean to be rude, but I'm curious as to what you are doing at my aunt's house. Are you here as reporters or as friends?"

Jack and Enid exchanged glances. "Both, actually," Jack said. "How long has it been since you talked with Catherine?"

"A few years back we talked at least once a week, but then I got busy and we drifted apart. I feel really bad about that, because she doesn't have any other close family. I haven't heard from her in months. For some reason she's been on my mind lately, and I haven't been able to reach her by phone." Roo glanced at her watch. "I'm sorry but I've got an appointment I need to get to. I just came by here since I was in town. You know, work-related." She pulled two business cards from her canvas messenger bag and gave one to Enid and one to Jack. "If you'll give me your cards, I'll contact you tomorrow. I'm staying at the Glitter Lake Inn. Do you know it?"

Jack smiled. "Yes, I'm the owner. The manager is a great guy named Theo."

"Cool. I'll be in touch."

CHAPTER 13

When Enid and Jack arrived at the Glitter Lake Inn, Theo greeted them, as usual, with hugs. "Please come in. I know you're here to meet with Miss Murray, and she's in the library. I have coffee, tea, and croissants set out on the balcony table. It's still cool enough to sit outside, unless you'd rather me move you inside?"

"The balcony is perfect," Enid said.

"Before we leave today, I'd like to talk with you," Jack said to Theo. "You know, some inn business."

"Of course." Theo led them to the library, where Roo was sitting outside, gazing at Glitter Lake. The early morning sun cast jewels of light across the water rippling in the breeze. She stood when Enid and Jack appeared. "Good morning. I never thought I'd find a place as beautiful as Charleston, but I believe I have. This is magnificent."

Theo beamed. "Yes, it's like heaven here." He opened his arms toward his guests. "Is there anything else I can get you now?"

"No, we're good. Thanks," Enid said.

Jack and Enid sat down with Roo at the small table. Jack and Roo drank coffee, while Enid poured a cup of Lady Grey tea.

"Thanks for coming out here, although I would have been happy to come see you at the newspaper office," Roo said.

Jack wiped croissant crumbs from his mouth and laughed. "Are you kidding me? Give this up for bad coffee at the office?"

"How long will you be here?" Enid asked Roo.

"I had actually planned to go home late yesterday, but after meeting you two, I wanted to have time to talk." Roo sipped her coffee. "Why don't we start by you telling me why you were checking on Aunt Cat?"

"I can answer that," Enid said. "I was contacted by Roscoe at the Madden Historical Society. He worked for Miss Murray as an intern while he was completing his master's thesis on small-town historical preservation. He had planned to leave for a full-time job, but Catherine never returned, so he's been covering for her. Now he's worried because she hasn't contacted him. Do you know Catherine's friend Karla, a Native American woman?"

"I met her long ago. Aunt Cat hinted they were related by marriage but hadn't stayed in touch until recently. Aunt Cat married young and her husband died. I don't know anything about him or his family—that was before my time and my mother, well, she wasn't one to dwell on family ties. Aunt Cat has never talked to me about that time in her life, but I'm happy my aunt has such a good friend. Why do you ask?"

"When I met with Roscoe, Karla was there also. She describes herself as an intuitive, and I have to admit that there is something special about her. She helped me with an investigation last year, and her abilities are uncanny. She said she dreamed about Catherine calling out for help."

Roo gasped. "I'm certainly not an intuitive, and I'm not usually a dreamer, but I keep having these weird feelings that

Aunt Cat is in some kind of trouble. Maybe it's just guilt because I haven't stayed in touch."

Jack put his napkin on the table. "Do you know of any other acquaintances that might know where Catherine is?"

Roo shook her head.

"Where would she go if she just wanted to get away?" Enid asked.

"See, that's the odd thing. I've never known Aunt Cat to take a vacation or travel, other than maybe a day trip to Charleston to see me, and that was only once or twice. Sometimes she'd go visit a historical site, but that was usually in the state."

"You said she doesn't have any other relatives," Jack said.

"She's got a few distant cousins, but as far as I know none of them live around here."

Enid pulled Ruby-Grace's card from her worn leather tote, a gift from her ex-husband years ago. "Since you're an insurance investigator, are you looking into your aunt's disappearance in any kind of official capacity?"

"Oh no, not at all. I work as an independent investigator, mostly for smaller insurance companies who don't have their own on staff. I work mostly suspicious death claims and fraud. For years, I worked at a large insurance carrier and was moving up the ladder, as they say. But when my boss got too touchy feely, I filed a sexual harassment charge against him, and that was the end of my illustrious career. I opened my own investigative services company a few years ago. But back to your question. I'm here strictly as a family member." Roo's cell phone vibrated and she pulled it from her pocket. "Sorry, I need to take this." She left the balcony and stepped into the library.

While she was inside, Jack turned to Enid. "I'm going to give the inn to Theo."

Enid sat up straight. "What? But why?"

Jack smiled. "Well, you know he can't afford to buy it. Besides, I really don't want to profit from property I shouldn't even have. When Cassie died, I wasn't able to find any of her family, so I kept it, hoping the right solution would come along. I just want it to go to the right person, someone Cassie would approve of."

The mention of Cassie's name evoked painful memories for Enid. She and Cassie had grown to be close friends, and Jack might have been married to her now, had Cassie's life not ended so tragically.

Before Enid could respond, Roo returned. "Sorry, that was my biggest client. I've got to get back to Charleston. Unfortunately, this is one of my busiest times. But let's stay in touch, and I'll let you know if I hear from Aunt Cat."

CHAPTER 14

After Roo left, Enid stood beside Jack in the library. "I'm going to wait here while you talk to Theo," she said.

"That's not necessary. I have no secrets from you."

"Actually, I don't think I'm ready to accept that you're giving the inn away. I keep thinking of Cassie and what she would think."

"You don't think she would be happy that I'm deeding the inn to someone who has made more profits since he began managing it than any of the other innkeepers before him, including Cassie? If I tried to run the inn myself, it would fail miserably. Is that what you want?"

"No, of course not. But why do you need to change the arrangement you have with Theo now? He gets paid well, plus a percentage of the profits, and the inn makes enough to cover maintenance. What's wrong with that?"

"I'm afraid Theo might return to Boston. After all, he was a chef in a Michelin-rated restaurant. He mentioned he wants to secure his daughter Harriett's future. She's an only child, and he's a single parent. If he moved, I'd have to sell the inn to someone who is far less deserving of it."

Enid cocked her head sideways. "How did you get to be so wise?"

"Just lucky I guess," Jack said, laughing. "Come one, let's go talk to Theo."

As they were leaving the library, Theo approached them. "I just checked Miss Murray out. Is this a good time to talk?"

"Absolutely. Can we just sit here in the library? I've invited Enid to join us."

"Of course." Theo motioned for them to be seated on the huge sofa, and he sat in the chair next to them. "I trust you're happy with the inn's performance?"

"You have done amazing things with this place," Jack said. "You have increased the occupancy rate and stay booked at capacity most of the time. The inn has become a sought-after wedding and shower venue, and your art shows, afternoon teas, and other events are all successful. Your Friday night dinner reservations sell out every week. The guests love you, and you make my life as the inn's owner easy. I appreciate all you've done."

"If you'd like to take over managing the inn, I would certainly—"

"Whoa. Let me stop you right there. I own the local newspaper, a horse ranch, and this inn. I don't need anything else on my plate. Besides, you are irreplaceable."

Theo glanced at Enid for some explanation.

"Jack, tell Theo about your plan, so he can stop wondering what this is all about," she said.

"Sorry, I wasn't trying to be mysterious," Jack said. "Theo, I'd like to deed the inn to you. I'll need to charge you a dollar to make it legal, but the inn would be yours, as long as you agree to stay here and run it."

Theo stared at Jack. "But . . . I'm honored, but I can't afford to buy it."

"Theo, he's giving it to you, with the condition that you stay here," Enid said.

Theo buried his face in his hands. "I'm sorry, I'm just overwhelmed." He wiped his eyes. "Perhaps we can agree on payments over time. I can't let you just give it to me."

"I've been looking for a solution to this situation ever since Cassie passed and willed the inn to me. She has no relatives that I can locate, and even if she did, you're far more deserving than someone who has no interest in preserving the inn. I assume Cassie willed it to me so the inn would be in good hands. She always said she was the steward of it, not the owner. I don't want any of the profits. You hold onto them for future maintenance. You'll need it. But I will put a provision in the contract that in the event you decide later than you want to sell it, I get first dibs on buying it back at current market value."

"I would just give it back to you if that ever happened."

"No, it's your inn, for you and Harriet's future, assuming you want it. You've poured your heart and soul into this place, and it's paid off. You've earned it, Theo."

"Is this what you want?" Enid asked Theo. "Don't do it for Jack. Do it for you and Harriett, if this is what you want."

Theo shook his head.

"Are you saying no?" Enid asked.

Theo threw up his hands. "No, I mean yes. I was shaking my head in disbelief. I can't . . ."

Jack jumped up from the sofa and held out his hand to Theo. "Congratulations to the new owner of the Glitter Lake Inn. I'll have the paperwork drawn up this week."

Enid hugged Theo. "I'm happy for you, and for Harriet." Cassie's image suddenly appeared in Enid's memory. She was smiling. "Cassie would be happy, too."

As Enid and Jack drove back to the newspaper office, they rode in silence until they reached the Madden town limits. "You're a good man, Jack Johnson. And you're right. Cassie would be happy about your decision to give the inn to Theo. I feel like she's truly at peace now."

Jack laughed. "Make a note. You know, that I was right for once."

CHAPTER 15

That afternoon, Enid was sitting at her desk at the newspaper office when her cell phone vibrated. It was Josh.

"Hi, babe," he replied when she answered. "You busy?"

"No, I was just trying to wrap up a few things before I left. I've been wanting to call you to find out about your meeting with the governor, but I didn't want to bother you."

"You are *never* a bother. How about dinner tonight? We can catch up."

"That would be great."

"I'll bring everything to your place and cook. I've got a great new pasta recipe and a bottle of wine I've been saving."

. . .

After dinner, Enid started clearing dishes, and Josh put his hand on her arm. "Let's leave these. I'll help you clean up later. It's cooled down enough to go outside." He took Enid's hand and led her to the screened porch on the back of the house. They sat together on the wicker sofa, holding hands.

"Thanks for cooking dinner. It was delicious. One day, maybe I'll learn to cook more than just roast chicken."

Josh took her hand and kissed the back of it. "You're perfect, even when you burn toast."

"I do not burn toast. Well, okay, maybe I have a few times when you distracted me. That doesn't count. Anyway, tell me about your meeting with the governor."

"I start next week. It's a twelve-month assignment, for now at least."

"Are you looking forward to it?"

"Yes and no. It will be a good change of pace, but I'm afraid it will be very political. I'm not too good at doing dances."

Enid squeezed his hand. "You're perfect just the way you are. Besides, as you said, maybe the spotlight will be off us for a while."

"I hope you're right. I've missed you."

"Same here." Enid eased her hand away from his. "Can I talk to you about Miss Murray?"

Josh laughed. "Still at work, I see."

"This is more personal than work."

"I didn't mean to make light of it. What's going on? Has she shown up yet?"

"No, and I'm worried about her." Enid told Josh about the meeting with Ruby-Grace Murray.

"Well, at least Ruby-Grace is an investigator. Maybe she can find something out."

"Hmmm. Maybe. She's a one-person company and stays busy just making enough to pay the bills. After we met her, I checked her out, and she's legit."

Josh took Enid's hand again. "There's something else bothering you. What is it?"

"Do you think something has happened to Miss Murray?"

Josh shifted in his chair so he could look into Enid's eyes. "I think you're letting your imagination run wild. We've got no reason to think she's been abducted or that anything bad has happened. I know you're worried about her, but let's not assume the worst without any reason to do so."

Enid nodded but felt uneasy. "Let's clean up the kitchen, then we can relax. I hope you brought your toothbrush."

Josh grinned. "Left an extra one here last time."

Enid poured a cup of coffee for Josh, who was sitting at her small dining table looking at his phone. "So, what's on your agenda for today?" she asked. When he failed to answer, she sat down beside him. "That's rude. I hate it when people check emails at the table."

Josh looked up. "Sorry. Looks like I've got another meeting with the governor today. So much for starting next week." He laid the phone on the table. "What about you? What's your day like?"

"Oh, just another day of solving crimes the police couldn't. Or wouldn't."

"Ouch, that hurts." Josh pulled her over and kissed her. "But coming from an award-winning journalist, I'll have to concede defeat."

"Would you like some burnt toast?" Enid asked.

Josh's eyebrows shot up. "Does that mean you want me to distract you?"

Before she could answer, Josh's phone rang. He listened without saying anything until the end. "I'll be there shortly. Make sure you secure the scene." He leaned over and kissed Enid again after ending the call. "Sorry, but I've got to run." He stood to leave but turned back to her. "A body was found near the old barn in Miss Murray's neighborhood, but stay away from there."

Enid's hand flew to her mouth. "Oh, God, no. Please tell me it's not Miss Murray."

"Don't know yet. I'll call you later. Just stay away from the scene, and I'll tell you what I can later. Please."

. . .

Enid drove to the newspaper office and practically ran inside, nearly colliding with Ginger. "Well, aren't we in a hurry this morning," Ginger said.

"Sorry, Ginger. Oh, you're back. Thank goodness. How was your vacation?" Without waiting for a reply, Enid headed down the hallway. "Is Jack in his office? I didn't see his car."

Ginger called out after Enid. "The vacation was great. Thanks for your sincere interest in my life. No, Jack is not here, and with you being a hotshot investigative reporter, I thought you'd already know that."

Enid walked back toward Ginger. "Sorry, I'm a bit distracted this morning. Do you know where he is?"

Ginger shrugged as she walked back to her desk. "Something about a doctor appointment. Said he'd be in later."

"Crap. I was hoping he could go to a crime scene."

Ginger scanned Enid from head to toe. "Something wrong with you that you can't go?"

"No, but . . ." Enid stopped short of telling her Josh had commanded her to stay away. "You're right. There's no reason I can't go. After all, I am a newspaper reporter."

Ginger looked at her. "Yeah, well?"

Enid called out over her shoulder. "Tell Jack to call me when you hear from him."

"Sure thing, Princess."

. . .

As Enid approached Miss Murray's neighborhood, she tried to push from her thoughts what Josh's reaction would be. He wasn't going to be happy, and she'd have to make amends later. At least he wouldn't be sheriff after this week, and maybe their jobs wouldn't cross as often. Whatever concerns she had about upsetting Josh were supplanted by her need to do her job unrestricted.

From all the sheriff's deputies at the old barn, finding the scene was probably going to be easy. She didn't see Josh's black SUV with "Bowman County Sheriff" in white letters across the back. Breathing a sigh of relief, she parked her car a block away and pulled her notepad, pen, and phone from her tote.

As she got closer to the barn, a voice called out to her. "Ma'am. You can't be here. What's your business?"

Enid produced her press card for the deputy.

"Oh, hey, Miss Blackwell. I didn't recognize you. Not that we've ever met, but I've read all your articles." His jaw tightened. "But you still can't be here. Sheriff Hart said no reporters."

So Josh had expected her to ignore his order to stay away. That made Enid smile slightly. "I won't go any closer or contaminate anything, and I'll stay here and observe, you know, as a private citizen. Besides, the body wasn't actually found in the barn, was it?"

"No, ma'am. I mean, I can't talk to you, that is to a reporter, about it." The deputy looked uneasy. "Just stay here. No closer."

Enid glanced at the nametag on the deputy's uniform. "Thank you, Deputy Truluck. I promise not to cause any problems."

"I appreciate that, ma'am."

Truluck walked back toward the barn. He had confirmed the body was not actually there, so where was it? She put her hand over her eyes to shade them from the morning sun and caught a glimpse of a reflection in the woods behind and to the right of the barn. It appeared to be the glint of sun on a windshield. She looked around to see how the vehicles would have gotten to the area. No other roads were evident, other than the one she was parked on. They likely drove through the neglected, overgrown pasture.

"Excuse me," a voice called out from behind Enid, causing her to jump and turn around abruptly. "Sorry, didn't mean to scare you." The woman was in what Enid's mother used to call a house dress, which her mother explained was just a comfortable dress worn at home. It wasn't suitable, at least not by her mother's standards, for wearing outside the house. "I live down the road just over there." She pointed to a small white house. "Do you know what's going on?"

"I'm sorry I don't." Which was true enough. "I'm a reporter just trying to find out myself. Enid Blackwell," she said, holding out her hand.

"Hey, I'm Sylvia."

Enid tried to remember where she had heard that name. "Are you Miss Murray's neighbor?"

Sylvia took a step back. "How would you know that?"

"Miss Murray is a friend of mine, and I asked Sheriff Hart to check on her. He mentioned he had talked to you."

Sylvia squinted her eyes slightly. "Oh. I see. Well, I didn't know much to tell him."

Enid glanced toward the barn. Nothing seemed to be happening, at least not that she could see from this vantage point. "Would you mind if we talked a bit, about Miss Murray, that is? I'm really concerned about her. Especially now."

Sylvia glanced toward the barn herself. "Well, okay. You want to talk here or at my place? We can sit on the porch. Not too hot yet. Now, later in the day, well forget it, especially if you try to sit on my metal chairs."

"That would be nice. I'll follow you." Enid walked slightly behind Sylvia, trying to let her feel like she was in charge. Perhaps that would make her feel a bit easier about talking to a stranger.

After they walked the half block to Sylvia's house, she motioned toward the two metal gliding chairs on the porch. "They're not great, but they're pretty comfy."

"This is fine. Thanks." Enid was glad to sit, as her leg was throbbing again.

"You need some water or anything? I'll go get you some."

"No, I'm fine. And I won't keep you long." Enid's chair glided backward and her feet flew out in front of her as she sat down. "We used to have chairs like this when I was a kid. I forgot that there's a trick to sitting in them gracefully."

Sylvia sat down with an ease that came from practice. "I reckon so."

"When was the last time you talked with Miss Murray, and do you mind telling me what you talked about?"

Sylvia threw back her head and laughed. "I like that about you. You're nosy and don't mind me knowing it. But then, you're a reporter, so I guess that's natural. Let me think a minute." She looked across the street at Miss Murray's house, as though the view would jog her memory. She stopped her glider suddenly by planting her feet firmly on the porch floor. "You know, I had forgotten this, but we talked . . . No, wait. That wasn't the last time we talked. This would have been before that."

"That's fine. What do you remember?"

"Catherine brought some papers over for me to witness her signature. 'Course, she had already signed them before she came over."

"What kind of papers? Do you remember?"

"She never said. Just asked me to witness her signature."

"Was it a lot of papers or just one or two pages?"

"Oh, it was just a few pages."

"But you never saw her sign them. Did you recognize her handwriting?"

Sylvia stopped gliding again. "What are you asking? If I did something wrong, do I need a lawyer?"

"No, you didn't do anything wrong. I'm just trying to figure out what's going on. I didn't mean to alarm you. Like you said, I'm a reporter, and I ask nosy questions. My apologies."

Sylvia smiled. "I like you, Miss." She had apparently already forgotten Enid's name. "You got spunk, but you're nice about it. Anyway, you got me thinking now." She squinted again. "I'm beginning to worry about her myself. Not like her to leave this long without telling me."

"Are there any other neighbors she might have told?"

"Not likely. The rest of the neighbors are all young folks. Look at how they're fixing up these houses." She pointed down the street. "That one added a top to the house, a second story." She pointed to another house. "That one added a whole new kitchen to the back. Pretty soon, it won't be the same around here. Those distribution center folks are moving in and taking over everything."

A young man walked out the front door as they were talking. "Hey," he said to Sylvia. "What's going on?"

"This here is a reporter. She's asking about Catherine across the street," Sylvia said. "And this is my grandson Robert," she said to Enid.

Enid held out her hand, "Pleased to meet you, Robert."

Robert took her hand. "Pleased to meet you, ma'am." He appeared to be either shy or nervous. Enid couldn't decide which, but he was pleasant enough.

"Robert here, he's been keeping up Catherine's yard." Sylvia squinted when she looked up at him. "Haven't you?"

"Yes, ma'am. Been trying to keep the place nice for her. You know, for when she returns."

"I'm sure she'll appreciate that," Enid said. "Did she mention her plans to you at all before she left?"

"No, ma'am. I helped her with a few things on her computer, but she didn't mention anything like that to me."

Enid pulled two business cards from her purse and gave one to each of them. "My mobile number is on here. Please call me if either of you think of anything else, no matter how small the detail." She smiled. "We nosy reporters need all the help we can get from responsible citizens like you." She stood to leave.

"You know what's going on at that barn, don't you?" Sylvia asked.

Enid didn't want to alarm her, but it hardly seemed fair to withhold information since Sylvia was trying to help her. "It's not confirmed, but I believe they found a body near there."

Sylvia jumped up from her chair. "I'm going inside then. Robert, you oughta come in too." Robert glanced at Enid, smiled slightly, and then followed Sylvia. Enid could hear the door lock engaging as they secured themselves inside.

CHAPTER 17

As Enid walked along the edge of the road toward the barn, she could see Josh standing there, looking in her direction, his arms across his chest. She knew that posture. It wasn't a good sign. His official SUV was now parked behind hers. She already knew what he would say: *What part of don't go there did you not understand?*

She kept walking toward him. When she was within earshot, she called out, "Josh, I know you're going to be upset."

As she got closer, he broke out into a loud laugh, causing two of the nearby deputies to look toward him. "Hell, no. I'm not upset. In fact, I appreciate the fact that you have confirmed the order of the universe once again. The sun rises in the East and sets in the West. Hot's on the left and cold's on the right. And Reporter Enid Blackwell does exactly what she wants to, despite my specific request that she not come here. So, thank you, Miss Blackwell. All is well in the universe. Order is maintained."

Enid glanced at the two deputies who were snickering to themselves. "Glad I could be of service, Sheriff. Can you give me an official statement on what you've found?"

Josh relaxed his stance a bit. "No statement at this time."

"Look, Josh, Sheriff Hart, I know you're upset, and if I were anything other than a reporter, you'd have a right to be. But this is my job. You have your job to do, and I have mine."

Josh glanced toward the deputies. "Let's walk down the road a bit." They walked nearly to Sylvia's house before Josh stopped and turned to face Enid. "You're right. I had no right to expect anything different. I shouldn't have told you about the call, but I'm not good at lying to you or withholding information. I apologize for my outburst. I guess this transition is already getting to me."

"This whole thing is hard on both of us. Can you at least tell me whether you're here as the governor's gang liaison or as the sheriff?"

"It's going to be another scorcher today." Josh wiped his forehead and glanced at the sky. "But to answer your question, I came as sheriff, but this looks like it might be a gang hit."

"I haven't mentioned this to you, but when I was checking around the barn a couple days ago, a person in a hoodie was watching me. I think it was a male, but I can't be sure. He never did anything threatening, but it was creepy."

"You should have told me earlier. And you need to be more careful about where you're snooping around. Since this place is abandoned and looks like it might be a hangout for the local kids, the person you saw may have seen something that could help us. We'll check it out. Then you've got to leave. I'll get one of the deputies to take your statement about the person you saw."

"When are you going to issue a statement to the press? I'd like to get a jump on the *State* reporters if I can."

"Here's my statement, and you can use it. 'The body of a young white male was found in Bowman County today. He had no identification on him. We are unable to release the cause or details of his death at this time, pending further investigation.' Will that hold you for a little while?" His voice was much softer now.

Enid finished scribbling in her notepad. "Thanks. I'm relieved it's not Miss Murray, and I'll try to stay out of the way after I give my statement."

"The sheriff's department wants to maintain good relations with the press." He motioned toward the barn. "I think you may be overly anxious about Miss Murray. She's likely just visiting someone. I need to get back. We'll talk later."

Enid wanted to follow him, but she had pushed the boundaries of their relationship as far as she could. No need to make his job any harder than it already was. The sound of an approaching vehicle behind her made her turn around. The county coroner's van was driving toward the barn. As it got closer, it veered to the right across the open pasture, where Enid had seen vehicles earlier.

Even though the body was a young male, Enid was uneasy about the possible gang activity so close to Catherine's home. Looking back toward Sylvia's and Miss Murray's houses, the neighborhood appeared to be one in transition, but at least it looked safe. So much for appearances.

CHAPTER 18

When Enid pulled into the newspaper parking lot, she saw Jack's pickup. Inside, she confronted Ginger. "Did you forget I asked you to have Jack call me?"

"No, I did *not* forget. I told him, but I can't *make* him call you."

Instead of replying, Enid walked past her toward Jack's office.

"He asked to see you when you got back," Ginger called out.

When Enid walked into Jack's office, he was on the phone. He held up a finger to indicate he'd be with her in a minute.

"I'll be there tomorrow," he said, turning his attention back to the call. "How quickly can you take care of it?" Jack took a few notes and then hung up. "Sorry to keep you waiting. I just needed to set up an appointment."

"Ginger said you had gone to the doctor. Is everything okay?"

"Of course. I just need to have a few tests run."

Even though Enid was concerned, she knew that asking more questions would violate the unspoken boundaries she and Jack had established. While they were colleagues and friends, they both knew when to back off. "Do you have a few minutes? I'll tell you about my morning."

Jack pushed back in his chair and smiled. "I can't think of anything else I'd rather talk about right now."

Enid filled him on the discovery of the body. "I've got a statement from Josh, but it's not much." She left out her confrontation with Josh. "By the time we go to print in a couple days it will be old news."

"That's one of the disadvantages of being a weekly newspaper. On the other hand, we write stories that the dailies don't have the space or resources to cover. Don't worry about being the first out the gate with this. Just stay after it. That's what makes you a great reporter—hanging in there when others move on to the next big thing. Sticking with it is what you do best."

"Josh hinted this might be a gang-related killing. Perhaps I could tie it into the research I'm doing."

"Sound good. The sheriff's office will be issuing more information. Let's just make sure we're in the loop. I'm not worried about the *State* newspaper's coverage. They'll quickly move on to the next story." He paused. "It scares me to death to think that you could have been a victim. That's where you cut your leg, right?"

Enid nodded. "I thought of that too." Enid stood to leave when Jack stopped her.

"Have you got a minute?"

She sat down again. "Sure."

"I wanted to make sure you were still feeling good about my giving the inn to Theo. I know it's important to you, and to me, that I do the right thing."

"If there's anyone I can trust to make the right decision, it's you. And I know you trust Theo to preserve the inn and its legacy."

Jack leaned forward in his chair. "Trust is a funny thing. We all want it, but when we get it, it can be a burden. There's so much responsibility that comes with being trusted. When Cassie left the inn to me, I knew she knew that I would try to do what was best. I didn't make this decision about the inn lightly. I've been thinking about it for almost a year. And then . . . well, I decided I'd better stop thinking about it and get it done."

"Sounds like you've already put the gears in motion."

Jack looked puzzled. "Oh, you mean that phone call. That was something else. I'm having my will redone and I need an executor and a power of attorney. I don't want to burden you, but I trust you more than anyone I know. Would you be willing?"

"I . . . I don't know what to say. Don't you have a relative you'd rather appoint?"

"I know it's asking a lot, but I don't really have a lot of choices, as you know. You can think about it."

"No, it's not that. Of course I'll do it."

"Thanks, I'll see my attorney tomorrow to get the papers drawn up. And, just so you'll know, I will have provisions in my will for you. I'd like for you to take the paper, you know, just in case I get hit by a train. Then you can decide whether to sell it. If you do, make sure you get a good price."

"Don't joke about things like that." Enid wanted to ask more questions but stopped herself. Now was not the time.

"Sorry." He raised his hand. "Now go on back to work. I've got things to do too."

CHAPTER 19

When the governor's assistant showed Josh into the office, Governor Larkin was sitting at the large mahogany desk. "Come on in, Josh." He stood and held out his hand. "Good to see you. Have a seat."

Josh sat in the large chair in front of the desk. "Good afternoon, sir."

Instead of sitting back down, Larkin walked from behind his desk and sat in the chair beside Josh. "Thanks for coming in. I know it's a little drive for you to get here. The traffic in Columbia seems to get worse by the day."

"No problem, sir. It was a pleasant drive, actually." Josh didn't explain that anytime he could be alone, even for an hour, was a welcome relief.

"We're both busy men, and you're going to get even busier soon, so I'll get to the point of why I summoned you here." Larkin's jaw tightened.

"Yes, sir."

"There are two things, actually, but let's start with the most important. I heard about the killing in Bowman County. I believe the body was found this morning. Why don't you fill me in on the details."

"We got a call from a citizen walking his dog. When the dog started barking, the man followed him to the site where the body was found. It was a young male, and he was . . ." Josh paused, unsure how much the governor really wanted to hear. "The body was impaled with a large piece of metal that looked like a piece of ornamental fencing, the kind with a pointed top."

Larkin was leaning forward, expressionless. "Go on. I want to hear whatever you know."

"The body was on a makeshift altar of wood pallets."

"Why did you say an altar?"

"For one thing, it was built up to about three feet high. And there were candles around it, along with a few headless chickens." When Josh worked in New Mexico, he had been to several similar scenes.

"Sounds like you are suggesting some kind of satanic worship." Larkin sat back in his chair. "Go on."

"Perhaps. Or just someone trying to make it look like that." Josh paused. "I assume this information will stay with you, sir. There are certain details we wouldn't want to get out yet."

Larkin smiled. "As a sheriff working for the governor of South Carolina, you probably didn't get too much direction, or interference, from me." His smile faded. "But this assignment is different. I expect full disclosure from you. And I know how to hold information close to the vest."

"Sorry, sir. I didn't mean to imply anything, it's just that, well, I'm trying to figure out this new role."

"We'll have to figure that out together. Now go on."

"The victim had the number 14 carved on his stomach. There was so much blood that I didn't see it, but the coroner confirmed it as I was driving here."

Larkin stood up and returned to his seat, the wide desk between them again. "I assume you suspect that's a gang tag for their fourteen-word creed. I can't remember it precisely, but I imagine you've seen it."

"Yes, sir. I'm familiar with it. In fact, the old barn nearby had the 14 tag on it, so I assume it's either a gang hit or someone wanting to throw us off track. It could be a satanic group wanting us to think it's a gang hit, or vice versa. Or it could be both. Some of the gangs, especially Mara Salvatrucha, MS-13, practices such things. They feel the devil is their ally."

Larkin glanced at his watch. "It's sad what this world is coming to. Well, stay on top of it. Your replacement will assume the local investigation. That's no longer your responsibility. But I created this new liaison role because I need direct eyes and ears on these escalating gang activities. It's hard to get unfiltered information when you're the governor. Everything becomes political. We've got to put a stop to these gangs before they get a firm foothold. It's a moral and an economic issue. No one will want to relocate their companies to an area controlled by gangs. That area is prime for new businesses. In fact, the state development council is in conversations now with a large manufacturing company looking for affordable land like the acreage near that barn."

"I understand. Shall I release all my other work to my replacement now also? Sounds like I'm already in the new role."

"That's correct."

Josh was half out of his chair when the governor spoke. "Wait, I said there were two things I wanted to talk to you about."

"Sorry, sir." Josh sat back down in his chair and waited.

"What is your relationship with Enid Blackwell?"

"Sir?"

"I believe you two are in a relationship. Is that correct?"

"We've been seeing each other for more than a year. Has there been some kind of complaint made?" Josh tried to conceal his irritation.

"No, just idle chatter at this point. But I don't have to remind you that while Ms. Blackwell is a small-town newspaper reporter, she has achieved some prominence, some might say notoriety, with her articles on police corruption."

"Sir, I assure you my relationship with Ms. Blackwell has not interfered with or compromised my work in any way, nor will it. In fact, she and I have had this conversation and we are both aware of the potential *appearance* of conflicting interests." Josh paused. "What exactly are you asking me to do? I'm not good at reading between the lines, sir, and that's what this conversation feels like. If you have doubts about me being in this role, I will be happy to step aside and let you find someone you have more confidence in."

Larkin held up both hands. "Whoa, let's not get ahead of ourselves. I appointed you because I know you have the skills and experience to work with me and others working to eliminate this growing cancer in our state. I'm simply asking you to be hypervigilant regarding this situation." Larkin stood and held out his hand. "Now I'm sure you need to get back to work, and so do I. My office will provide you with a list of upcoming task force meetings and other events you'll need to attend. In fact, you may want to consider moving closer to Columbia, but I'll leave that decision to you."

CHAPTER 20

It was nearly nine that night when Enid's cell phone rang. She didn't recognize the number on the screen and decided it was another junk call, which she seemed to be getting a lot of lately. But when she heard the notification that she had a voice mail, she listened to the message. *"Miss Blackwell, this is Sylvia, Catherine Murray's neighbor. I just got a text from her. She said she's visiting a relative and not to worry about her. You asked me to let you know, so that's why I called so late. Goodnight."*

Enid tapped in Sylvia's phone number. After several rings, Sylvia answered. "Hello."

"Sylvia, this is Enid Blackwell. Thanks for calling me. Are you sure it was Catherine who texted you?"

After a brief silence, Sylvia replied. "Well, I guess it was her. Except that . . ."

"What is it?"

"Well, I've never gotten a text from her. I didn't even know she had a pocket phone. But she put her name at the end of the text, so why wouldn't it be her?"

"Can you look at the text and give me the phone number?"

"Sure, hold on." She gave the number to Enid. "That area code, 854, is from around here."

"Thanks. Do me a favor. Can you forward that text to me?"

"Sure. How do I do that?"

Enid explained it to Sylvia. In a few seconds, the text appeared. "Got it. Thanks."

"You don't think it was her?"

"I have no idea, but I'll check it out. Thanks, Sylvia. You've been a big help."

Enid hesitated calling so late, but then again, she needed to know if Catherine Murray was indeed alive and well. When she called the number Sylvia gave her, a different one from the one Roscoe had given her, she got a mechanical voice recorded message with no name. That reporter's instinct she and Jack often joked about told her not to say anything, so she ended the call. Instead, she opened her laptop and logged onto the newspaper's search service and input the number for a reverse search. Nothing came up. She put in Catherine Murray's name and address into the search field. Her land line number, which Enid recognized, was the only phone listed. The tightness in Enid's chest got worse. It was too late to call Roo, but she would do so first thing in the morning.

. . .

After tossing all night, Enid got up early, before the alarm sounded. Then, after a couple hours work at home, she drove to the newspaper office and parked her car. Instead of going inside, she walked down to the historical society.

Roscoe came to the door when she rang the bell. "Oh, Ms. Blackwell, I was just going to call you." He stepped back and gestured for her to come in. "We can sit in here." He pointed to the small sitting room.

Enid sat on the antique velvet sofa. She could feel the springs and was glad she didn't have to sit there long. "Do you have news on Miss Murray?"

Roscoe straightened his maroon and navy bow tie. "There was a message on the phone when I got in this morning. I saved it for you if you'd like to hear it."

"Yes, of course."

Roscoe stood up and motioned for Enid to follow. "Come on back to the office."

Enid was glad to get off the sofa. She followed him to a small back room. It was filled with filing cabinets, a large wooden desk, a banker's chair, and boxes stacked against the wall.

"Sorry for the mess in here. Not much storage in these old buildings." Roscoe played the message of the female voice for Enid.

"I'm calling for Catherine Murray. She asked me to let you know she is unable to return to the historical society at this time and appreciates Roger taking care of everything for her. Please make sure he gets this message."

Enid took her phone from her tote. "I'd like to record that message, if you don't mind. Can you please play it again?" She held the phone closer as Roscoe replayed it. "She called you Roger. That's odd."

"I thought so, too, but then maybe when Miss Murray asked her to call that lady just heard the name wrong."

Enid put her phone away. "Perhaps. But we're making the assumption that call is legitimate. Why didn't Catherine call herself?"

Roscoe's hands flew to his mouth. "I knew it. I knew something was wrong. It is, isn't it?"

"We don't know for sure, but this call came from the same number of a text message her neighbor got last night. But it's a different number from the first text you got. This message was left about ten minutes after the one sent to the neighbor. Makes you wonder why they called you so late. I guess to be sure they didn't have to talk to anyone."

Roscoe clasped his hands together. "What should we do?"

"I'm going to call Roo, that's her great-niece, and see if she knows anything. I'll let you know what I find out. In the meantime, let me know immediately if you get any more messages."

"I will. Oh, Lordy." Roscoe put his hand on his stomach. "I'm feeling sick."

"Try not to worry, okay? I'll be in touch." Enid walked to the front door but then turned back to Roscoe. "How much longer will you be in Madden? I know you need to move on to a full-time job."

"The mayor is still paying me a stipend. She says if Miss Murray doesn't return soon, the historical society will fire her. Imagine that. Miss Murray is an institution in Madden." He clasped his hands again. "They can't just up and fire her. That wouldn't be right."

"Well, maybe we can clear this up soon." Enid smiled, hoping to convince Roscoe that her own worries were unfounded.

CHAPTER 21

When Enid returned to the newspaper office, Ginger was standing by her desk with one hand on her hip. "Where have you been? I saw your car when I came in but couldn't find you anywhere."

"Sorry," Enid said. "I had to run an errand first." She reached into her tote for her notepad. "Can you see if you can find out anything about this phone number?"

Ginger wrote down the number. "Yes, ma'am. I'm on it." She nearly ran back to her desk. Enid made a mental note that she needed to involve Ginger in more research, as she seemed to enjoy it. And she was pretty good at it. Enid walked down the hall toward her office. Jack's office door was shut, which was unusual unless he had someone in there with him. She put her ear to the door but didn't hear anyone, so she tapped on the door. "Jack, are you there?"

She heard the doorknob turn and then the door opened. "Hey, come on in."

"Are you sure? I don't want to disturb you."

"No, it's fine." Jack returned to his desk. "What's up this morning? Ginger was running around here trying to find you. I told her you might be at Sarah's having breakfast."

"No, I went to the historical society. Can I fill you in?"

"Sure."

Enid told Jack about the text to Sylvia and the message for "Roger" left for Roscoe. "I'm going to call Roo in just a few minutes to see if she's learned anything else about what's going on."

Jack rubbed his neck, a tell that he was worried or anxious. "Good idea."

"You haven't been yourself for a while now. I'm starting to worry."

Jack smiled slightly. "It's nice to have someone worry about me, but I'm fine."

Enid glanced at his desk. It was filled with legal documents, long paper with a blue backing. "Are those your new wills?"

Jack glanced at the papers. "Yeah, just going through them. After they're executed, I'll give you a copy since you're my executor. Thanks again for taking on that responsibility."

"Of course. I'm happy to." She stood. "I'm going to call Roo now."

"Sure," Jack said.

Enid returned to her office, trying to push her worries about Jack out of her mind. He was probably just busy and tired. Besides, estate planning wasn't exactly a happy task, which is why she had been putting it off. Now that she was divorced, she needed to have her own will redone. Sadly, she didn't have any close heirs, but she also didn't own much either. There was something to be said for living simply.

She called Roo's number. "Hi, Roo. This is Enid Blackwell. Do you have a minute to talk?"

"Sure, but I'm on my way to Aunt Cat's house. I'll be there in about thirty minutes. Do you want to talk there? I found her house key."

Glancing at the clock, Enid hesitated. She had a story to finish before the end of the day and needed to settle down and complete it. But she wanted to talk to Roo. "Sure, I'll leave now and meet you there."

Enid gathered her things in her tote and told Ginger on the way out where she was going. "You can let Jack know. He looks busy, so I don't want to bother him."

"Do you think Jack's alright?" Ginger asked.

It was unusual for Ginger to express concern, which set off alarms in Enid's head. "I'm sure he's fine. Probably just a lot on his mind."

"He's going to the doctor again this afternoon. And he told me not to mention it to you."

Enid forced herself not to react. "Thanks for letting me know. And let's not jump to any conclusions, okay? If he's like me, he puts everything off for a while and then has to catch up on seeing everyone. I think one of the reasons medical care is so expensive is that there's a specialist for every part of your body."

"I hear you."

C H A P T E R   22

When Enid arrived at Miss Murray's house, Roo was sitting on the front steps on a phone call. Enid stood back to avoid eavesdropping, but Roo motioned for Enid to come sit on the porch.

"I see," Roo said to the person she was talking to. "So there's nothing else you can tell me then?" Roo rolled her eyes upward, looking disgusted. "Can you at least let me know if you hear from her again?" Roo then punched the cell phone to end the call. "Grr. . .!"

"Is everything okay?"

"No. I mean, I don't know. That was Aunt Cat's attorney. He's also an old family friend. When I got here and found out the locks had been changed, I got worried, so I called him. I thought he might know something. I didn't think about calling him earlier."

"Karla mentioned the locks. She said something about Catherine having them changed after some repairs were done. Does the attorney know where she is?"

"I don't think so, but I'm not sure. He said any conversations with her or about her were confidential. But he did tell me he's no longer her attorney. He said he got a letter from her stating that she had retained a new attorney to update her estate planning documents *and* to name a new power of attorney."

"Would he tell you who the new attorney is?"

"He claims he doesn't know, and I doubt he'd lie to me. He's an attorney, right? I just can't believe Aunt Cat would make someone else her POA. She really doesn't have any other close relatives. Just a few distant cousins here and there, and she always said they were bottom feeders."

Miss Murray had always seemed so proper, and it was difficult for Enid to imagine her using that phrase. Apparently, there were a lot of things about Catherine Murray that were a surprise. Enid pointed across the street to Sylvia's house. "I talked to her neighbor, and she remembered witnessing some legal documents for Catherine a few weeks ago, right before she . . ."

Roo threw her hands up. "I know, right? Do we say she's missing or what? All I know is I'm really starting to worry now. First, she changes the door locks, and then she replaces me with god-knows-who as her medical and personal power of attorney." Roo jumped up from the steps. "Come on."

"Where are we going?" Enid asked as she followed Roo to the back of the house.

Roo was digging around in her messenger bag. "I know I've got . . . Wait, here it is." She pulled out a metal tool several inches long.

"Please tell me that's not what I think it is."

"It's a hook pick. Usually works pretty good on these old locks. I kept telling Aunt Cat to put deadbolts on her doors."

Enid glanced around. "We can't break in. What if we get caught?"

Roo looked up at Enid. "You can leave." She put the pick in the door and jiggled it around a few times until it clicked. "That was easy." Roo turned the door handle. "You coming in or leaving?"

"Roo, I don't know about this. Even if we find something, we'd have to admit you broke in."

Roo laughed. "And here I thought you were this brave investigative newspaper reporter." She walked inside the kitchen. As Enid followed Roo inside, she tried not to think what Josh would say if he knew she was an accomplice to breaking and entering. Roo flipped the light switch but there was no power. She stepped over to the refrigerator and opened the door. "Ugh." It was full of spoiled food.

Enid took the tail of her blouse and pushed on the back door to close it. If this became a crime scene, no point in leaving prints.

"Come on, let's look around," Roo said. She was already down the hallway before she finished talking.

Enid used her blouse tail again to turn the lock on the kitchen door. After all, a killing had taken place just up the road, and whoever did it was still out there. She could hear Roo walking around the house on the shiny, waxed hardwood floors. Enid walked toward the dining room. It was a small area with a maple dining table, six chairs, and a large matching china cabinet. The pattern on the dishes was a familiar one from the 1950s: tiny pink roses with bits of green leaves and gold around the edges of the plates and saucers. Her mother had owned a similar pattern. Enid often used her dining table for multiple uses, like eating, conferences, and paperwork, so she assumed Catherine might do the same. Pushing aside her concerns about leaving prints, Enid pulled open a large drawer in the china cabinet. It was stuck and hard to pull. As she tugged on it, the china pieces clinked against each other. She lifted the drawer slightly by the handles and pulled again. This time it opened.

Inside the drawer was a mixture of tarnished silverware, a cork from a wine bottle, and a stack of papers. Most looked like old, paid bills. She lifted out a stack carefully and laid the papers on the table.

"Enid, come here," Roo called from one of the back rooms. "I found something."

"Coming." Enid placed the papers back in the drawer and with both hands was able to get the drawer shut again. "Where are you?"

"In the bedroom. Down the hall."

Enid walked past one bedroom that appeared to be a guest room. Roo was in the bedroom next to it, sitting on the bed. She was holding a small box in her hand.

"What is that?" Enid asked.

Roo was holding a small, metal file box. She lifted the lid. "This is proof."

"What do you mean?"

"This box is where Aunt Cat kept all her important papers. You know, life insurance policies, her will. Things like that. But it's empty." Roo frowned. "I can still hear her saying to me, 'Ruby-Grace, if something happens to me, everything you need to know is in this box.' Well, now I need to know and there's nothing here."

"And what about Catherine's mail? Have you seen any?"

"No, I checked the mailbox and looked around the house. Even if I am a relative, I know the post office won't tell me if she's having it forwarded."

"We need to go to the police. I know the sheriff. Well, he was the sheriff. But he can still tell us what to do."

Enid put her arm around Roo's shoulders. "Maybe we'll find her soon, and she'll laugh and apologize for making us worry."

Roo pulled away from Enid and turned to look at her. "You don't really believe that, and neither do I."

Enid nodded. "You're right. Things aren't looking good here."

CHAPTER 23

Enid unlocked the front door of her house and directed Roo to the multipurpose room used as a guest room and home office. "It's not fancy, but the sheets on the futon sofa are clean and there's plenty of space in the closet for your things. The guest bath is right there in the hallway," she said, pointing.

"It's really nice of you to let me stay here. After we talk to your sheriff guy tomorrow, I'll head back to Charleston. I am a working girl, after all. Got a couple of urgent messages I need to return soon."

"You're more than welcome. Besides, I enjoy the company. I love the peace and solitude here, but it gets a little too quiet sometimes. Just make yourself at home."

"Thanks."

"I need to check in with the office and then finish an article." Enid glanced at the time on her cell phone. "It's due in an hour."

"This looks like where you work. I'll go sit on the porch and get out of your way."

Enid laughed. "No, I'm fine. I've learned to work anywhere I can plug in my laptop. Just let me know if you need anything. We'll grab something to eat later."

"That's okay. I don't eat dinner too often. If you've got a cold glass of tea and some saltines and cheese or peanut butter, I'll be fine."

"Sounds like my kind of food. We'll talk later."

Enid sat at the small dining table and finished the article. She uploaded it for Jack to edit and then called Ginger. "Hey, just thought I'd check in."

"Where have you been? Never mind, I know where you said you were going but you've been gone a long time."

"Sorry. Anybody looking for me?"

"Not really. Jack didn't come back after he saw the doctor. He's working from home."

Enid sat up straight. Jack usually didn't work at home because his internet service was so slow. "Why is that?"

"No idea. I'm getting ready to lock up and leave unless you need something."

"That's—"

"Wait, sorry to interrupt, but I almost forgot to tell you. You know that phone number you gave me to check out? Well, it's a burner phone."

"A burner? You're sure?"

"Yep. I've got my sources."

"Okay, thanks for checking it out. Let me know if you hear from Jack."

"Enid, someone's at your door," Roo called out from the hallway.

"Gotta go," Enid said to Ginger." Then she called out to Roo, "Thanks, I'll get it." Enid walked to the door and peeped out one of the translucent glass panels that framed it. She pulled the door open. "Jack? What a surprise." He looked even more tired than he had this morning.

"Sorry to drop in unannounced, but . . . I didn't know you had company." He motioned toward Roo who was standing behind Enid. "Hi, Roo. Nice to see you again."

"Hi, you too."

Enid gestured for Jack to come inside. "Roo's just staying here a couple days."

"Mind if I come in? There's something I need to ask you."

"I'm going to head back to my room," Roo said.

"Thanks, Roo," Enid said. "Would you like a glass of tea or wine?" she asked Jack.

"You got any of that expensive Texas bourbon left?"

"You mean the one you gave me to keep here in case you needed it? As I recall, you instructed me not to give it to you unless it was a front-page-news day." When she saw Jack's expression change, she was immediately sorry she had said it. "Want it with water or soda?"

"On the rocks." Jack sat on the sofa.

Enid poured a jigger of Garrison Brothers Balmorhea Bourbon in a glass and added a few ice cubes. For the most part, she didn't drink liquor, but she had to admit this prize-winning bourbon tasted more like bourbon candy: a combination of amaretto coffee, chocolate, and pecan brittle. She poured another glass for herself. If this was going to be a headline-news night, she needed fortification.

"Thanks," Jack said, taking the glass from her. Enid sat down beside him and waited while he sipped the caramel colored liquid. "Ah, that's good," he said. "I would never pay what this cost. Thank goodness it was a gift from one of my wealthy acquaintances." He sat his glass down on the table. "First, I want to hear what's going on with you."

Enid filled him in on what they had discovered at Miss Murray's house, and the red flag Roo raised with the empty documents box.

"I admit, those are not good signs."

"I forgot to mention that Roo found out she was no longer Miss Murray's power of attorney. The former attorney told Roo about the change. Well, sorta off-the-record told her."

Jack sipped his bourbon. "We need to have more of these kind of nights." His smile faded. "But the POA info changes Catherine's situation." He sat his glass on the table. "As I understand it, Miss Murray takes off and leaves Roscoe hanging at the historical society. Then you find out she's left for who-knows-where, and all of her important papers are missing. And she changes her attorney and her power of attorney." He exhaled loudly. "Taken all together, I agree with you and Roo. This doesn't look good. One thing in particular concerns me, and that's the change of power of attorney. That person, at some point, may have total control over her and her finances. You have to be careful that you select someone who will not breach that trust. And if what Roo says is true, the only person close enough for Murray to trust is Roo. Or, what about Karla? Have you talked to her again? Maybe Miss Murray made her the POA."

"I haven't heard from Karla, but that's not so unusual. She's a free spirit that drifts in and out. But I do need to talk to Karla, Roo, and Roscoe together, so we can compare notes. Maybe we can meet at the historical society tomorrow, although I have no idea how to reach Karla. Miss Murray was always the one who arranged my contact with her. I'll ask Roscoe if he knows how to reach her." Enid sipped her bourbon. "I could get addicted to this. It would be great drizzled over Sarah's homemade peach ice cream."

Jack laughed. "Now you're making me hungry."

"Don't you think we need to report Miss Murray as missing? I was thinking of asking Josh to help."

"I think there's enough evidence to indicate something is not right, and I agree that you and Roo need to report it, get it on record. By the way, I got your article on Josh's appointment to his new position. It'll run in tomorrow's paper."

"So you got the paper ready?"

Jack made a face at Enid. "Of course. Did you think I wouldn't? When have I ever missed an edition?"

Enid blushed. "Sorry, it's just that Ginger . . . Well, I'm just glad everything is okay." She had promised Ginger not to mention Jack's doctor appointments.

Jack cleared his throat. "Well, that's what I wanted to talk to you about."

Enid felt the air leave her lungs. "What's wrong?"

Jack rubbed his neck and looked at the floor. "There's no easy way to say this. I have stage three prostate cancer."

Enid's hands flew to her mouth. "Oh, no. Jack, how . . .? Are they sure? You're too young, aren't you?"

Jack took her hands in his. "Leave it to me to beat the odds. My father got it at an early age also. I'm just lucky it was caught, since they don't usually screen for it until you're at least fifty."

Enid squeezed Jack's hands. "So how did your doctor find it?"

"I was having some problems, and lucky for me, the doc wanted to do a complete screening of everything."

"Thank goodness." Enid pulled her hands away gently. "I don't know what to say. How will they treat it?"

"There're all kinds of drugs they can use to suppress testosterone production. Please don't worry. They can work miracles these days, and it was caught before becoming stage four. That's a miracle."

Enid wiped away the tears streaming uncontrollably down her cheeks. "What can I do to help you?"

"Just continue being the good friend that you are. By the way, I feel bad about not telling you all this before you agreed to be my executor and POA. If you want to change your mind, I'll understand."

"Don't be silly. I'll do anything I can to help you." She paused. "But what would I do if something happened to you? You're my best friend, my mentor, my . . ."

Jack pulled her closer to him. "Please don't cry. I can't stand to see you upset. Everything will be fine. The odds are really good these days. I promise."

Enid nodded, not trusting herself to speak.

"But I will miss some time from work here and there for treatments and appointments. I'll try not to slack off too much." He wiped an errant tear from her chin. "I'll tell Ginger and others. I'm not trying to keep it a secret. People have a right to know, especially if it affects them. I just wanted you to know first."

"I appreciate that. Do you have someone who can help you run the paper?"

Jack smiled. "Remember that conversation we just had about trust? You're the only person I trust to run the paper if I'm not there."

"I'm a reporter, not an editor, and I certainly don't have any experience running a newspaper. Wouldn't you feel more comfortable getting someone with experience?"

"It's not like I'll be incapacitated. I'll be there to help you when you need it. We'll make it work. Together."

"As I said, I'll do whatever I can to help. I just don't want to let you down." She leaned over and kissed Jack on the cheek. I love you, dear friend. Please get well."

CHAPTER 24

The next morning, Enid and Roo arrived at the Madden Historical Society just as Roscoe drove up in his green Mini Cooper. "Hello, ladies. Come on in," he said as he unlocked the front door.

Enid and Roo followed him inside. "Thanks for meeting with us on short notice," Enid said. She introduced Roo and Roscoe.

"Isn't that cute, Roo and Roscoe," Roscoe said. "Sounds like a, well, actually, I'm not sure what it sounds like, but it's cute." He grinned. "Don't you think?"

"Do you always smile that much?" Roo asked him.

Roscoe looked shocked. "Yes, I suppose I do. I mean, why not?" He turned to Enid. "Do I smile too much?"

Enid laughed. "No, Roscoe, you're perfect just as you are."

"I was just asking," Roo said. "Didn't mean to hurt your feelings. Sometimes I'm too outspoken. My apologies." She stuck out her hand. "Friends?"

Roscoe shook Roo's hand. "It's okay. I'm just a bit sensitive. At least that's what I've been told. Anyway, want coffee or tea?" Both Enid and Roo shook their heads. "Okay, then let's go in here to talk."

After they were all seated, Enid turned to Roscoe and told him what they had discovered at Catherine's house. His eyes widened and he put his hands to his mouth. "Oh, my. This doesn't sound like Miss Murray at all."

"Do you have any way to get in touch with Karla?"

Roscoe appeared to be thinking. "I don't think so. She just showed up here that day, the day we talked about Miss Murray's . . ." He paused. "Is she really missing?"

Roo stood up. "I'm tired of tiptoeing around this subject. Yes! She is missing, alright?" She sat down again. "Sorry for the outburst, but I'm really worried now." She turned to Enid. "I haven't told you yet, but I talked to a friend of mine at one of the life insurance companies where I do contract work. He wouldn't confirm whether Aunt Cat had changed her beneficiary, but he didn't deny it either. You know, ethics, confidentiality, and all that."

Roscoe was swaying back and forth in his seat. "Oh, my. Oh, my," he repeated.

Roo said to Enid, "I'll try to find Karla Burke. That's what I do, find people. Well, one of the things I do. But, as I said, I don't know much about her."

"If Karla is a psychic, we could sure use her help right now," Roscoe said.

"She told me she doesn't have any psychic powers," Enid said. "She just intuitively knows things. But not everything, and not all the time."

"Sounds like a psychic to me," Roo said. "Does she take clients? If so, she'll have a Facebook page, maybe a website. Anyway, I'll start trying to find her."

"And I'm going to meet with the sheriff, well, used-to-be-sheriff Josh Hart. He can give us some guidance."

"What can I do?" Roscoe asked.

Roo spoke up. "Look through everything you can find of Aunt Cat's. Correspondence, emails, address books, that kind of stuff."

"I couldn't do that," Roscoe said. "That's snooping."

Roo cocked her head and looked at him. "For real? If you find anything interesting, let me know." She pulled a crumpled business card from her pocket. "You can reach me here."

CHAPTER 25

Josh was walking just outside the perimeter of the crime scene when he got the text message to call Enid. She would have to wait, because another body had been located several miles from the old barn. This time it appeared to be female. The body had been burned and mutilated nearly beyond recognition. As an undercover cop in New Mexico, Josh had seen a lot of violence and hatred, but now he feared the entire world was losing its humanity.

"Any idea who she was?" he asked the new Bowman County Sheriff, John Stanholt.

Stanholt stared at Josh a moment before responding. "Looks like the governor thinks it's a gang hit. Otherwise, why would you be here?"

Of all the people Josh would have picked to replace him as county sheriff, Stanholt would have been near the bottom of the list. Josh had recommended a deputy who had a master's degree in criminology and had been certified in computer forensics, but Governor Larkin had the final say, and he had picked an old friend and political ally. "Just doing my job. I'm not here to interfere or get in your way."

Stanholt pointed toward the body in the black coroner's bag. "Probably some guy offed his old lady."

"She looks like early thirties, from what I can see."

"Hard to tell. She could be younger but just had a hard life. Part of her clothing was torn off before they, well, as you can see, they cut her up bad. That outfit doesn't look like something a housewife would wear. Probably worked the streets."

Josh glanced back at the nearby neighborhood. "Anybody reported missing?"

"We're looking into it. Anything in particular I can help you with?"

Josh pointed toward the 14 that had been sprayed on the ground in that orange paint that landscapers use to mark plant beds. "You seeing that 14 tag around anywhere else lately?"

Stanholt looked at the numbers. "No, can't say I have. What's the significance of 14?"

Josh explained the gang's fourteen-word creed. "Could just be a prank, but if you would, keep an eye out for this or any other gang tags you see." Josh handed him a business card. "Here's my new phone number. Give me a call if you see anything."

Stanholt slipped the card in his pocket without looking at it. "Sure thing. Now I need to get back to work."

Like the killing near the old barn, this appeared to be a gang hit, confirming Josh's fears that WS14 was active in this area. With nothing else he could do here, he decided to visit Sylvia again while he was nearby.

He parked in front of Sylvia's house and walked to the front door. There was no answer and no sign of activity. Her old Impala was still parked in the driveway, and all the blinds were closed. He knocked on her front door, then waited and knocked again. "Ma'am, it's Josh Hart. We talked about Miss Murray. Could I speak to you?" He put his ear to the door but heard nothing.

He walked past the car toward the back of the house. A five-foot cyclone fence surrounded the back yard and there was a padlock on the gate. Josh returned to the front of the house and knocked again.

With no answer, he decided to walk over to Miss Murray's house. He was nearly across the street when a white van nearly ran him down. "Hey, watch it," he yelled. He couldn't see the driver's face. From his brief glimpse of the profile, it could have been a woman or a thin man with long hair. There was a blonde passenger who was clearly female. She gave him a middle finger salute as they sped away. "Idiots," Josh shouted at them. But by then, they were halfway down the block.

He walked to the front door and rang the doorbell. He didn't expect anyone to answer, but it was worth a try. The blinds were all closed, so he couldn't see anything inside. He walked around to the back of the house, and his hand instinctively went to his gun. The back door was standing wide open. The upper half of the door was glass, and the thin floral curtain over it blew in the breeze. "Anybody here?"

Josh stepped inside the small mud room area that was between the back door and the kitchen. When he stepped inside, the floorboard squeaked. He froze and waited. "Is anybody here?" he called out again.

When he first stepped into the kitchen area, nothing seemed disturbed. He pulled a rubber glove from his pocket and opened the refrigerator door. It was nearly empty, other than a package of some kind of meat that looked spoiled. He turned to look at the wall behind him, where a large white porcelain sink overlooked the backyard. When he looked out the window, he had a clear view of a small white storage building near the end of the property. Across the front, 14 was sprayed on the double doors in red paint.

CHAPTER 26

Before Josh could call Sheriff Stanholt to tell him what he had found, his cell phone vibrated. He looked at the screen: Enid. She had called earlier, and it was unusual for her to call twice, so he answered. "Hi, sorry I haven't had a chance to call you back."

"And I'm sorry to bug you, but we need to talk. Soon."

"I'm at a crime scene." Josh immediately regretted saying it. But Enid couldn't stop being a reporter, any more than he could stop being a cop. "I can't tell you any more right now." Governor Larkin's warning about Enid was still on his mind. "I'm not sure when I'll leave here, but I'll check with you later."

"What kind of crime scene?"

"Please don't ask. I'll tell you what I can when I see you."

"I have a house guest."

"Oh, well, I guess we could meet somewhere else." Josh tried to control his imagination. Was it Cade? Sometimes ex-husbands had a way of showing up.

"No, in fact, Roo and I both need to talk to you."

"Rude?"

Enid laughed. "No, R-O-O. Roo, you know, like kanga-roo. Remember Dr. Seuss? Never mind. Her name is actually Ruby-Grace. I'll fill you in when you get here."

Josh hated to admit he was relieved her guest was a female. He trusted Enid, but they had been drifting apart, and he couldn't blame her if she wanted to see someone else. And he had to deal with Larkin's admonishment at some point. But for now, he needed to report what he had found at Miss Murray's house.

Josh then called Sheriff Stanholt, who showed up within minutes. Josh waited on the front porch and watched as Stanholt got out of his vehicle. He didn't look too happy.

"I suppose there's a good explanation about why you wandered down here and checked out this house." Stanholt looked around the neighborhood. "This used to be a nice place. I remember the mother of one of my friends lived here."

"There's not much industry around here to keep folks from moving away. Most of what's left are retired widows."

"And you're here for what reason?" Stanholt asked.

"This house belongs to Catherine Murray. She's the town historian for the Madden Historical Society. A couple of her friends asked me to do a welfare check on her, you know, when I was still sheriff. So I checked it out."

"I take it you're still looking for her."

"She hasn't shown up yet. I don't know if she's missing or just failed to let her friends and great-niece know where she is." Josh pointed across the street to Sylvia's house. "That's where one of Murray's friends lives, over there." Josh decided not to offer that he had just been to her house.

"You said you found evidence of gang activity at Murray's house, so let's take a look at it." Stanholt headed to the front door. "This isn't a crime scene, is it? I don't want to contaminate it."

"I didn't search the whole house. You're the local in charge, and I didn't want to step on your turf. But with the two gang-style killings just up the road, this doesn't look good."

"I'm going to get gloves from the car. Need some?"

"Got some here." Josh patted his pants pocket.

Stanholt returned and tried to open the front door. It was locked. "How'd you get in?"

"Back door."

Stanholt walked down the porch steps and around the side of the house. Josh followed behind him. The sheriff glanced at the open back door and radioed for one of his deputies to come take photos.

Josh pointed toward the shed in the yard and the 14 symbol sprayed on it. "There's the tag."

"I'm going to check the rest of the house first." Stanholt led the way into the kitchen and pointed toward the back door. "You stay here and watch my back."

Josh positioned himself so he could see out the back window while watching the door. He glanced around the kitchen area but nothing looked unusual. No dishes were in the sink, and nothing appeared to be out of place, other than the door frame was damaged. Whoever came in used a crowbar or something similar to pry open the old lock. If Catherine Murray was on a planned trip, she either forgot to empty the refrigerator first or ended up staying longer than she'd planned. She was at the age where people sometimes forget things. Although it was hard to explain why the electricity was turned off, unless the bill just hadn't been paid.

A few minutes later, Stanholt joined him. "Nothing unusual that I could find."

"We need to secure that back door. Otherwise, we'll have squatters in here soon."

Stanholt nodded and waved his arm. "All of this looks like juvenile vandalism to me. They probably broke in, didn't find anything of value, and then tagged the shed out there as a prank."

"Maybe. Let's go check the shed."

This time the sheriff followed Josh. The wooden storage building was approximately twenty feet from the back of the house. A lock hasp was on the double doors but there was no padlock and nothing to suggest it had been forcibly removed. Josh put one hand on his holstered gun and opened the door with the other. As sunlight filled the space, a stack of cardboard boxes and rusted garden tools came into focus. "Looks like junk," he called out to Stanholt. "If you don't need me here, I've got something to take care of."

"We got this. You go on." Stanholt looked happy Josh was leaving.

CHAPTER 27

Sitting in the rocker on his front porch sipping bourbon, Jack watched the fireflies light up the night. He thought of the Balmorhea he had shared with Enid. It would be too easy to lean on her emotionally, but she didn't need that. Neither did he.

When his wife died of cancer years ago, he thought his world had ended. And it did, for a while. Slowly, over several years, he had rebuilt his life, mostly by throwing himself into his work at the newspaper. At that time, it was the *Madden Gazette,* a weekly publication covering mostly local events. A couple years ago, he bought two ailing weeklies in bordering counties and transformed the newspaper into the *Tri-County Gazette,* a weekly paper with broader coverage. Did he do it to keep Enid around? He had asked himself that question several times. With her journalist and investigative skills, she wouldn't stay at a small-town paper very long. Or did he do it for himself? He had to admit he had become bored editing the *Madden Gazette* that covered only the small town.

What would happen to the newspaper if he had to give it up? Enid had no interest in running it, and he couldn't blame her. She loved reporting, and the administrative work would eat up her time. He'd worry about the newspaper later. The doctor had encouraged him to carry on his life as usual, with a few precautions: plenty of rest, exercise, healthy foods.

Tomorrow, he would sign the inn over to Theo. At least he could feel good about that. When Cassie died and left it to him, he vowed to keep the old inn going as long as he could. He was lucky Theo came along when he did. He was made to be an innkeeper and had shown good business acumen as well.

Jack took another sip of bourbon. Trust was a funny thing. A person was lucky if he had one person he could trust with his life. Jack knew he could trust Enid and Theo, if the need arose.

The stillness of the night was pierced by his cell phone's ring. Cade Blackwell's name appeared on his screen. "Hey, buddy. How are you?" Jack asked. He listened as Cade talked. "Sure, I'd love to have you visit. Everything okay with you?" Jack smiled as Cade invented an excuse to come visit. Enid must have told him about Jack's cancer, and his long-time buddy Cade was coming to cheer him up. Jack smiled. "I look forward to seeing you."

Jack went inside and pulled the door shut behind him.

CHAPTER 28

Roo checked with most of Catherine's known, distant cousins and anyone else who might know where she could be. Nobody knew anything. There were a couple cousins she had heard of, or vaguely remembered from long-ago reunions when Roo was much younger, but she couldn't find them. She couldn't even remember the last names of some, as they were like strangers to her. The sad fact was their family just wasn't close. Even she and Catherine had drifted further apart in recent years.

While Roo was telling Enid about the list of people she had contacted, they nibbled on a tray of snacks Roo had pulled together. Unlike Enid, Roo was at home in the kitchen, but made no pretense of being fancy about it and often served food in the plastic containers from the grocery store.

Enid pushed thoughts of Jack out of her mind. "I wish we could find Karla Burke."

"Why is that? Do you think she knows something we don't?"

Enid laughed. "Well, I guess that would be true since she's an intuitive."

Roo threw up her hands, laughing with Enid. "Of course!"

"It's good having you here," Enid said. "I wish it were under happier circumstances."

"Do you get lonely living in this small town?"

"I really hadn't thought about it until Jack . . ."

"Your boss?" Roo slapped her hands on the table. "No way. Are you two, well, you know . . ."

"No, we're just friends. But he's my best friend, and he's having some health issues right now."

Roo took Enid's hands in hers. "I'm so sorry. You must be worried to death."

"I'm trying to stay positive about it." The sound of a car in the driveway interrupted them. "That must be Josh. I'm anxious for you to meet him."

"Wait, you've got two men?" Roo winked at her. "You vamp, you."

"Oh, please. Stop it." Enid opened the front door and Josh was standing there. "Come on in."

Enid introduced Roo and Josh. Afterward, Roo stood back and studied him, then looked at Enid. "Well, he's eye candy, that's for sure, but I'll let you know later if he's good enough for you."

Josh blushed. "Thanks, I'll do what I can to pass your test." He followed Enid and Roo to sit at the dining table. "What's all this?" He pointed to their notes scattered across the table.

"These are the people Roo has already contacted, and now we're making a list of hospitals to call." Enid saw the change in Josh's expression. "What's wrong? Have you found out something about Catherine?"

Josh looked at Roo. "We found some vandalism at your aunt's house earlier today."

"We were just there and didn't see anything," Roo said. "It must have been done after we left. What kind of damage was it?"

Josh described the broken lock on the back door and the 14 sprayed on the storage building.

Enid gasped. "Oh, no. That's the gang tag you found at the old barn. You don't think . . ." She stopped and looked at Roo. "Let's not jump to conclusions. Whoever did it probably just discovered no one was at the house and decided to play a prank."

"Or a gang has taken over Aunt Cat's house," Roo said.

Enid turned to Josh. "What are you going to do?"

"The sheriff, John Stanholt, is in charge of the investigation," Josh said.

"But isn't there something you can do?" Enid asked.

Josh dropped his head and then looked up at Enid. "I can't get involved. The governor is already upset that you and I have a relationship. In fact, he's warned me against seeing you."

"That's a bunch of crap!" Roo yelled. "Sorry. As I told Enid, I get excited easily."

Josh laughed. "I'll remember that. And, while we may all think it's crap, he's my boss. And not just any boss, he's the governor, so I don't want to get on his bad side."

Roo stood up. "I have some work to do for a client, and I think you two need time to catch up and figure all this out."

After Roo went to the guest room and shut the door, Josh suggested they sit on the porch. "It's cooled down enough."

"I'll get us a glass of wine and be there in a minute."

When Enid joined him a few minutes later, Josh had leaned back in the rocker with his eyes closed. "Are you tired or is it something else?" she asked.

Josh sat up and took the wine glass. He then proposed a toast. "To us. May we find a way to survive all this crap." They tipped glasses.

"Maybe I shouldn't ask this, but are you sorry you took this new position?"

"I'm not sure I'm ready to answer that. It's way more political than I ever imagined, and now it's yet another barrier for us."

"I hate to add to your already gloomy mood, but I need to tell you something."

Josh leaned back and rocked gently, so as not to spill his wine. "Go ahead. I'm braced."

"Jack has cancer."

"What?" Josh sat up quickly and spilled his wine on his trousers.

"Let me go get a towel. Be right back." Enid hurried into the house and came back with a dish towel in her hand. "Hold still." She blotted the wine, removing as much as she could. "Maybe the dry cleaners can get the rest out."

Josh took her hand. "Sit down and tell me more about Jack."

Enid sat on Josh's lap and laid her head on his shoulder. "He's got stage three prostate cancer."

"I thought he'd be too young for that."

"That's what I said, but it does happen. I'm just glad they caught it."

Josh stroked Enid's hair. "What's his prognosis?"

"It's good. He'll start treatment soon. And . . ."

"And what?"

"He's asked me to help manage the newspaper, if it becomes necessary." Enid kissed Josh, and he wiped the tears from her face.

"I know you're worried about him. I am, too, but let's not assume the worst."

Enid nodded. "I agree. Between Catherine's disappearance and Jack's cancer, I'm just feeling a little emotional right now. Not to mention that your boss has forbidden you to see me."

"We'll just have to be more discreet." Josh stroked her hair again. "How long will Roo be here?"

"Just a couple days. She's got a lot of work to do around Charleston. I'll help her as much as I can. I'm also going to talk to Jack about doing an article on choosing the right power of attorney. I never realized how much control the person you appoint has over your life until Jack asked me to be his. It's kinda scary."

"Not if you choose the right person, but I agree you have to be careful."

"Should I report Catherine's disappearance to the sheriff's office?"

"I think you should." Josh looked at his watch. "As much as I hate to, I've got to go. I have to write a report tonight."

Enid held him closer until he kissed her and gently pulled away. "I really do have to go."

As Enid watched Josh leave, loneliness overcame her with nearly the same fierceness as when her mother died. Everyone she was close to seemed to be drifting away.

CHAPTER 29

Roo led the way to the information desk at the Bowman County sheriff's office. "I'm the relative, so I need to do this."

"Can I help you?" the female deputy asked Roo.

"We, that is me, I would like to file a missing person's report."

"Does this person live in Bowman County?" the deputy asked.

Roo glanced at the name on the deputy's shirt. "Yes, Deputy Wallace, she lives in your county. Otherwise, we wouldn't be here."

Enid stepped up to the desk, giving Roo a sideways glance. "Ruby-Grace is naturally worried about her great-aunt. If we could talk to someone and file a missing persons report, we'd appreciate it."

Roo turned her head to look at Enid and then looked back at the deputy. "Yes, we *would* appreciate it." She flashed an exaggerated smile.

The deputy looked at Roo, then responded to Enid. "Have a seat, and I'll have someone help you."

"Thanks," Enid said.

After they sat in the metal chairs against the wall, Enid turned to Roo. "I'm sorry to have stepped in, but you know how the saying goes. 'You catch more flies with honey than vinegar.'"

"I know, I know. It's just that her stupid question irked me. Does she really think we drove all the way from another county to report it?"

Enid saw Deputy Wallace glaring at them. "Shh. You're not making any friends here."

Roo flipped through several years-old *Good Housekeeping* magazines, while Enid looked around the waiting area. If Josh could have handled this report, it would be so much easier. But things had changed.

"Ruby-Grace Murray," the deputy called out. "Follow this officer," she said, pointing to a young male deputy.

Enid and Roo followed him down the hall to a desk he pointed out. They sat in two chairs, just like the metal ones in the waiting area. Less than a minute later, a tall deputy with silver hair greeted them and introduced himself. "I'm Deputy Hyatt. You want to file a missing person's report?"

"Yes, that's what I told—"

Enid kicked Roo's foot. "Yes, she would."

"Which one of you is filing this report?"

"I am," Roo responded. "I'm her great-niece."

The deputy turned in his chair slightly so that he was facing the computer screen. "Your name?" Roo spelled her name, emphasizing it was hyphenated. She answered a series of routine questions, like when she last saw Catherine Murray and whether there had been any life events that might have caused her to leave voluntarily. Roo shook her head and then told him about Roscoe at the Madden Historical Society.

Enid gave the deputy the address and phone number there. "She wouldn't leave Roscoe hanging like that. She was, is, the most responsible person I know."

"Anything else?" Hyatt asked Roo. Before she could respond, he said to Enid, "By the way, do I know you from somewhere? You look familiar."

"I don't think so, but it's possible." She hesitated before adding, "I'm a reporter for the *Tri-County Gazette.*"

Hyatt snapped his fingers. "Oh, yeah. Now I remember. You're dating Sheriff Josh Hart."

Enid winced. "Yes, we're close friends."

Then Hyatt's eyes appeared to take in every detail of Enid's face. "He was a good sheriff."

"He still is," Enid said. "He's still the sheriff."

"Oh, he won't be back here. They never come back after those high-falutin' assignments. The big boys take care of their own."

Enid wanted to declare that Josh wasn't one of "them," but she refrained. "Miss Murray and I understand that we have no way of knowing whether Catherine Murray is actually missing or just away. We've tried to find her, but after the apparent gang murder just a short distance away from her house, we've become worried something may have happened to her. Now we understand someone has broken into her house and tagged it. So naturally, we're very concerned."

"I understand, ma'am, and I'll get this filed right away. We'll have someone go to her house, check the hospitals, and . . ." He paused. "And the morgue, of course."

"As I told you, I'm an insurance investigator," Roo said. "I've already done all that."

"We'll contact you if anything comes up. I think this is enough to get us started." He leaned in toward Roo. "You realize that it's possible she doesn't want to be found. Happens all the time. There's no evidence of foul play here, and the fact that someone broke into her abandoned house is likely a crime of opportunity. You understand that, right?"

Roo leaned toward him. "And do you understand that Aunt Cat's behavior, her just up and leaving without telling anyone, is *not* typical? Something is not right here, and I expect your office to do a complete investigation."

Enid stood and pulled up on Roo's arm. "I'm sure they will. Come on, let's go." She looked at Hyatt. "Thank you. We appreciate whatever you can do to help us find my friend's great-aunt."

CHAPTER 30

Jack was at his desk when Enid arrived at the newspaper office the next morning. "Hey, sunshine. You're in early."

"I wanted to recommend an article, see what you think."

Jack pulled off his reading glasses and laid them on the desk. "Sure. Let's have it."

Enid sat in the chair across from him. "After you asked me to be your power of attorney, and after we found out Catherine had changed hers, I've been thinking about doing an article. After all, people really need to choose wisely. That's a lot of power over your life to hand to someone."

Jack rubbed his neck. "That's not a bad idea. The article, I mean." He reached into his desk and pulled out a business card. "Here's a friend of mine, an attorney who handles estate planning. He's in Columbia, and I'm sure he'd be happy to talk with you."

Enid wrote down the attorney's phone number and email address. "Thanks, I'll contact him." She handed the card back. "How are you? I mean, are you feeling okay?"

Jack smiled. "Cancer generally doesn't hurt, at least not until it's too late."

Enid remained silent.

"Sorry, bad joke. I'm just trying to ease the tension. I'll be fine. If I know you, you've already done your homework and found that the odds of beating this thing with the proper treatment is nearly a 100 percent five-year survival rate. I'll take those odds any time, so please stop worrying. Promise me."

Enid nodded. "Okay, then I'll let you get back to work." She stood to leave. "Have you signed the inn over to Theo yet?"

"It's in the works now. Should be finished in a couple days. Theo was obviously very happy, and I'm happy for him. I know Cassie would be pleased, too." Jack raised his hand. "Wait, I almost forgot. Cade is coming in later today. He's going to stay with me a couple days so we can catch up."

"Tell him I said hello."

"You can tell him yourself. He mentioned he wanted to see you."

"Perhaps," Enid said as she left Jack's office. She wasn't in the mood for an ex-husband reunion. Distracted, she nearly ran into Ginger in the hallway.

"What's up with you?" Ginger asked. "You look like you lost your best friend."

Enid cringed. "I'm fine." She started toward her office but then turned back. "Would you like to help me with some research? You seem to enjoy it." Then she added, "And you're good at it."

Ginger's face lit up. "Sure. Whatcha need?"

"I'm helping a friend find her aunt. She may have been hurt and might be hospitalized. Her name is Catherine Mur-ray, she's the—"

"I know. She's at the Madden Historical Society. We're in the same romance novel book club."

"You're in a romance book club? With Catherine?" Enid tried to conceal her shock.

"Well, we were, but then she just stopped coming."

"When was that?"

"She's missed at least two meetings. Maybe more. I had to miss one or two myself, so she could have been gone longer. Do you think something happened to her?"

Enid was still trying to imagine Catherine reading a romance novel. "We're not sure, but now someone has broken into her house. We need to let her know." Enid looked in her tote and pulled out a stack of papers. "Here are the hospitals in South Carolina, North Carolina, and Georgia. They won't give you any information on patients but ask to speak with a patient named Catherine Murray. If she's not there, they'll tell you they don't have anyone by that name."

Ginger flipped through the pages. "How many hospitals are there?"

"Nearly three hundred in the three states. Start with South Carolina. Focus on the larger ones and those near highways. Roo and I will do North Carolina and Georgia. I know it's a lot to ask, but just do what you can. Don't let it interfere with your other work."

"Got it." As Ginger headed back toward her desk, Roscoe walked into the newspaper office.

"I need to see Miss Enid. Right now, that is, if she's not busy." Roscoe straightened his yellow and charcoal bow tie.

"I've seen you around town, but who are you?" Ginger asked.

"He's taking Catherine's place at the historical society while she's gone," Enid called out. "Come on back, Roscoe." He followed Enid to her office and stood until she invited him to sit. "What's going on? You look anxious."

He handed her a large brown envelope. "Here. You asked me to look through Miss Murray's things, and I found this."

Enid looked inside the envelope and pulled out some papers. "What is this?"

"Miss Murray apparently had a DNA test done, and then she did some genealogical research. There's some correspondence in there. Since you asked me to see what I could find, I read it."

Enid smiled. "It's okay. We're only snooping to try to find her." She looked at letters from a woman named Belinda. Her return address was a post office box in Winnsboro, South Carolina, a small town not too far away. But in her last letter, she also gave Catherine an actual address, also in Winnsboro. "Looks like she and Belinda planned to get together." She looked up at Roscoe. "Good job. This might be exactly where she is."

Roscoe beamed. "Thank you. I'll keep looking, but I wanted to share that with you. I'll go now." He held up his hand. "'Bye."

Enid grabbed her tote and walked to the front of the office where Ginger was staring at her computer screen. "Focus your search on hospitals that service the Winnsboro area. I'm going to head up there now to this address. Just tell Jack I had to go out if he asks."

CHAPTER 31

Enid put the address in her phone and started the navigation guidance. The destination was less than an hour's drive from Madden, but most of it was secondary roads. She called Roo and updated her. Roo had never heard of anyone named Belinda in the family but admitted she didn't know the distant relatives very well. "I'll let you know what I find out," Enid said.

About forty-five minutes later, she was going down Congress Street in Winnsboro. She recognized the clock tower from an article one of their reporters had written on its history. Dating back to 1837 or thereabouts, it was the oldest continuously running public clock in the United States.

Sadly, like many other small towns, Winnsboro had fallen on hard times. The textile mill and nearby nuclear power plant closings had erased many of the local jobs. But the town was filled with good people who were trying to bring life back to it.

On Enid's drive through town, she passed small, mill-village style homes that looked a lot like the one Catherine lived in: wood siding, one story, small porch in front. When Siri announced Enid had reached her destination, she checked the address again to see if she had made a mistake. The address belonged to an abandoned service station just outside of the town limits. An elderly man had a small beach umbrella set up in front of it, along with a table of fresh produce. Enid parked in the open area beside the building and walked over to him.

"Excuse me, sir. May I ask you a few questions?"

"Certainly, Miss. How can I help 'ya?"

Enid showed him the paper with the address she was looking for. "I'm looking for a person at this address. Does anyone live here?"

"You mean in this here buildin'?" He pointed behind him.

"Yes."

"Nobody lives here. I don't know if anybody ever has. This here was Edwin's, or was it his brother Calvin's, can't remember. Anyway, one of them boys ran this place for a while. It was an Esso station, sometime in the 1970s."

"What happened after it closed?"

"Well, it didn't exactly close. Some fella from Georgia bought the place and ran it for a while. It changed to Exxon a couple years after he bought it. Can't remember his name."

Enid wanted to hurry him up, but she had learned that small-town conversations had their own pace and rhythm, and if you attempted to alter it, you shut it down. "But you're sure no one stays here or perhaps uses this place as a garage or workshop?" She tried to consider why anyone might use this mailing address.

"I come out here two, maybe three days a week to sell produce. Been doing it for years. When I come depends on the weather, my crop that week, or my arthritis. Sometimes it gets so bad I can't make it over here. You see, I live *way* over there." He pointed west. "My customers know to come back the next day if I'm not here. I got some real good folks that buy my produce regular like."

"So you never see anyone else here?"

"Well, like I just said, not when I'm here. But I'm not here *every* day. You know, just a couple of days a week, and not much in the winter."

Enid reached for the wallet in her tote. "I'd like to buy some tomatoes from you."

"That all? I mean, look at them cucumbers. I like to cut them up and—"

"You're right. I'll take some tomatoes and cucumbers." She handed him a ten-dollar bill. "Will that cover it?"

"More than. What else do you want? How about some fine okra?"

Enid had never learned to like the slimy vegetable. "Just give me ten dollars' worth of your best vegetables."

"You know the tomato is actually a fruit."

Enid took the bag from him. "So I've heard. Thanks for your help. Do you mind if I look around the building a bit?"

"It's not my building. Like I said—"

Enid threw up her hand. "Thanks again. I'll just put this in my car first."

"Don't leave them in that hot car too long. Won't be fresh then."

"Thanks." Enid put the brown paper bag in her car and walked to the front door of the abandoned building. She was glad when another car stopped at the produce stand and diverted the elderly man's attention.

When she pulled on the front door of the building, it was stuck but didn't appear to be locked. With both hands, she tugged harder, and it opened. Inside, the musky smell nearly took her breath away. The floor was concrete with patches of square red linoleum tiles that had survived years of abandonment. A ray of sunlight shone through the hole in the roof, and dust particles danced in the shaft of light. After poking around a little, she found nothing to suggest anyone had occupied the space in the last few decades.

She pulled the front door closed behind her and glanced at the produce stand. Two cars were parked beside hers, and the elderly man was busy helping them. She walked around to the back of the building, carefully stepping over broken liquor bottles and fast food wrappers. Someone had even tossed a soiled baby diaper into the tall weeds.

When she got to the back of the building, she stopped in her tracks. About fifty feet ahead was a small, overgrown cemetery with a few graves. The area had long ago been claimed by age and weather. The old wire fence around the small cemetery had rusted, and the narrow gate was leaning to one side. She tugged on it until it opened enough to get through.

Carefully watching her step, she walked over to a row of graves. The first one was a child who had lived less than a year, and the small grave was overgrown by weeds. Next to the child was a larger grave. Erosion of the granite made it difficult to read some of the names and dates. She leaned down and ran her hand across the stone, brushing away some of the dust and dirt. The last name appeared to be Byrne. She walked over to the other graves. One was part of the same family, and the fourth stone appeared to be older than the rest but was too eroded to read. Apparently, this was an old family cemetery. The fifth stone looked a little less weathered than the others. It was simple and plain, with none of the intricate carvings of the older ones. Oddly, there was no name on it and no footstone. Why would someone put a blank headstone here? And why was someone with this address corresponding with Catherine?

CHAPTER 32

Enid took a photo of the blank headstone and nearly ran back to her car. The old man called out to her, "You okay, Miss?"

Enid waved back. "Fine. Thanks. Got to get these veggies home while they're fresh. I appreciate your help." She slammed her car door without waiting for his response.

The drive back to Madden seemed to take forever. The air conditioning was trying hard, but failing, to cool the hot, sticky air in the car. Someone had been corresponding with Catherine using the mailing address of the old cemetery. She needed to go back and study the ancestry report that Roscoe found more closely.

Her cell phone rang, and she pushed the green button on her steering wheel. "Hello." There was no immediate answer. "Hello," she repeated.

"Oh, hi. I couldn't hear you for a moment."

"Cade, is that you?"

"Yes. Where are you?"

"I'm doing some research. Are you at Jack's?"

"Nearly. I'm taking him out to dinner tonight. Why don't you join us?"

"Thanks, but I think I'll pass. I need to work on a few things. I know you two would like to catch up."

"Well, if you change your mind, just call me. We won't be leaving until six or so. I'll see you before I leave tomorrow."

"You're only staying one night?"

"Yeah, I had planned to stay longer, but I got a new assignment I've got to start on."

"I guess that's the price for being a hot-shot Associated Press reporter." Enid immediately regretted her tone. Cade was living his dream, and she was happy for him. It was just that the AP brought back memories of happier days when she and Cade lived and worked together. While Enid had no ill feelings toward her ex, she wasn't in the mood for him.

"Right. Let's have breakfast in the morning at least. I'll text you later. Bye." He hung up before she could protest.

By the time she got back to the newspaper office, the back of her blouse was soaked with perspiration. Ginger said Jack had gone for more tests, and she was leaving for a dental appointment, so Enid would have the office to herself for the remainder of the day. She went to the restroom and put wet towels on her neck to cool herself down before she settled at her desk.

The DNA report on Catherine didn't reveal much, so apparently she had done some research on her own to find the relative she had been corresponding with. Enid looked at the letters again. Since it was done by regular mail, there was no way to know what Catherine had written to the other person. The letter from her relative, written a couple months ago, was signed "Belinda" and had a certain tone of familiarity. They must have talked by phone in addition to corresponding. Or perhaps Catherine already knew Belinda and had simply lost touch with her and was getting reacquainted.

Enid tapped on Roo's phone number. After three rings, it went to voice mail. "Hey, Roo, this is Enid. Call me if you get a chance. Otherwise, I'll see you in a couple hours at the house."

After doing an internet search on Belinda Murray, Enid found a number of people with that name across the country. It could be any of them. Or none of them. She looked at the stack of messages on her desk. It was time to push Catherine's disappearance aside, if it was that, and focus on her own work. With Jack expecting to be away from the office more often, she would have to stay focused on her work at the newspaper.

Her desk phone rang. It was one of the paper's other reporters. "If you need Jack, he's not in right now."

"He told me to call you if I had any questions."

"Me? Why? Never mind, what do you need? I'll try to help."

"I need to expense something. Can you approve it?"

Enid groaned. "Are you serious? You can't make that decision on your own? Or wait for Jack to return?"

"Well, it's a bit unusual."

Enid knew the reporter had not been out of school more than a year, and she remembered her own uncertainty when she was learning the business of working for a newspaper. "What do you need to buy?"

"A new iPad. I lost mine."

"What do you mean you lost it? Maybe you just misplaced it."

The reporter sighed. "I'm sure I lost it."

The *Tri-County Gazette* paid for a reporter's monthly cell phone bill but did not furnish iPads. "If this was your personal property, I don't think we can cover that. Check with your insurance company."

Another sigh from the reporter. "It'll be way below my renter's insurance deductible. I figured the paper wouldn't cover it, but I was there working a story. Shouldn't the paper cover it?"

This time Enid sighed. Was this what running a small-town newspaper office was all about? "Put your request in writing and send it to me. I'll see what Jack says." Jack would likely pay for it. He had a soft spot for young reporters trying to find their way into the business. Most of them worked a year or less, and if they were any good, they moved on to bigger papers and more money. Jack had even helped a few of them find better jobs. He had the patience and compassion for dealing with the daily employee issues. Enid doubted she had those same qualities.

"Right. Will do," the reporter said. "And thanks."

Enid returned all the other messages on her desk and wrote a short piece for the next edition. As she uploaded it to Jack, she tried to imagine herself running the paper, even temporarily, if Jack was unable to . . . She couldn't bring herself to finish the thought. Jack *would* be okay.

Her cell phone rang. It was Roo. "Hey, I'm headed home in about twenty minutes," Enid said. "We can talk then."

"That's why I'm calling. I need to get back to Charleston for a few days, so I'm leaving now."

"Well, be careful driving back." Enid had gotten used to having Roo around and would miss her company. But Enid also needed some time alone to sort through all that was going on.

CHAPTER 33

After staying up late doing research and then tossing and turning most of last night, Enid was in no mood for Cade. He texted he would meet her at Sarah's Tea Shoppe for breakfast, and no amount of protesting could dissuade him.

When she got to Sarah's, the usual breakfast crowd of retirees and newcomers filled the place. A couple years ago, mostly Madden's older gentlemen came in to discuss the weather, taxes, and local news. The men insisted that they only shared news, not gossip. Now that the distribution center had brought new residents to Madden and the surrounding areas, the mix was about half newcomers and half town folks.

Enid walked to the table where Cade was sitting. "Have you been here long?"

A brunette walked up behind her. "No, he just sat down. Want your usual Lady Grey?"

Enid sat across from Cade. "Yes, Cindy. That would be nice. And an order of—"

"I know, toasted whole grain, no butter. Got it coming."

"Thanks," Enid said.

"It never ceases to amaze me how you've made yourself a home here," Cade said.

"You say that every time you visit me. You should be used to it by now. How was your dinner with Jack last night?"

"Good. It would have been better with you there, though."

Enid leaned back in her chair. "That's a nice thing to say to your ex-wife."

"Just stating the obvious." He sipped his coffee. "I know you're worried about Jack, but other than the cancer, he's healthy. He's also a fighter. He worries about you more than himself." Cade rested his hand on Enid's. "I think he's in love with you."

Enid pulled her hand away. "Is that what you wanted to tell me?"

"Yes and no."

Enid massaged her temples with her fingers. "I'm not in the mood for riddles."

"I think you need to be aware of Jack's feelings—"

Enid interrupted. "Did you two talk about me last night?"

Cade grinned. "Yes and no."

Enid gathered her tote and started to get up.

"Wait, I'm sorry to tease you. Remember how I used to when we were first married? You loved it then. I made you laugh."

"I'm sorry for being so irritable, but I'm tired, and we've both changed a lot. Please just tell me what it is you want to say. I need to get to work."

Cade sighed. "You're right. We've both changed." He sipped his coffee. "No, Jack and I didn't specifically discuss you last night, but your name came up. Often, actually."

"I'm not happy that you two were discussing me."

"Whoa, now, let's not lose perspective here. We both care about you, and when I told Jack about my plans, he expressed concern about you. That's only natural, and actually it's quite gentlemanly."

Enid set her tote down again. "What plans?"

"I'm being transferred to London for at least a year, maybe more. It depends on how Brexit goes. If it's as big a mess as everyone thinks it will be, then I might be there longer. This whole thing has the potential to wreck Britain's economy."

"But you're not a financial or an economics reporter. You write about corruption."

"Exactly. There's a question about whether the Vote Leave process was corrupted, and some people think the UK democracy is crumbling. The environment is ripe for all kinds of voter fraud, under-the-table deals, bribes, payoffs, you name it."

"Sounds a bit familiar." She sipped her tea to buy some time. How should she feel about Cade's leaving? Would she be relieved to have her ex-husband out of the picture, at least for a while? Or sad because, like it or not, she knew he was always there if she needed him. "I'm not sure what to say. I guess congratulations are in order. This is a big assignment."

Cade looked up at the ceiling, as if searching for words, before looking into her eyes. "Come with me. I'm sure we can get you assignments either with the AP or a newspaper that needs London coverage." He held up his hand. "Wait before you protest. It might be good for us to see if we still have a chance. We can get a two-bedroom place if that's more comfortable for you. And if we decide it's not going to work, Jack would take you back at the *Tri-County Gazette* in a heartbeat."

Enid put her hands on Cade's. "As you said, I have a life here, and I think we've passed the point of getting back together. Don't you?"

"Maybe. Maybe not. But we might not ever find out once I leave."

"When *are* you leaving?"

"Day after tomorrow."

Enid felt the air leave her lungs. "Wow. That's pretty fast. Did you tell Jack?"

"Yes. That's one of the reasons he was worried about you. If I'm gone, and he's, well, if he gets worse off . . ." Cade held up his hand again. "And before you say anything, I know, and Jack knows, that you're perfectly capable of taking care of yourself."

"Then why worry about me?"

Cade cleared his throat. "Because we both love you, maybe in different ways. Worry just comes naturally with love."

"Aren't you both forgetting about Josh?"

"No, but unless you find a way to reconcile your career paths, well then, you're going to have to stay away from each other or lead secret lives. Neither of those options sounds promising. I still care about you. And I know we'd still be married if I had been a better husband. I put myself and my career first and ignored your needs. I'm not proud of that. But I can't fix the past."

"You're not to blame. We both changed. As for Josh, we'll figure it out."

Cade looked at his Apple wristwatch. "I'm sorry. I don't want to leave it like this, but I've got to get back to Charlotte to pack. Just think about what I've said. You don't have to come now. The invitation remains open."

After paying the bill, Cade walked with Enid to her car. "If you need me, change your mind, or just want to talk, I'll always be there for you. They have planes from London to America, you know." He took her hands and squeezed them gently. "I'm so proud of what you're doing. In many ways, I envy you. Stay true to yourself and be happy. But remember, my offer stands."

Enid wrapped her arms around Cade. "Best of luck to you. I'll be fine, but thanks for the offer." She got in her car and watched Cade walk to his rental vehicle. Would she see him again? Would he find someone in London and stay? Why does this feel so final?

C H A P T E R   3 4

When Enid arrived at the newspaper and headed to her office, Ginger followed close behind. "You need to let me know when you're going to be late. People are looking for you."

Enid spun around to face her. "I had business to attend to. Who's looking for me?"

"Me, for one." Jack's voice came from behind her. "Just come see me when you get a minute." He had dark circles under his eyes and looked pale. When Jack returned to his office, Enid asked Ginger, "Who else is looking for me?"

"Some woman named Ruby-Grace. Her phone number is—"

"I've got it." Enid smiled. "I apologize for being snappy. Lot on my mind."

Ginger looked like she wanted to say something else but instead replied, "No problem."

Enid walked down the hall to Jack's office. "Is this a good time?"

Jack took off his reading glasses and put them on his desk, then rubbed his eyes. "These drug store glasses don't seem to work anymore. I need to get my eyes checked." He motioned toward the chair across from his desk. "I'd like to talk if you've got a minute."

"Are you okay?" she asked.

Jack waved his hand as if dismissing the comment. "I'm fine. Just wanted to let you know I'll be spending some time in Columbia at the Cancer Center for treatment. I'd like to train you on how to get the paper out."

"Sure." This day was not going well.

"I know this is not what you want to do, but it's an important job, and I need someone I can trust to do it, temporarily at least. Since we've gone to digital printing, it's not nearly the headache it used to me. Although, I miss the old printing process. With any luck, I'll be back in the saddle before too long."

"I hope so." Enid paused. "I had breakfast with Cade. He told me about moving to London."

"How do you feel about that?"

"Honestly, I'm not sure. It's a good career move for him. If there's corruption there, he'll find it." For the first time, she realized it could also be a dangerous assignment, as journalists now have a target on them. Money not only corrupts, it kills. "And before you ask, I declined going with him."

"He pretty much said you would."

"The next time I hear from him, he'll probably be inviting me to his wedding." Enid tried to force a smile.

"Maybe. How's the article on the power of attorney topic coming along? I'd like to feature it soon."

"Working on it now. Is there anything else?"

"No, other than to say thanks for your support and especially your friendship."

Enid couldn't think of words that wouldn't seem trite, so she just stood up. "You can look at my calendar and schedule the training when you're ready."

"Thanks. I've already let most of the reporters know you'll be helping me. They all know my situation."

"We'll get through this."

Jack smiled. "Yes, we will."

. . .

When Enid got a call from Roo, she wasn't prepared for the abrupt tone. "I don't want to talk now," Roo said. "Meet me at your house in two hours."

"I thought you needed to stay in Charleston a few days." Then Enid realized the call had ended. She held her cell phone, staring at it, not sure what had happened. She was tempted to call Roo back and tell her she wouldn't be home until later, because she had plenty of work to do at the newspaper office. But the urgency in Roo's voice was disturbing.

She had promised Jack an article on the practical and legal implications of powers of attorney, so she called the estate attorney Jack had recommended. After talking to the office manager and using Jack's name, Enid was transferred to the attorney. "Hi, my name is Enid Blackwell, and I work with—"

"I don't mean to interrupt, but I know who you are. Jack told me you'd likely call. What can I do for you?"

"I'm doing an article on power of attorney. You know, the benefits and dangers, what to be careful of."

"I can sum that up pretty quickly for you. It's important to have someone you trust who can act on your behalf if you become unable to do so yourself. Otherwise, the court will appoint someone, and you don't want that."

Enid scribbled in her notepad. "So how do you pick a good power of attorney?"

"I know this will sound obvious, but pick someone you trust with your life. If you become incapacitated, this person will have the right to pull the plug on your life support, access your finances and basically control your life."

"That's pretty scary."

"Well, it's damned if you do and damned if you don't. If it weren't for client confidentiality, I could tell you some hair-raising stories about POA abuses."

"How do you rescind a power of attorney once someone is appointed?"

"If you're of sound mind, you just amend your POA and name a new person. But if you wait until you've lost your mental capacity, say in the case of Alzheimer's or dementia, then it's too late."

"What could you do then?"

"Pray that you have made a good POA choice. If not, then pray there's another person who steps in and petitions the court to get involved. I won't kid you. It can get real messy from a legal standpoint."

"If I have any further questions, can I call you back?"

The attorney chuckled. "Of course. I'd do anything for Jack Johnson. He's one of the good guys."

After the call, Enid stared at her notes and thought of her own life. Who would she trust to make those decisions on her behalf? Jack was the easy answer, but now might not be the time to appoint him. Cade? That prospect made her uneasy, especially if he remarried. And her relationship with Josh was too uncertain right now. She had a few long-lost cousins, whom she'd have to track down, but otherwise no close family. That feeling of being alone in the world, the same feeling she had after her mother died, threatened to overcome her, so she refocused her attention on the article. What she needed was someone with personal experience to add to the article. She would start asking around.

After finishing a few more items on her daily reminder list, she realized she needed to head to her house to meet Roo. Enid packed her laptop and notes in her tote and headed to Ginger's desk. "I'm going to work from home. Let Jack know if he looks for me. Thanks." She left before Ginger could fire back.

CHAPTER 35

Enid had barely walked inside her house when Roo came rushing in the front door. "Sit down, we've got to talk."

"Hello, Roo. Good to see you, too." Enid sat on the sofa.

"Sorry. How are you?" Before Enid could reply, Roo flopped on the sofa beside Enid. "I found her."

"Who? Catherine?"

"No, silly. I found the real Belinda. You know, Belinda Murray, the one Aunt Cat thought she had written to."

"Wait, are you saying—"

Roo waved her arms. "Yes! I'm saying that the person Aunt Cat contacted was *not* her. Well, she was herself, but you know what I mean."

"How do you know the so-called real Belinda is real?"

Roo stood up quickly and headed to the kitchen. "I need a Coke Zero. You got one?"

"No, but there's some Pellegrino in the fridge."

"Note to self," Roo called out from the kitchen. "Stock real-people food in Enid's kitchen." When Roo returned, she was drinking the sparking water straight from the large bottle. "This isn't half bad, but it lacks the bouquet and re-finement of Coke Zero." She took another gulp before flopping on the sofa again. "What did you ask?" She waved her arm in the air. "Never mind, I remember. You asked how I know this Belinda is real." She took another long swallow from the bottle. "She is Aunt Cat's third cousin.

And I actually met her a long time ago at a family reunion. Or maybe it was at a funeral. They're practically the same thing in the South."

"Has Catherine ever met her?"

"Aunt Cat, oddly enough considering her interest in history, didn't attend most of the family functions. It's weird."

"But what makes you think she's the real Belinda?"

Roo pulled a handful of papers from her laptop backpack that was on the floor by the sofa. "In one of these letters, the fake Belinda claims they share twenty-five percent DNA."

Enid waited for Roo to continue. "And?"

"Third cousins typically share less than one percent DNA. So fake Belinda was lying."

"And how do you know so much about DNA?" Enid asked.

"I had this insurance death claim I investigated once . . . Never mind, it's not important."

Enid laid her head back on the sofa. "Here's what I don't get, though. Catherine was a historian and a pretty smart lady. Wouldn't she have known about the DNA percentages?"

"Not necessarily. Aunt Cat was a town historian, not a genealogy expert, and, like I said, had little interest in family until recently. And she never got any formalized training in being a town historian. She just kept records of Madden better than anyone else. Kind of a self-appointed authority."

Enid sat up again. "How did you find the real Belinda?"

Roo rubbed her hands together. "Okay, here's where it gets really interesting. Apparently, the lawyer, the one who used to be Aunt Cat's attorney, felt like something might be off with her changing her attorney, her executor, and her power of attorney. He checked out the address Aunt Cat gave him and found out it was a bogus address."

"Wait, how would he have that information if he was no longer Catherine's attorney?"

Roo threw her hands up in the air. "Exactly. I asked the same thing. He said she gave him the information for the person to replace me as her executor. But he got suspicious and started asking questions, told her he wanted to be sure she was making the right decision before he made the changes. After all, he's a family friend, not just her attorney. Catherine got upset with him and told him she should have used the attorney Belinda recommended. Aunt Cat left his office, and he never heard from her again."

"It's a good thing he at least got that bit of information."

"No kidding. Anyway, he went down the list of people named Belinda Murray in North Carolina, South Carolina, Georgia, and Virginia. He started with the closest addresses and worked his way down. When he found the real Belinda, the woman who actually *is* related to Aunt Cat, she got worried. The attorney told her to contact me, since he could no longer be officially involved. Belinda waited a while, thinking maybe she should stay out of it. But then she called me yesterday from Virginia. Even though she didn't really know Aunt Cat that well, she felt she was already involved, I guess because her name was used. She offered to help any way she could."

"Seems like fake Belinda has given out a few bogus addresses." Enid told Roo about going to Winnsboro to check out the location that turned out to be an abandoned building. "Behind the gas station was a small family cemetery.

One of the headstones had no name, no date, or anything inscribed on it."

"That's creepy. What do you think that's about?"

Enid shrugged. "I have no idea."

"Oh, I also did some checking on Karla Burke. She's staying in Cassadaga, New York, which is only a mile or so from Lily Dale."

"You mean the medium village in upstate New York?"

Roo jumped to her feet. "Yes, exactly!" Roo sat down again, this time with her legs crossed under her. "Lily Dale is *the* psychic capital of the world. Well, maybe not the world, but at least in this country. It's a really cool place, if you're into that sort of thing. There are about fifty mediums who live there year-round, and every year they have this big festival. More psychics pour in and thousands of people come for readings. Most of them want to connect with dead people."

"But Karla claims she is not psychic. And how do you know so much about Lily Dale?"

"I had a friend who went there every summer to talk with her dead mother. Maybe Karla is trying to connect with Catherine." She paused. "Oh, I guess that would mean she thinks Aunt Cat is dead."

"Let's not jump to conclusions. By the way, how did you find Karla?" Enid asked.

"I told you, this is what I do for a living."

Enid laughed. "In other words, I shouldn't ask."

Roo grinned. "The problem is that I can't find a way to contact Karla. No phone, no cell number, no email. I do, however, have an actual address of where she's staying."

"Are you planning on going there?"

"I've always wanted to see Lily Dale, but I can't take off for New York right now, much as I'd like to. I just got two new insurance cases to investigate, so I sent Karla a snail-mail letter and asked her to get in touch with us immediately."

"I'm not sure about Karla. I mean, she helped me with research on a previous assignment. In fact, she was very helpful. She and Catherine seemed to be close, and when I met with her and Roscoe at the Madden Historical Society, she seemed genuinely concerned. But then she just disappeared."

"Are you thinking she had something to do with all this?"

Enid rubbed her temples. "I don't know. It's just all so bizarre."

"Tell me about it."

"We need to let the sheriff's office know about Belinda. Something's not right."

CHAPTER 36

Enid and Roo signed the visitor's register at the Bowman County sheriff's office and asked to see Deputy Hyatt. After a few minutes' wait, they were escorted to his desk.

"We've got more information about Catherine Murray," Roo said.

Hyatt squinted. "She show up?"

Roo frowned at him. "No, she did not. But we know something is not right. You see, up until recently, I was my aunt's executor for her will and also her personal and medical power of attorney. I found out that she has also changed her attorney and that someone else is now taking care of all that."

"She's entitled to make changes, you know," Hyatt said. "No crime in that."

Roo frowned again. "I *know* that, but we located some correspondence between my aunt and someone who claims to be Belinda Murray, her third cousin. However, I've been in contact with the *real* Belinda Murray. She doesn't know anything about all this." Roo's hands flew up in the air, startling Hyatt. "Can't you see? Someone has scammed my great-aunt and has done who-knows-what to her!"

Enid put her hand on Roo's arm, giving her the calm-down look. "There's something else you need to know," Enid said. She and Roo exchanged glances. "It's a bit complicated."

"How's that?" Hyatt sounded skeptical.

For the next ten minutes, Enid told him about going to Winnsboro to check out Belinda's address and finding the small cemetery and the blank headstone.

Deputy Hyatt pushed back slightly from his desk. "That's some tale. But it doesn't mean a crime has been committed. Maybe somebody was supposed to be buried there but changed their mind." He looked at Roo. "Nothing you've told me seems related to your aunt, but that would make a helluva movie plot if it was. I'll add this information to your report, and we'll check out this Belinda Murray thing. But before you go, is your aunt wealthy, by any chance?"

"Why?" Roo asked.

"Because money is often at the root of these kinds of crimes, assuming of course, a crime was actually committed." He squinted.

"She was a frugal woman," Roo said. "She saved money, and she also had an inheritance from her parents' estate. They were both killed in an accident. I think she also got some money from her husband who died."

"What kind of money are we talking here?" Hyatt asked.

"When Aunt Cat and I went together to her attorney's office, which was several years ago, she told him her worth was about two million dollars. She invested wisely, and I doubt she's spent much of it, so it may be worth closer to three million by now."

Hyatt leaned back in his chair. "That's what we call motive." He squinted at Roo. "By the way, are you an heir to your aunt's estate?"

Roo frowned at Hyatt. "She was leaving the bulk of her estate to charities, not me. And, if you think I would hurt my aunt in any way, then you can . . ."

Enid grabbed Roo's arm. "Thank you, Deputy. Let us know if you find anything."

CHAPTER 37

Josh sat outside the governor's office, waiting to be summoned inside. Some days he felt like a new puppy on a leash. Anytime Josh wandered away slightly, his owner yanked the leash to pull him back. The cryptic message left on his phone last night was a clear indication he had been pulled back into line.

"You can go in now," the governor's aide said.

Josh took a deep breath, gave the aide an obligatory smile, and walked inside the paneled office. "Hello, sir."

Governor Larkin looked at the aide still standing by the office door. "Bring us some coffee, will you? And hold my calls."

Josh sat down across from him.

"I'll get right to it, if that's okay with you." He continued without waiting for Josh to reply. "The acting Bowman County Sheriff, John Stanholt, tells me you've been interfering in his investigation."

Josh shifted in his chair. "That's not exactly what happened, sir."

Larkin motioned for the aide to come in with the coffee tray. After coffee was served and the aide left, Larkin focused again on Josh. "Then why don't you tell me why you were canvassing the neighborhood of a crime scene."

Josh set his coffee cup back in the saucer. "Before I was appointed to this position, I was investigating the disappearance of Madden's historian, Catherine Murray, who lives in Bowman County. I got involved doing a welfare check on her, but she wasn't there."

"I see. And has Miss Murray been found?"

"Not that I'm aware of, sir."

"And has anyone filed a missing persons report with the sheriff's office?"

"Yes, I believe that it has now been done." Josh didn't want to bring Enid or Roo into the conversation if he could avoid it.

"Do you think it has anything to do with gang activity in that area?"

"I don't know, sir. It's certainly possible. Gangs are fairly indiscriminate in choosing their victims, especially if they kill to gain favor with the gang or to be initiated. They operate by a different moral compass. But they also like bragging rights. If they were involved in any way, we'd probably have heard about it by now."

"But, as I understand it, neither you nor the sheriff's office has found any evidence that Murray is a victim of foul play."

"Other than her house being vandalized, no. But her friends and a relative, as well as her neighbor, are sure she wouldn't take off without telling them. And she wouldn't just leave the Madden Historical Society unattended like that."

Larkin took a long, slow sip of coffee. "I understand one of those 'friends' is that newspaper reporter friend of yours, Ms. Blackwell."

"With all due respect, Governor, I'm not sure why that's relevant. We have a respected, senior member of the community who has disappeared without a valid explanation, and we have a gang murder practically in her backyard. Not to mention that someone spray painted her storage shed with a gang tag." Josh lowered his voice. "Since you like to get to the point, I will too, sir. If you put me in this position as window dressing, then I'm not your man. And Ms. Blackwell, friend or not, is a concerned Bowman County citizen who came to the sheriff's office for help. She is now working with Sheriff Stanholt's office."

Larkin smiled, but his eyes didn't. "Just to clarify my expectations, I want you to leave the local investigations to those in power, namely Sheriff Stanholt and his deputies. Otherwise, you'll get your directions from me. Does that clarification address any misunderstanding you and I may have had?" He forced another smile.

Josh stood up. "Yes, sir. Your message is clear."

CHAPTER 38

After Roo had settled into the guest room for the night, Enid called Josh. "Hey, babe," he answered. "Good to hear your voice."

"Can you come over? Roo's in the guest room, but we can talk on the porch. I guess I just need to see you."

"I can be there in about an hour. That too late?"

"No, I've got an article I can work on until then."

About forty-five minutes later, Josh pulled into the driveway. Enid tapped on Roo's door. "Josh and I will be outside. I wanted to let you know in case you heard voices."

"Don't worry, I've gone deaf suddenly," Roo called through the closed door. "I can't hear a thing you're saying."

Enid smiled. Roo was like the sister she had always wished she had. A little impetuous, but that was part of her charm. Enid opened the door and wrapped her arms around Josh. "Oh, God, I've missed you so much."

"I've missed you, too. Come on, I've got a six pack of Coors in a cooler on the porch."

"Sounds good. Want me to bring anything to munch on?"

"No, beer and you. That's all I need right now, but not in that order."

They settled into the two wicker chairs on the small porch. Josh pulled Enid's chair as close to his as he could and then popped the lid of a beer and handed it to her. "I know beer's not your favorite drink, but it's all I had."

She sipped the foam from the top of the can. "Tonight, it's perfect."

Josh took a long drink and laid his head back in the rocker, closing his eyes.

"You look tired. Is it the new job?"

Josh sat up and smiled. "More like the new boss."

Enid took Josh's hand. "It's me again, isn't it? Otherwise, you'd just brush it off."

Josh pulled her hand up to his face and kissed it. "I have a feeling if it wasn't you, there'd be something else." He paused. "I may have made a mistake taking this job."

"I suppose it's too late to tell the governor you've changed your mind. The last thing I'd want to do is become a problem for your career, but if you're not happy, you need to get out."

"And do what? I don't think the acting sheriff will just move aside so I can go back to my old job." Josh turned up his beer can and finished it off and then took another one from the cooler. "It's at least a two-beer night. But I'm tired of talking about my situation. I'll figure it out. You sounded upset or worried when you called. What's going on?"

She told Josh about Belinda and her and Roo's conversation with Deputy Hyatt. "I know you can't get involved, but I just don't have a good feeling that the Bowman County sheriff's office will make this a priority. Have you heard anything that would suggest Catherine could be a victim of a gang?"

"Larkin asked the same thing. My gut tells me no. When the first murder happened, that young man, he was left on full display. That's more their style. The gangs use fear as a controlling force to discourage anyone that might challenge them. They would have no reason I can think of to abduct Catherine and then hide her-or kill her. What would be their point?"

Enid chewed her bottom lip. "Which means someone wants the killing to appear as if it's gang related."

"That thought crossed my mind." Josh hit the arm of the rocking chair with his flat palm. "Damn. I can't stand having my hands tied like this." He slapped the chair arm again. "I took the job thinking it was a good career move and that it would ease the conflict of interest between us. What a mess I've made."

"Please don't blame yourself. You had no way of knowing how all this would turn out."

"Maybe we should both leave and start fresh—something new for both of us."

Before Enid could respond, her cell phone vibrated in her pocket. She was tempted not to answer. "Just let me see who this is. I won't answer unless it's important." She pulled her phone from her pocket. She didn't recognize the number, but that little voice told her to answer anyway. "Hello." Then a moment later, "Thanks. I'll be right there." She ended the call and turned to Josh. "Jack's in the hospital. I've got to go."

Josh jumped up. "Come on. I'll go with you. It's too late to drive alone. Where is he?"

"They took him to Columbia by ambulance." She checked her phone. "Oh no, Jack called earlier` and I missed his call, but he didn't leave a message. I'll let Roo know what's going on."

. . .

Enid and Josh approached the reception desk at the hospital. "We need to see Jack Johnson. Is he still in the ER?"

The older woman with a "Volunteer" patch on her coral-colored smock studied her computer screen. "No, honey. He's not here. Not in ER. He's in Room 223." She handed Enid a photocopy of the hospital floor plan and circled a spot on it. "Take that elevator, which is right down the hall there, and follow the signs to his room number."

Enid grabbed the paper and called out "Thanks for your help," as she and Josh raced to the elevator. The room was just a short distance down the hall on the second floor. When they got to the room, the door was closed. Enid tapped on the door and then turned to Josh. "Maybe you should go in first, just in case he's not covered."

Josh nodded and slowly cracked the door open. "Jack, it's me, Josh." Josh turned back to Enid. "He's sitting up and presentable. Come on," he said, motioning for her to follow him.

Jack was propped up in bed with several pillows. An IV stand was next to the bed and tubes were taped to his arm. "Come on in."

Enid rushed to his bedside. "What happened? Are you okay?"

Jack patted her hand. "I'm fine. Just had a reaction to one of the treatments they gave me today. Didn't mean to scare anyone."

"Well, you did," Josh said. "How do you feel now? Better?"

Before he could answer, Enid interrupted. "If you're really fine, why did they admit you?"

Jack laughed softly. "Always the investigator. They're keeping me for observation. I'll probably get released in a day or two."

"Well, you can stay with me when they let you out." She turned to look at Josh. "Don't you think that's a good idea?"

"What about Roo?" Josh asked.

Jack jumped into their exchange. "Now wait a minute. I get a say in this, too. I'm not going to stay with anyone, and I'll be fine. Quit worrying about me."

"I'm so sorry I missed your call earlier," Enid said. "I could have brought you here."

"Actually, my call had nothing to do with coming here. I was just going to talk about your article on power of attorney. I didn't leave a message because I wasn't feeling great and decided to go home and rest. Once I got home, I got really sick. I just called 911, and here I am."

"But why didn't you let me know—"

Josh put his hand on Enid's arm. "He's not a child, so stop treating him like one." Josh asked Jack, "Is there anything we can do for you tonight?"

"Oh, no, but thanks. I've got all the old TV shows to catch up on, and the nurses come in every few minutes to make sure I don't have a chance to sleep."

"Hospitals are definitely not the place to get rest," Josh said. "We'll check on you tomorrow." He turned to Enid. "Come on. There's nothing we can do here. Let's let him rest."

"But—" Enid protested.

Josh took Enid's arm and guided her toward the door. "'Night, Jack."

As they walked toward the elevator in the parking deck, Enid pulled her arm from Josh's grip. "Why did you pull me out of there? You know he has no one nearby to stay with him."

Josh kept walking, leaving Enid a few steps behind him. "Come on. I'll take you home, so you can throw Roo out and make a place for Jack."

Enid jogged to catch up with him. "That's not fair. I just forgot about Roo momentarily. I wouldn't throw her out, although she'll likely be going back to Charleston soon."

Josh just kept walking. After they got in his pickup, they rode silently all the way to Enid's house.

"Are you coming in?" she asked. "It's not too late."

"No, I've had a long day. I'll talk to you later." Enid started to get out of the pickup, when he reached out to stop her. "You know, one day, you're going to have to figure out what role Jack plays in your life. He's a great guy, and I know you love him."

Enid pulled her arm away. "Loving someone and being in love are two different things." She got out and slammed the door behind her.

CHAPTER 39

Enid was sitting at the small dining table sipping tea the next morning when Roo sat down in the chair across from her. "You said last night you'd tell me this morning what happened with Jack. So, what happened?"

"He had a reaction to one of the cancer treatments. Something experimental they're trying. They're keeping him for observation."

"Then what?"

Enid set her tea mug on the coaster. "What do you mean?"

"Is he going back to work? Coming here?"

"I don't know yet."

"I'm going back to Charleston later today. There are some things I need to check out that I can't do remotely."

"You're welcome to stay as long as you like."

Roo stirred two teaspoons of half-and-half into her coffee. "I'd rather enjoy my coffee and die younger."

Enid nodded. "I know what you mean."

"It's none of my business, but you seem upset this morning. Is there something about Jack you're not telling me?"

"It's not about Jack. It's about me."

Roo sat up. "What's going on? Man problems with that handsome guy of yours?"

Enid blinked away the tears. "Yeah, something like that."

"I don't want to pry, but if you need a sounding board, I'm actually a pretty good listener, contrary to popular belief." Roo went to the kitchen to get a paper towel and handed it to Enid. "Here, wipe your nose before you get snot on the table."

Enid laughed. "You are such a brat." She blew her nose with the paper towel. "I was so insensitive to Josh last night." She told Roo about Josh's meeting with Governor Larkin and then the scene about Jack at the hospital. "What was I thinking?"

Roo reached out and took Enid's hands in hers. "Here's what you were thinking. That the three most important people in your life are slipping away. You're angry and you're scared. Does that about sum it up?"

Enid nodded. "You think I'm being silly, don't you?"

Roo leaned back in her chair. "Not really, but I can understand why Josh is jealous of Jack. There's a comfortableness there that I'm sure is threatening to him." She grinned. "After all, he's a man, right?"

"I don't want to lose Josh . . . or Jack. And I'm not sure how I feel about Cade. I mean we're never going to get back together, but it was nice having him nearby. It's complicated."

Roo made a dismissive wave. "Exes are always complicated."

"Were you married?"

Roo nodded. "It didn't work out well. That's one reason I moved to Charleston, to get away from him."

"Where is he now?"

"Far as know, he's in Georgia, but I'm always afraid he'll show up one day." Roo sighed. "You know, I've been thinking about Aunt Cat. Like I said, she never came to the family reunions or funerals. But in the past two years, she took an interest in connecting with family. She asked me to show her how to use one of those apps on my laptop. I think it was Family Search. She was never technologically skilled, but she knew enough to do the basics. I told her I'd come visit later and help her with her search, but I never did."

Anxious to shift her thoughts from her own situation, Enid got up to get the folder Roscoe had found at the historical society. "After I couldn't go to sleep last night, I went back through Catherine and Belinda's correspondence. I think I remember seeing some references to the family tree in here." She shuffled through some papers and held one up. "Here is it. Family Search, that's how she and Belinda got connected. Fake Belinda mentioned in her letter that she had tried to reach Catherine online after seeing her name on their family tree. She had enough information to convince Catherine to write back. It looks like they wrote back and forth a few times, but right before Catherine disappeared, she told Belinda she had set up an online account with Family Search and would check out the family tree."

"I guess either someone helped her with the app, or she figured it out herself. But why would Fake Belinda target Aunt Cat?"

"Is there any way Belinda could have known that Catherine had a sizeable estate?"

Roo rubbed her neck, a gesture that reminded Enid of Jack's habit. "Aunt Cat was a private person, so I can't imagine she would have freely provided that information."

"I certainly had no idea she had that kind of money." Enid took her teacup to the kitchen sink. "I've got to get to work, but I'm going to try to talk to Sylvia again. Something in my gut tells me she may know more—or may have seen more than she realizes."

"I'll probably be gone when you get home. Before I leave here, I'm going to follow up with the sheriff's office to make sure they're actually doing something. They can probably get more information from the hospitals than I was able to find."

"Plus, there are urgent care centers and other emergency facilities we don't even know about. I just can't believe she wouldn't contact you or Roscoe or someone to let us know she's okay."

"If she hasn't contacted us, it's because she can't," Roo said. "I just don't feel good about any of this."

CHAPTER 40

Before leaving for the newspaper office, Enid called Jack at the hospital using the direct room number. No answer. Perhaps he was having some tests done. She called his cell number to leave a message and was startled when he answered. "Hey, what's up?" He sounded cheerful for someone in the hospital.

"I didn't expect to get you."

"Then why did you call?"

"I meant I called your room and there was no answer."

"That's because I'm not there."

"I feel like we're playing riddles. So, where are you?"

"Sorry, I'm just trying to keep everything light and cheerful. And I am cheerful because I'm home."

"You're home? How did that happen?"

"Well, after you left last night, the nurse came in and said they were cutting me loose in the morning."

"Please don't tell me you took Uber to get home."

Jack laughed. "No, I wouldn't even know how to use one of those ride-sharing services, and I don't ever plan to. I don't trust getting into cars with strangers. Even if they're not sinister, how do I know if they drive safely?"

"I'm waiting. So how did you get home?"

"Actually, Josh called me last night, right after the nurse came in, and he offered to take me home."

"Josh? Why . . .?"

"He said he was just checking in. I thought it was unusual, since you two had just left, but I'm not going to read anything into it."

"I'm headed to the office now. Can I bring you anything?"

"No, I'll see you there later."

"Jack—"

"Don't start mothering me. It's not becoming of you. Besides, I've been released to return to normal activities. It was just a drug reaction. I'm fine. Go on to work now, that's what I'm paying you for. I'll see you later."

"Right, no more mothering, so unless you need me in the office, I'm going to see Catherine Murray's neighbor, Sylvia. I'm not sure why, but I want to talk with her again."

"That's fine. Follow your instincts. That's why you're a good reporter."

. . .

It was nearly nine o'clock when Enid got to Sylvia's house. It was a bit early to visit, especially since some retirees sleep later than the average working population. Enid walked across the street to Catherine's house to see if there had been any further vandalism done to the house.

The front door was still locked, which was a good sign, and none of the windows appeared to be tampered with. She peered inside and saw nothing unusual, so she walked around to the back of the house. Nothing had been done to remove or cover the 14 sprayed on the storage building, and the back door was closed but not locked. She opened it slowly and looked around inside the kitchen. The refrigerator door was open, and someone had emptied it. Even so, the odor of spoiled food hung in the air. A few flies buzzed around her. A cockroach scurried across the white porcelain sink. Bugs and insects have an uncanny sense of knowing when a house is unoccupied and then move in to claim it.

Glancing at her watch, it was nearly nine thirty now, so she'd see if Sylvia was up. Enid left by the back door, closing it behind her. She would talk to Roo about getting a new lock installed.

After two knocks on Sylvia's door, Enid was ready to give up and leave. She had turned to walk back to her car when she heard, "You're that reporter lady." Sylvia was standing in a bathrobe at her half-opened door.

"I'm sorry to bother you so early, but I was in the area and wanted to check on Catherine's house. Would it be possible to talk for a minute?"

Sylvia looked across the street and then to her left and right. "I'm not dressed much, but come on in," she said as she opened the door and then tugged on the sash around her robe. Motioning for Enid to follow her, Sylvia led the way to the kitchen in the back of the house. Her floor plan was nearly identical to Catherine's. Four chairs surrounded a small white-painted table in the kitchen area. "Coffee?"

"No, but thanks." Sylvia had the *Tri-County Gazette* spread on the table. "I see you subscribe to the paper. I hope you find it informative."

"I like to keep up with what's going on. Just read your article on that power of attorney thing. I don't have one, and maybe it's a good thing. That's pretty scary stuff, especially for somebody like me. I got one grandson, Robert, you met him. He's a charmer, but he'd just as soon rob me blind as talk to me. After my son's wife died, he left Robert with me and moved to Alaska. My son wanted to live off the grid. I guess that means no electricity. Anyway, he got killed in a bar fight in Anchorage. My grandson has moved out now, but he comes around occasionally. Most of my other kin folks are buried or gone."

"I'm sorry for your loss. I didn't mean to alarm our readers when I wrote that article, but choosing the right executor and power of attorney is important."

"I was actually thinking Catherine would be a good one for me, but since she's up and gone, well . . . Besides, she's older than me, so I'd probably outlive her."

"Catherine is why I stopped by. I guess you haven't heard anything from her."

"Nary a thing."

"Did Catherine ever talk to you about searching for her relatives online?"

"Yes, she did, actually. Not long before Catherine left, she asked me if I could help her find some information on a relative on some kind of website. I'd nearly forgotten all about it until just now. I couldn't help her, but Robert was here, and I asked him to help her. He's always on his phone or playing games on that computer of his. He went over to her house and helped her."

Enid didn't recall seeing a computer or laptop at her house. "Do you think it would be possible for me to talk to Robert?"

"Why? Do you think he did something wrong?" Sylvia tightened the sash on her robe again.

"No, not at all. In fact, I appreciate that he helped her. But he may know something that will help us find her. I gave him my business card earlier." Enid stood up. "I won't keep you any longer, but please let me know if you see anything unusual across the street."

"I don't venture out much, what with all the killings and stuff going on around here."

"I'm sure it's scary, knowing that a young man was killed up by the old barn."

Sylvia shook her head. "A crying shame. You know, he was a friend of Robert's."

Enid wasn't sure she had understood her correctly. "You mean Robert knew the person that was killed?"

"Yes siree. They was in high school together, at least."

"He didn't mention it when we talked earlier. Does your grandson have any idea why his friend was killed?"

Sylvia shook her head. "I didn't ask, and he didn't tell."

"It's really important that I talk to him. Can you please ask him to call me?"

"I'll pass the message on, but I can't guarantee he'll call."

"Thank you." Enid's mind was racing as she walked to her car.

CHAPTER 41

When Enid got to the newspaper office, Jack had already left. Ginger said he was resting and would try to come in later. Enid didn't want to disturb him. "Ginger, can you do a little online research for me? I need to find a guy named Robert."

Ginger picked up her notepad and then looked up at Enid. "Last name?"

"Ryce, I think, assuming he has the same last name as his grandmother."

"Why didn't you ask her?"

Enid cocked her head sideways. "Thank you for that bit of advice. But Sylvia is suspicious of me, and I'm sure a lot of other people, so I didn't press her for more info or she would've clammed up. I can't blame her. Her friend has disappeared, and her grandson's high school buddy was murdered in a gang-style killing just up from her house. I'd be jittery, too."

Ginger threw up her hand. "Okay, just saying. I'll see what I can find."

"Thanks. I'm going to make some calls."

Enid went to her office and looked at the stack of messages on her desk. More than half were from other *Tri-County Gazette* reporters who had questions about their assignments, expenses, or other newspaper related issues. She glanced through them. None seemed urgent, so she pushed them aside for now.

Her first call was to the Bowman County sheriff's office. She asked for their public relations officer and was referred to someone who sounded like he was a teenager. "I'm Enid Blackwell, with the *Tri-County Gazette*. I'd like an update on a young man that was murdered." She provided the address and all the information she had on the incident, and then she was put on hold for several minutes. When the man returned, he gave her the name of the victim. "Is this being investigated as a gang killing?" She knew he wouldn't tell her, but it was worth a shot. "Is there anything else you can give me?" She noted a few other details he gave her. "Thanks, I appreciate the information."

Enid looked at her notes. The young man's name was Daniel Boodemore, age twenty-two. A quick online search revealed that he had been a former star high school running back and had received a scholarship. But in his freshman year at college, he got into trouble and was expelled. Public arrest records showed he had been charged with possession and drug dealing. "What a shame," she said aloud, shaking her head. A knock on her office door startled her. It was Ginger.

"I found the name and a phone number. I just emailed it to you."

"Thanks. I appreciate—" Before she could finish, Ginger had turned on her heels and left. Enid laughed at herself when she thought of Ginger as an impertinent kid, since she was only a decade younger. Having always been polite and respectful all her life, Enid had a hard time identifying with some of today's youth. Although, she had to admit Ginger

was smart, hardworking, and a whiz at research. Just no social skills.

Enid opened her email and found that not only had Ginger given her the name, address, and phone number, she had
researched his criminal record also. Like his murdered friend
Daniel, Sylvia's grandson Robert had been charged with
possession and distribution of drugs. He had also been
charged with vandalism twice.

Enid picked up her cell phone to call Josh but stopped
herself. Josh wasn't working Catherine's case and had been
warned to stay out of it. Trying to pull him into it would be
irresponsible. Instead, she tapped on Roo's number. "Roo,
it's me."

"Hey, you. I was just going to call you to let you know
I've got to go out of town for a week or so to investigate a
death claim. Their local person is out on maternity leave, so
I'm going to help out. What's going on?"

"Nothing that can't wait. I've uncovered some information I was going to share with you about Catherine. Well,
maybe it's connected. Maybe not." Enid told Roo about
Robert helping Catherine, his connection with the first murder victim, and their similar criminal backgrounds. "It's
possible they were in something illegal together."

"I'm sorry I can't come to Madden to help you. Here it
is, I'm the investigator but you're doing all the work."

"I know you don't have much free time, so don't worry
about it. I'll keep you posted if I find out anything relevant."

"I just keep hoping that Aunt Cat will show up and apologize for scaring us all to death."

"Perhaps she will. Safe travels."

Enid had just hung up when someone knocked on her office door. It was Roscoe from the Madden Historical Society.

"Ms. Enid, I'm sorry to bother you, but I just wanted to let you know I'll be leaving Madden tomorrow."

"Does that mean you've heard from Catherine?"

"Oh, no, ma'am. The truth is, I've been fired. Well, not exactly, but the mayor told me she doesn't have the funds to pay me any longer. I'm not an employee, and they don't pay volunteers. She's been generous to give me a stipend to help a little. But I need to move on anyway. I've already lost one job by staying here."

"What will happen to the historical society?"

"The mayor said it would be closed until they find another historian, which probably won't happen."

"I'm so sorry this whole thing has interfered with your getting on with your life. You have your master's degree now, and so much to look forward to. Hopefully, we can find Catherine soon and put this all behind us. Best of luck to you, Roscoe. Please stay in touch."

"I will. You take care, Ms. Enid. When I get settled in somewhere, I'll contact you."

After he left, Enid thought of how sad it would be to see the Madden Historical Society shuttered, and sadder still to think she might never see Catherine or Roscoe again. The intellectual part of Enid accepted that change is part of life. But that didn't make it any easier.

In a defiant move against Governor Larkin, Enid called Josh. When she got his recorded voice message, she just tapped the red icon to end the call. What message could she leave? That her world was changing too rapidly? That she was angry their jobs were interfering with their lives? With no adequate words coming to mind, she made herself a cup of tea, hoping the British remedy for everything wouldn't let her down.

CHAPTER 42

Catherine's head was spinning as she tried to open her eyes. Instead of trying to take in everything at once, she picked a dark brown spot on the ceiling tile overhead, probably caused from a roof leak, and focused on it instead. Her head throbbed and her throat was parched. "Where . . ." The words stuck to her mouth. *Where am I?*

Slowly, she tried to raise her arm. It was heavy and she couldn't move. She tried her leg and was able to bend it but she didn't have the strength to try the other one. *Someone help me. Please.*

For what seemed like an eternity, she stared at the brown spot and kept trying to wiggle her toes and move her limbs. The effort exhausted her.

"Well, well, the great lady is awake again."

Catherine shifted her focus to the woman standing at the foot of her bed. Did she say "again?" Had she seen this place before now? If so, she didn't remember it at all. Everything seemed strange, dream-like. She managed to get her arms in position to sit up slightly. Her head felt like a bass drum player was banging away. *Boom, boom, boom.*

The woman walked to her bedside and leaned over her. Her breath smelled like cigarettes. "Like I told you before, if you're good, we're good. So you be good and lay down." She put her hands on Catherine's shoulders and pushed her back into the mattress. "There you go." The woman took her pulse and noted it on a clipboard that was never left in the patient's room. "Worthless old bag," she muttered. She pulled up Catherine's gown and yanked the adult diaper off her. "And I'm tired of cleaning up after you." The woman slung the soiled diaper into a trashcan in the bathroom. Without wiping Catherine clean, the woman put a new diaper on her and pulled the covers up. When her cell phone rang, she didn't answer it. "Yeah, yeah, I'm coming."

Catherine didn't try to sit up again. The effort was too much. She watched the nurse prepare a syringe and stick it in her arm, which was black and blue with bruises and painful to the touch. In less than a minute, she drifted back into a deep sleep.

The nurse walked out of Catherine's room, slamming the door behind her.

CHAPTER 43

Enid checked on Jack, who insisted she stop worrying about him. He would be back in the office tomorrow. "I've read all the coverage I could find in the *State* newspaper and the other dailies around here," she said. "Surprisingly, there's not much information. I think the sheriff is downplaying the gang connection."

"I haven't seen many of the reporters around town lately. I think they've moved on to other stories, for now at least. But we'll keep monitoring their coverage."

"I agree." After talking with Jack, she finished her article assignments. She was anxious to end the depressing day and prepared to go to bed early.

Right after she turned out the bedside lamp, her cell phone rang. Josh had probably seen where she had tried to call. She sat up in bed and looked at the screen. It was an unknown number. "Hello."

"Enid, this is Karla."

Stunned, Enid was unable to speak momentarily.

"Karla Burke."

"Karla," was all Enid could say.

"Did I wake you?" Karla asked.

"No, it's fine. Where are you?"

"I don't mean to barge in on you, but I'm right outside your door."

Again at a loss for words, Enid stammered, "You mean here? You're at my house?" Enid walked to the front door and looked through the peep lens Jack had installed for her when she moved in. Karla was standing there, phone against her ear. Enid opened the door. "Come on in. I'm sorry I'm not dressed. I was just preparing for bed. Your call caught me off guard."

Every time Enid had seen Karla, she appeared to float instead of walk. Tonight was no exception. Karla's long flowing skirt billowed out behind her as she walked into the house. "How long have you been back in town?" Enid asked.

"I just drove in from New York."

"You must have gotten Roo's letter."

"Do you mean Catherine's great-niece Ruby-Grace?"

"Yes, she wrote to you in New York."

"Yes, I got her letter, but that's not the only reason I'm here. Perhaps she is the other person's presence I felt when I talked with Catherine."

The hair on Enid's neck prickled. "You've talked with Catherine? When? Where?"

Karla smiled. "Mind if I heat some water for my herb tea?" Without waiting for an answer, Karla floated into the kitchen as though her skirt were a magic carpet.

Enid followed Karla into the kitchen. "Here, I'll do that for you." She filled the tea kettle with water and turned on the gas burner. "Please have a seat." She motioned toward the small dining table.

"I'm sure you think I'm trying to be mysterious." Karla smiled slightly. "I'm not trying to be. It's just that I get lost in my own world at times. I have not seen Catherine in the way you mean, but I did communicate with her. In fact, she came to me while I was trying to connect to another friend, someone who had recently passed."

"So that's why you were in Lily Dale?"

"Yes."

Having worked with Karla before and trusting that she did indeed have some kind of intuitive gifts, Enid pushed her skepticism aside. "Is Catherine . . ." Enid couldn't bring herself to finish the sentence.

"I got the impression she is still alive, if that's what you're going to ask. Although, at times, when I've worked with a medium, I've communicated with people who have passed and they talk to me as though they are still alive. So I can't be sure."

Enid poured the boiling water over the teabag in Karla's cup and then made herself a cup of Lady Grey. No point in avoiding caffeine. This was going to be a sleepless night.

"What did she say? Or would you prefer not to discuss it?"

Karla laughed. "If I wanted to keep it private, I wouldn't be talking to my favorite reporter."

Enid nodded. "Fair enough."

With a now-serious expression, Karla continued. "As I said, I was working with a friend who is a medium at Lily Dale. I assume you're familiar with the community in upstate New York."

"Somewhat. I remember seeing a TV show about it, and Roo filled me in also."

"As the medium was trying to connect me with my late friend, Catherine came to me instead. I don't have visions, so I can't tell you where she was or anything like that. I only sensed that she is in big trouble. And there was a younger, kind spirit there also, perhaps it was Ruby-Grace. They were not connected, but they were trying to reach out to each other. Your spirit seemed to be connected somehow to the younger person's."

"That's probably because Roo and I have been working together to find Catherine." She filled Karla in on Roo's finding the real Belinda.

"That's not like Catherine to be so gullible. She's is in danger. Of that, I am sure. Have you checked the hospitals?" Karla sipped her tea.

"We did, and now the sheriff's department is also checking, although I didn't get any sense of urgency from them. I'm not even sure they believe anything is wrong. They think the house being vandalized was just random, because it was empty, and has no connection to Catherine's disappearance. It's frustrating."

"I'm not sure this will help, but I'd like to go to Catherine's house in the morning. Can you arrange that?"

"Of course. Roo is out of town, but I'll let her know we're going there, just in case something comes up. And you're more than welcome to stay here with me."

"Thanks, but I have a place to stay. I'll be back here tomorrow. I know you have a job to do, so we can go early if you like."

"Sounds good." Enid walked Karla to the front door. "I'm glad you're back."

Karla nodded and walked into the darkness.

. . .

Karla showed up at Enid's house early the next morning, just as Enid was putting away her breakfast dishes. Karla declined the offer for anything to eat or drink, wanting to get an early start. "I find that early morning and late at night, I am more intuitive. I think there's something about the distractions during a busy day that make it hard for me to focus," Karla said. "Or perhaps I'm just getting older and more scatter-brained."

On the drive to Catherine's house, Karla kept her eyes closed, so Enid turned off the car radio and drove in silence. When they pulled into Catherine's driveway, Karla got out of the car and looked toward the old barn a few blocks away. "Something happened there," Karla said, pointing.

Enid told her about the murder. "No one seems to think there's a connection between the killing and Catherine, but the young man who was murdered went to high school with the grandson of the woman that lives across the street." She pointed toward Sylvia's house and noticed someone had pulled the curtains slightly aside in one of the windows.

"Could be coincidence. This is a small town."

"Come on, I'll take you inside." After breaking into Catherine's house, Roo had the locks changed and had given Enid a key. For extra precaution, Roo had also emailed a note permitting Enid to enter the house, in case anyone questioned her being there.

The air inside was stale and the smell of spoiled food still lingered. "Would you like for me to stay here and just let you roam?" Enid reached her arm out against the wall to support herself.

"Are you alright?"

"It's just my leg. I cut it on a piece of wire fence, and it's still painful at times."

"I hope you heal soon. As to your question, I can tune you out if you're around, no offense meant, so it's up to you."

"None taken," Enid said. "But I'll just sit here. Take your time." She wanted to keep an eye on Sylvia's house. Perhaps whoever was watching them was harmless. Probably just Sylvia. "Oh, I forgot to mention the gang tag on the storage building outside was discovered after the killing at the old barn up the street."

Karla just nodded and began walking toward Catherine's bedroom.

Enid pushed the front curtain aside slightly and looked across the street. No one seemed to be looking back. The only car in Sylvia's driveway was the same one she had seen before.

After a few minutes, Karla walked down the hall and began going into the other rooms, one by one. When she ended up in the kitchen, she opened the back door and went outside to the storage shed. Enid stayed inside and watched as Karla ran her hand across the 14 painted on the wooden siding. In a few minutes, Karla came back inside and went back to Catherine's bedroom.

After nearly five minutes of silence, Enid went to check on Karla. She was lying on Catherine's bed with her arms and legs spread slightly. Then she curled up into a fetal position and began making noises. Enid remained silent until it became clear that Karla was crying, nearly sobbing now.

"What's wrong?" Enid asked.

Karla appeared not to have heard her, so Enid just watched. Karla began shaking her head, side to side. "No, please no." She then grabbed her own forearm and kept shaking her head. "Please."

Enid didn't know what to do, but she didn't want to break whatever connection or intuitive message Karla was getting. In a few minutes, Karla sat up on the edge of the bed. She seemed startled to see Enid standing there. "I hope I didn't frighten you." Karla wiped the tears from her face. "Sometimes, I just feel what someone else is feeling. It can be disconcerting for others to observe."

"Was it Catherine?"

"I think so."

"I saw you grab your arm. Do you know what that was about?"

"I just remember it felt like someone was sticking me with something very sharp."

"What about the storage shed, did you get anything from that?"

Karla began walking back toward the kitchen. "I can't tell you why, because I don't know, but the negative energy from that shed seems very close."

"This place is starting to give me the creeps. Are you ready to go?"

Karla nodded.

As Enid and Karla were leaving the house, the car across the street sped away. It was hard to get a good look, but one thing Enid was sure of: it was Sylvia's car, but the driver wasn't Sylvia.

CHAPTER 44

Enid waited until the car was out of sight before backing into the street.

"You seem anxious," Karla said.

"The person in that car was not Sylvia. It may have been her grandson."

"You said earlier he was friends with the murdered boy."

"That might not mean anything. This is a small town, and everyone goes to the same high school. Knowing each other could just be a coincidence. But he also helped Catherine with an online ancestry search." She paused. "Would you mind terribly if we don't go straight back?"

"I'm in no rush."

"I'll just call the office and let them know where I am." Enid tapped on Ginger's number. "I'll be in shortly. Is anyone looking for me?"

Ginger's voice filled the car. "Only the whole world."

Enid glanced at Karla, who was smiling, and rolled her eyes. "Could you just name a couple of the people who are looking for me?"

"Well, Jack for one, but then he's used to you disappearing. And then one of the reporters wants to talk to you about benefits. I think she's pregnant."

Enid groaned. "Fine. I'll be back before lunch. And tell Jack I'll talk with him later."

"I'm sure you will," Ginger said before ending the call.

"Some days she can be hard to take," Enid said to Karla.

"Where are we going, by the way?" Karla asked.

"I want you to see the graveyard I told you about. Just to see if anything comes to you."

"Good. I'd like to see it. But, as I said, I'm not psychic, so I may not get anything, or something may come to me later in a dream."

"What do you know about Catherine's family?"

"Not much, but what do you mean?" Karla asked.

"It seems as though Roo, Ruby-Grace, is her only close relative. So why would Catherine replace Roo as executor and power of attorney?"

"She told me several years ago she had done her estate planning, and at the time, she seemed content that all of that was taken care of. But I also know scam artists are skillful at talking people into things, especially older people."

"I don't think I would want my family tree and other information on one of those ancestry websites."

"Ancestry research has brought families together, and in that sense, it's been a blessing to many. But I agree with you. It opens up the potential for victimizing unsuspecting people."

They rode in silence until they reached the cemetery just outside of Winnsboro. When Enid parked the car and got out, the elderly produce man threw up his hand. "Guess you liked my vegetables since you've come back for more."

"I'll get some before I leave. We're just going to look at something first." Enid motioned for Karla to follow her.

When they got to the back of the old service station Karla immediately walked toward the headstone with no name, the fifth stone.

"Watch your step," Enid said, being careful not to re-injure her leg as she stepped over the rusted wire gate still laying open from her previous visit. "I imagine this is a family cemetery, so we're trespassing." Enid glanced around to make sure no one was nearby.

Karla didn't seem to hear Enid as she knelt down beside the gray granite headstone. She closed her eyes, running her fingers across its cold surface. When Karla opened her eyes, she stood up. "I can feel a lot of sadness or anguish here."

"Is someone buried in that grave?" Enid asked.

"I can't tell, but there's definitely some strong energy centered here."

"Coming here, we passed a monument company just down the road. I'll bet they know something about this cemetery. Maybe we should pay them a visit."

Enid and Karla walked back to the front of the building. "You can wait in the car if you'd like. I need to get some tomatoes," Enid said. The last ones she bought were still sitting in her refrigerator, but she felt obligated to buy something from the old man.

Enid picked up three large tomatoes. "This will do me today."

"That'll be two dollars with your repeat customer discount."

"You don't have to do that," Enid said.

The old man smiled. "Anything for you, pretty lady. You enjoy those." He handed her the brown paper bag.

Enid started to walk to her car but turned back. "Has anyone else been here at this cemetery lately?"

"No, can't say that I've seen anyone. But then again, I can't say I haven't. Like I told you, I'm only here a few days a week."

"Well, thanks." Enid turned toward the car. She handed the bag to Karla. "Here. Why don't you take these. I still have the last ones I bought."

"I'll give them to the woman I'm staying with. She'll appreciate them."

A short drive later, they were at the monument company. The small building was surrounded by an overgrown yard. On one side, a few headstones were on display, and on the other side of the yard were statues of angels and various animals scattered around.

As Enid and Karla got out of the car, a middle-aged man came out to meet them. "Can I help you?"

Enid introduced herself and Karla. "I'm doing some research, and I ran across this headstone with no name in an old cemetery up the road behind an old gas station. Do you know anything about it?"

The man's eyes squinted slightly. "My great grandfather started this company, then my grandfather and father carried on after that. Now I guess it's my turn. I got three daughters, so not sure what'll happen when I'm gone. But, back to your question. What exactly do you want to know?"

"Who owns it? Is it a family cemetery?"

"There's a lot of those scattered around here. If it's the one behind the old Esso station, then it belongs to the Byrne family. An old Irish family."

"That's the name I saw on several of the headstones," Enid said.

"I haven't done any stonework there myself. My granddaddy and daddy did though, God rest their souls." He paused. "Reason I remember is my daddy used to tell some tall tales about the family. Scared me some when I was young. Those Irish folks, no offense intended in case you happen to be one, they're a bit different."

"My own ancestry is Welsh, so I know what you mean."

The man smiled. "There you go, you know what I'm saying. Anyway, my daddy told me about them putting a headstone there without a name on it."

"Do you mean someone was buried there anonymously?" Karla asked.

"No, ma'am. As I recall the tale, no one was buried there. Mr. Byrne wanted a place for all the wandering spirits to gather, in case they didn't have a resting place. He and his family owned the whole cemetery, so I guess they could do what they wanted. My daddy said they had more money than good sense."

"That's very odd," Karla said. "Although, I do know of families who put an alter for their dead ones in their house. Most people think it's for honoring the dead, and in a way it is. But the real purpose is to give the family spirits a place to gather so they don't wander about and cause any problems."

"Guess that makes some sense then," he said. "Like I said, the Byrne family was a bit different in their way of thinking. Nice people, though, according to Daddy. Paid on time, and all that."

The man took off his green John Deere baseball cap and rubbed the top of his head. Looking at Enid, he said, "Don't put my name in any article saying anything bad about the Byrne family. Wouldn't want to cause no hard feelings. Although I think most of the family has died out by now."

"I understand, and I'm not going to get you in trouble," Enid said. "We were just curious about who owned the cemetery and about the headstone with no inscription on it. That's all."

He put the cap back on his head. "I need to get back to work, unless you want to buy something."

Karla began walking back to the car, and Enid held out her hand to the man. "Thanks, we appreciate the information. I'm not from around here, but if I hear of anyone who needs a headstone, I'll send them your way. You do nice work."

The man tipped his cap. "Thanks, ma'am," he said before walking back to the small building.

On the drive back to Enid's house, she was the one who spoke first. "This whole situation just keeps getting weirder. I'll do some checking on the Byrne family, but I'm not sure that will help us much."

Karla nodded. "And I need some time alone to sort through all this."

CHAPTER 45

After dropping Karla off to get her car, Enid went to the newspaper office to face Ginger's wrath. "Sorry I'm late, I got tied up."

"Yup." Ginger turned her attention back to her computer screen. "He's waiting on you."

Enid dropped her tote onto her office chair and then walked down the hall to Jack's office. She tapped on his open door. "Got a minute?"

Jack took off his reading glasses and grinned. "You bet."

For the next half hour, Enid filled him in on her and Karla's visits to Catherine's house and to the monument company. She ended by saying, "I'm sorry this has taken so much of my time. I'll get my assignments done, I promise."

"I'm not worried about that. You're the most conscientious person I know. Just be careful."

"I wish Josh could help me, but I don't want to put him in a worse situation."

Jack slapped his forehead with the palm of his hand. "Oh, crap. I almost forgot. Josh called here looking for you. I told him you'd call him. Sorry I forgot to tell you earlier."

Enid turned toward the door. "I'm sure he's not sitting by the phone waiting for me, but I'll call him later." She paused. "I didn't ask how you're feeling. I hope you've fully recovered from that drug reaction."

"Fit as a fiddle."

Enid would have believed him had he not rubbed his neck immediately afterward, a telltale gesture when he was upset or worried.

CHAPTER 46

Not for the first time, Susan Everhart wondered if she had made a mistake coming to work for the nursing home. She had been a nurse's aide at Memorial Hospital but applied to the home because they paid more. Some of her friends had warned about the place being unethical and unsafe for patients. But in addition to higher pay, it was closer to Susan's home.

When she sat for the interview for this job, the woman seemed less interested in her experience and credentials than she was in Susan's ability to mind her own business and not engage in gossip. At the time, it seemed easy to assure her potential employer that she would comply, but now she was beginning to wonder about this place.

What bothered Susan most about the new job was how the patients were treated. An elderly man in a wheelchair was left alone in the courtyard one day. It started raining and no one went out to get him. Susan noticed him slumped over in his wheelchair in the rain and rushed out to bring him in. Instead of being acknowledged for her good deed, she had been reprimanded, as the elderly man was not one of her assigned patients. Later, when the man died of pneumonia, Susan was given a "bonus" of a week off that happened to coincide with the state investigator's visit to the center.

Since the employees were not allowed to talk about their employer, and in fact were rewarded for reporting anyone who did, Susan couldn't talk to anyone about her concerns. Most of the patients were adequately taken care of, but one thing Susan noticed was that most of them rarely had visitors. Maybe that was normal. Since she had never worked at a nursing home, she had nothing to compare it with. Susan hoped she didn't end up at a place like this when she became old and forgotten.

She walked into the next patient's room to drop off clean towels and change the bed linens. The patient in this room was known only as "121," her room number. There were no medical charts in the room, since all the records were digital, so there was nothing to indicate the patient's real name.

121 looked to be in her sixties. She had silver hair that needed trimming badly. When Susan first met her, about two weeks ago, 121 seemed to be less gaunt. Now, her eyes had dark circles under them and her cheekbones were even more prominent. Most of the time she was sedated. Susan knew for a fact that Nurse Louise administered the prescription drug to her twice a day.

121 appeared weaker each day, and though Susan was afraid she was sick, she knew better than to interfere with nursing matters. If there was one thing she had learned in working here, it was knowing her place. She was an aide, as she was often told, and should leave the nursing to the "professionals." The center did not have its own doctor, but if any of the patients required one, a young man with pale skin and slicked-back brown hair, who looked to be less than forty, showed up with his medical bag. He walked fast and always looked angry. He never stayed long with any of the patients. Those with more serious matters were taken to the hospital.

"How you doing today, Miss 121?" Susan asked. "I'm going to tidy up your room. Is that okay?" She didn't expect the patient to respond. She never did. "I'm going to put you in this chair over here so I can change your linens. Let's help you get up, so you don't fall. Careful, take it easy." Susan put her arms under 121's armpits and surprisingly, 121 was able to help herself move to the chair. "Well, aren't you the strong one. You must be eating your Wheaties for breakfast."

Susan liked to talk to the patients, even though most of them didn't respond. The banter helped her see the patients as human beings, not objects. She straightened 121's gown and made sure she was secure in the chair. "Now you just sit there while I change these sheets. You can look out the window. See that real pretty bird sitting in the tree? He's watching me to make sure I take good care of you, and I will."

Without warning, 121 grabbed Susan's slender arm with a surprisingly strong grip. She tried to talk but slurred her words.

"What's wrong?" Susan asked. "Are you okay?" She tried to pry the woman's hands from her arm. "You can let go now. I'm right here."

"Hellll . . ."

"Should I call the nurse to come check on you?" Susan asked.

121 shook her head. "Nooo. Hel mu."

"Are you in pain? What do you need?"

"Out . . ."

"You want out of your chair? Your room?"

121 shook her head again. "Call . . ." 121 pointed to the clipboard and pen that Susan had laid on the bedside table. It was a checklist for Susan's assigned patients and their room numbers.

"You want my work list?" Susan was confused but handed the clipboard to her. 121 pointed to the Bic ballpoint pen on the table and made a grunting noise. "You want the pen, too?" Susan handed it to her but watched 121 closely, because she recalled a movie scene where a prisoner stabbed and killed a guard with a pencil to his neck.

With the clipboard and pen in hand, 121 slowly wrote across the list of patient rooms. When she finished, she closed her eyes. "Pleee," she said softly.

Susan had to sign and turn in the checklist to her supervisor, so she wasn't sure how she was going to keep her from seeing what 121 had written. Instinctively, Susan knew the woman had confided something important to her, and Susan wasn't going to betray that trust. "I'll take care of this, and I won't tell anyone. You just sit here quietly and let me finish your room. Okay?" Susan didn't read the message, because she was anxious to finish the bed and hide whatever the note said before someone else saw it.

121 nodded slightly. "Tha ou," 121 said, her words slurring again.

After Susan finished, she got 121 back into her bed. This time the woman looked directly into Susan's eyes. "Ou goood gur . . ."

Disturbed by what had happened, Susan's mind was racing. She didn't see her supervisor or anyone else in the hallway, so she slipped into the locker room. Aides were required to lock their phones away while they were working and retrieve them at the end of their shifts. Susan spun the combination lock and quietly opened her half-length metal locker. She slipped her cell phone from her purse and snapped several copies of the note 121 had written.

Now she had to figure out how to destroy the checklist before someone else saw the message. Susan had no idea what it said, or even if it would make sense. But if she destroyed the note, what would she tell her supervisor when she asked for the checklist?

Trying to think quickly, Susan ducked into one of the bathrooms. She took the paper and ran water over it until the ink from the note 121 had written was running and illegible. She then took a paper towel and removed as much of the blue ink as she could. There. It was hardly noticeable. She would tell her supervisor she had accidentally knocked a patient's pitcher of water onto her clipboard. A scolding was inevitable, but she was willing to take that chance.

The rest of Susan's workday seemed to drag on forever, as she was anxious to get home and see what the note said. She laughed to herself when she thought that maybe the note would say "go to hell" or something else obnoxious. But deep inside, Susan knew the note was important to 121. And that made it important to Susan.

CHAPTER 47

It was nearly six o'clock that evening when Enid remembered Ginger's message to call Josh. Maybe she should wait until she got home, had a shower, and could settle down to talk. Lately, it seemed that their conversations were mostly about avoiding work issues or anything that could cause problems between them. She put a reminder on her phone so she wouldn't forget again and packed up her things to leave for the day.

When she arrived at her small bungalow, she braked suddenly a short distance from the house. The lights were on, and she knew she had not left them on that morning. Perhaps Karla had. No, she remembered Karla had gone straight to her car when Enid had dropped her off. Surely if someone was trying to rob her, or worse, they wouldn't announce their presence by turning on the lights. Even the porch light was on.

Enid proceeded slowly, wincing at the noise of her tires on the gravel driveway. No way to sneak up on whoever was there. She pulled up closer to the house and walked to the front door, giving it a little tug. It was locked. No signs of a break-in. She put the key in the lock and cracked the door open. "Who's there?" No answer. She reached into her tote and found the personal alarm Jack had given her. Although with no one close by, it wouldn't help much. Even so, she had it in hand, ready to activate. If it was as loud as Jack said, maybe it would scare her intruder away. Her 9mm gun was in the glove compartment, so she decided to go back and get it before calling 911.

She jogged back to the car, and just as she had her hand on the gun, she heard a voice behind her. "Enid. It's me." Josh's voice cut the stillness of the woods surrounding her. She breathed a sigh of relief.

"Josh, you scared me to death. I thought someone had broken in. Worse yet, I could have shot you."

He threw his arms around her. "Sorry, babe. I didn't mean to alarm you."

"Where's your truck?"

Josh released his bear hug on her shoulders. "I had to put my pickup in the shop, so I asked someone to drop me off here. Hope you don't mind. I left a message earlier today for you to call me. After Ginger said you were out, I didn't call your cell. Figured you were busy."

"I'm sorry I didn't call you. I was out most of the day." Had she avoided him? She pushed the unwelcome thought from her mind.

Josh took her hand. "Come on, I've got dinner ready. Hope you're hungry."

Enid followed Josh inside to the small dining area. A bouquet of roses was in the center. She looked at Josh. "What's this all about?"

With a boyish grin on his face, he pulled out a chair for her. "Let's eat first and talk later."

Josh had prepared baked chicken breasts, crusted with pecans and a thin sauce that tasted a little like bourbon and maple syrup. It was delicious. After they split a slice of chocolate cream cake from Sarah's, Josh suggested they go out on the screened porch to talk. Too many mosquitoes this time of year to sit on the open front porch.

They sat holding hands for several minutes before Enid spoke. "Where is your state vehicle? Or were you afraid for it to be seen at my place?"

Josh pulled her closer. "I just didn't want to be reminded of work."

"You don't really like the new job, do you?"

He shrugged.

"You can always quit."

"And do what? Pete is doing a great job in my old job as Madden police chief, and the mayor loves him. Stanholt has my sheriff's position, and I get the impression he's claimed it permanently. Not to mention the governor likes having a 'yes' man like Stanholt. Maybe I could go to work for the new distribution center, learn to drive a forklift, or better yet, operate one of those robots."

"So what will you do?"

Laughing, Josh asked, "Do you need an assistant?"

"I don't think Ginger would welcome you to our little office." They sat in silence for another few minutes. "You're leaving, aren't you?"

Josh sighed. "I don't want to, but I don't have another solution. Not yet, anyway." He pulled her close again. "But wherever I go, I'd like for you to go with me."

Enid pulled away and turned to look at him. "I'm sorry this new job didn't turn out to be what you wanted. And I support your decision to quit, if that's what you want to do. But I can't pack my bags and follow you. I have a life here. A good life. What happens if we settle somewhere else, and you stay in law enforcement and I work for another newspaper? We're back in the same boat."

"You make it sound hopeless for us. Is that how you feel?" Josh buried his face in his hands.

Enid pulled his hands away from his face and held them in hers. "Some days. But I don't want to lose you, either. I just don't have a solution. Maybe you should visit New Mexico for a while and reconnect with your sister. Perhaps getting away from here will help you clear your head so you can make a more permanent decision."

"I've considered that. But let me ask you something. Is Jack's illness what's keeping you here? You know he wouldn't want you to stay out of pity."

Enid leaned back in her chair. "Is it that hard for you to imagine that I really like my life and my work here? It's been years since I could say I'm truly happy. Twice, I gave up my dreams for other people, and I ended up resenting it. I can't do that to myself again. Even for you. And, no, I'm not doing it for Jack either. If I didn't want to be at the *Tri-County Gazette*, I'd leave."

Josh stood up. "Lately, I seem to have the knack for saying the wrong things to you. I didn't mean to minimize your job. I just don't want to leave without you." He started to walk away. "I'll clean up the kitchen. Then can you drop me off at my place?"

Enid shook her head. "No." She put her hand on his arm to stop him. "I want you to stay. Tonight, I mean. We'll deal with the rest of all this later."

CHAPTER 48

By the time Susan got home, she had nearly forgotten the note from the patient in room 121. Her two young sons were demanding something to eat, so she made them their favorite meal: mac and cheese in the blue and yellow box. It was nearly nine o'clock by the time she had gotten them to bed, cleaned the kitchen, and checked her emails. That's when she remembered the photo of the note on her phone.

She made a print on her old HP printer, praying that it would work this time. She made a mental note to check Walmart to see if they had one on sale she could afford. If not, she'd check Craig's List for a used one. Sitting at the kitchen table, she studied the note. The old woman had been medicated when she wrote it, so it might be nothing. Yet, 121 looked desperate.

She could clearly make out a word starting with "B" and the word "call." The "B" word could possibly be "Black-man." Yet, even in her drugged state, 121 had capitalized whatever the word was, so it had to be a name of something. Maybe it was a relative. Poor thing had not had any outside visitors since she came in. Nurse Louise had made it clear that she was related to the patient and that no other visitors were allowed. Susan wondered if there was some kind of rule against being the nurse for someone you were related to. Although Nurse Louise seemed to be close with the home's director, so the rules probably didn't apply to her.

Susan studied the note again. Ever since she had been a little girl, Susan had loved to solve puzzles. She read mysteries from the county library when she could get a few minutes to herself. This note was a puzzle. Well, maybe. Or maybe not. She cautioned herself not to let her imagination get the best of her. She glanced at the clock. It was approaching nine thirty, and she tried to get to bed by ten since she had to get up at five each morning.

She traced the note with her finger, trying to follow the flow of the letters. B-l-a-c-k-. Was the next letter a "w"? Blackwell? Maybe that was it. Susan didn't know anyone around with that name. It sounded British. Maybe 121 wanted a cup of tea. Susan giggled to herself at this preposterous idea. She had been watching too many reruns of *Downton Abbey*.

"Okay," she said aloud, "let's go with Blackwell." The problem was the person could live anywhere in the United States, or in the world for that matter. Given this possibility, she decided there was no point in searching online without more information.

Using the same technique, Susan traced the first word on the paper with her finger. Was that an "M"? No. The letters sloped down because 121 had problems writing. Susan held up the note and turned it to the left until it became an "E." Well, maybe. Susan rubbed her temples and looked at the clock again. It was time to go to bed.

After tossing an hour or more, Susan drifted into a restless sleep. She dreamed of trying to escape from a tangle of vines in a jungle. Then she went to sleep again and dreamed that she had fallen into a deep hole and couldn't get out.

Reluctantly, she got out of bed, accepting that there would be little sleep that night.

Sitting at the dining table, she studied 121's note again. "E Blackwell" was all she could get, and that could even be wrong. Whatever followed the E was totally illegible. Ellen? Eleanor? Esther? The possibilities were staggering. Susan turned on her laptop and waited. Just like her printer, it was old and took forever to boot up, but she couldn't afford a new one right now.

When she typed "E Blackwell" in Google, she instantly got back over two million hits. "Well, that's not very helpful," she whispered, careful not to wake the boys. She then added South Carolina to the search parameters, but that only increased the hits to more than eight million. Someone had told her once how to limit the scope of the search, but she had forgotten how. She would try a few more combinations and then give up. Maybe she could ask 121 what she had written, although that possibility seemed about as hopeless as her online search. Nurse Louise made sure 121 stayed incoherent, telling Susan that, if not kept medicated, 121 would have fits and could injure herself, other patients, or the staff. Even with Susan's limited medical training, she doubted 121 needed as much medication as she was getting.

"Okay," Susan sighed. "One more try, and then I'm going back to bed." On the fifth page, she saw a link to a news article from the *Tri-County Gazette,* which didn't cover her area but was just one county down the highway. In the article, reporter Enid Blackwell discussed the potential dangers of choosing the wrong power of attorney. Could this be the E Blackwell 121 had scribbled on Susan's clipboard?

But if Susan tried to contact Enid Blackwell, what could she say without sounding weird? The newspaper's website listed only one phone number, so Susan jotted it down. Chasing down one person out of eight-million possibilities seemed like a fool's errand, but she tucked the phone number in her purse and went back to bed.

CHAPTER 49

Sylvia paced her small living room, occasionally pulling back the curtain and checking to see if her grandson Robert had arrived. Just because he agreed to come over didn't necessarily mean he would. He had stood her up before.

This time might be different, though, because she had threatened to call the police on him if he didn't come to her house and talk. Maybe she shouldn't have been so forceful. She had nearly given up on his coming when she heard a car pull into the driveway.

After unlocking the front door and taking a deep breath, Sylvia sat on the worn brown plaid sofa and waited for Robert to come inside.

Wearing black jeans, a hoodie, and a deep scowl, Robert opened the door without knocking. Sylvia began to question her decision to confront him like this. But she had to. Things weren't adding up, or perhaps they were. Either way, she needed answers. She had prayed all night. After her daughter-in-law, Robert's mother, died of pneumonia, Robert's father, her son, left for Alaska, unable to deal with being a single parent. Sylvia took on the responsibility and promised God she would bring him up as a good Christian boy. She had tried her best.

He flopped into the chair across from her and pulled the hood off his head. "What's up?"

Hands shaking, Sylvia eased herself to the edge of the sofa. "Would you like something to eat?"

"Not hungry, and I gotta be somewhere."

"Well, then I'll just get to it. Do you know anything about Catherine Murray's disappearance?"

He shrugged. "Nope."

Angered by his attitude, she pressed further. "Don't lie to me, Robert. I can tell when you do. I've seen you charm people when it suits you. You made Catherine trust you. I know how you operate. Then you and that girlfriend of yours, you knew about her money and Catherine trying to find her family when you helped her on that computer program. Then your friend Danny got killed up there in the woods by the old barn. You seem to be the common thread in all this, but you haven't said a word. And as far as I know, you haven't talked to the police. How do you explain all that?"

"I didn't do nothing to her. Besides, they said a gang killed Danny." Robert glanced at the door, as though planning to bolt any minute.

Sylvia studied Robert's face, looking for telltale signs of what? Fear, deception? But he managed not to reveal anything. "She's a nurse, ain't she, that girlfriend of yours? How is it that she's interested in you? You got no job, you hang out with thugs, and you can't carry on a conversation."

Robert sat silently.

"Here's what I think. I think you and her cooked up this scheme to get that poor woman's money. I don't know how, but I think that little hussy of yours used you, convinced you to go along with her foolish idea. You best be careful or she'll outfox you. You might be the computer whiz and know how to play all those games, but she knows how to play people."

"She's not a hussy, and she's not playing me."

"Well then, there's that to be thankful for." Sylvia's anger overtook her fear. "I'll ask you again. Do you know anything about Catherine? Did your not-a-hussy girlfriend and you do something to her?"

"I don't need you to tell me how to live my life. We're saving money to buy a little farm in Kentucky and start a family."

Sylvia threw back her head and laughed. "Yeah, right."

Robert jumped up with such force that Sylvia pushed herself back on the sofa as Robert leaned over her, his six-foot frame bearing down. Suddenly, his hands encircled her neck, and he began squeezing hard. "You're an old bitch."

Sylvia struggled to get free, knowing it was futile. One of her flat-soled, patent leather black shoes came off in the struggle and went flying across the coffee table, knocking over a small porcelain figure of Jesus holding a lamb in his arms. As Sylvia took her last breath, she prayed for Jesus to take her into his arms.

CHAPTER 50

Enid was sleeping so soundly that she didn't hear the cell phone beside her bed ringing. But Josh did. "Do you want to answer that?" He handed her the phone.

She looked at the screen. "It's Jack. Why would he be calling me at 2:00 a.m.?" She answered the call. "Jack, are you okay?"

"Sorry to bother you, but there's been another murder. My contact at the sheriff's office just called. I thought you'd like to handle this one."

"Why? Who is it?" Enid asked.

"It's Catherine Murray's neighbor, the one you talked to, Sylvia."

Enid sat up and turned on the bedside lamp. "Oh, no. When did it happen?"

"Sometime this evening, apparently. One of the neighbors asked Sylvia to feed her cats while she was traveling. She said Sylvia always texted to say the cats were fed and safe. But when the cat owner didn't hear from Sylvia and couldn't get in touch with her, she got worried, especially with all that's happened in the neighborhood. The cat owner requested a welfare check and the deputy found the front door open, the house ransacked, and Sylvia strangled on her sofa."

Enid's stomach was in knots. "Oh, God. That's awful. I'll go there now and see what I can find out. Thanks."

"Be careful." Before Jack ended the call, he added, "Take Josh with you."

Enid put the phone on the bedside table. "Did you tell Jack you were coming here?"

"I told you I tried to find you, so I called Jack. I might have mentioned I was coming over."

Enid wasn't sure how to feel. These man-talks behind her back were annoying. Yet, she knew both of them were only trying to be helpful. But Sylvia's death was a much bigger concern right now. "Well, are you coming?"

. . .

When Enid and Josh arrived at the scene, a half dozen deputies surrounded the area and flashing blue lights lit up the neighborhood. Enid parked about two blocks from Sylvia's house. "If you don't want to be seen with me, you can stay in the car," she said to Josh.

"I think I'm past that," he said, opening the door.

They jogged up the street, getting as close as they could before someone stopped them. "Hey, wait, you can't . . ." The deputy pointed his flashlight at them. "Josh Hart, is that you?"

Josh nodded. "Hey, man. Good to see you. What happened here?"

"An old woman got strangled."

"Any signs of gang activity? Just asking because of the other incidents around here."

The deputy grinned. "That's right, I almost forgot. You're a big man with the governor's office now. Some kind of gang expert."

"Yeah, something like that."

"As far as I know, there's nothing here to indicate it."

"Gangs are not big into strangling," Josh said.

"Hey, look, it was good to see you, but I got to get back to work," the deputy said. "Stop by to see us sometime."

"Sure thing," Josh said. He and Enid walked a little closer to the house, being careful to stay outside the police perimeter. "Uh-oh. There's Sheriff Stanholt."

"It not too late for you to go back to the car," Enid said. "I don't think he's seen you."

"Screw that." Taking long strides, Josh headed straight for Stanholt.

"Oh, boy," Enid muttered to herself before she took off after Josh. This was sure to be an interesting confrontation.

Stanholt's face registered surprise when he saw Josh. "I don't recall anyone suggesting this could involve a gang," he said to Josh.

"I talked to this victim before I left the sheriff's office. I think she might know something about the woman missing from across the street, Catherine Murray."

"Oh, yeah. I think I heard that someone had filed a missing person's report." Stanholt looked at Enid. "You here as a reporter or did you just tag along with your boyfriend?"

Enid flashed her credentials. "Press. And he's with me."

"I'll be making a statement to the press later," Stanholt said to Enid. He turned to Josh. "And I suggest you stay out of the way. The governor might wonder why you're out here in the middle of the night. Don't you have early meetings in Columbia? You probably need your beauty rest."

Enid put her hand on Josh's arm as she spoke. "Thank you, Sheriff Stanholt. I look forward to your official statement." She tugged on Josh's arm as she turned to leave. At first Josh stood firm, and then he laughed at Stanholt and shook his head before walking away.

As Enid and Josh walked back to her car, she kept replaying all she had learned since Catherine's disappearance. "Something is not right."

"What do you mean?"

"I need to fill you in on what's going on. I was trying to avoid pulling you into all this, but I guess we're past that, too. Let's go back to the house, and I'll tell you all I know."

CHAPTER 51

With steaming cups of tea and coffee in front of them, Enid and Jack sat at her dining table. "There's so much that doesn't add up," she said.

"Why don't you just start from the beginning."

Enid dunked her tea bag a few times. "Catherine Murray disappears. She doesn't tell anyone other than poor Roscoe, and she leaves him stranded at the historical society. She knew he needed to leave Madden for another job. Then Ruby-Grace, Roo, finds out that Catherine has changed her executor and power of attorney without discussing it with Roo, Catherine's only close relative."

"People change their minds all the time. And she was probably embarrassed to tell Roo she had dropped her. Are you sure Roo is on the up and up?"

"I checked her out. She's who she says she is. Besides, she wasn't going to get much from Catherine, in case you're thinking along those lines. Catherine was leaving the bulk of her estate to charities, and Roo knew it. But here's the biggest problem. The person Catherine appointed as executor and power of attorney is not who Catherine thinks she is."

"I'm not following you."

"Roo is an insurance investigator and found out, through her sources, that Belinda Murray, the real one, has no idea that she was Catherine's newly appointed executor and power of attorney. Catherine apparently had been dealing with an impostor."

"Surely Catherine wasn't that gullible."

Enid shrugged. "That's what I said. But here's another weird connection. Sylvia's grandson, Robert, helped Catherine with her online family tree search. That's how she and the woman calling herself Belinda connected. And Robert and the first murder victim were at least acquainted."

"I wonder if Stanholt is checking all that out?"

"Catherine's family history was online for anyone to see, so it would be easy for someone to fabricate a false story to support the known facts."

"Didn't Roo get suspicious about this Belinda woman?"

"Roo and Catherine had not been that close lately, so Roo didn't know what was going on."

"Do you think Catherine was forced to make the changes against her will?" Josh asked.

"I don't think she was forced. Perhaps just conned. Sylvia witnessed Catherine's signature on some legal documents. But Sylvia didn't really look at the papers closely, so it could have been anything."

"And now, Sylvia is dead," Josh said.

"Do you think the first murder by the barn was actually gang related?"

"The governor has gone out of his way to assure everyone that it wasn't. I'm sure Stanholt was instructed to steer everyone in a different direction. While I don't think it was gang related, I don't think the possibility should be dismissed without a more thorough investigation. That's one of the things that got me on the wrong side of the governor."

"Why don't you think it was a gang killing?"

"I haven't done the investigation, but since the victim was into the local drug scene, that's more likely what got him killed."

"But the 14 spray painted on the barn and on Catherine's storage shed. Don't you think that points to a gang?"

"Maybe. But that tag is common knowledge. Anyone who wanted to throw off the investigation could have used it."

"Another strange thing is that the woman claiming to be Belinda corresponded with Catherine and gave her address as a small family cemetery in Winnsboro." Enid told Josh about her conversation with the stonecutter and about Karla's return to Madden. "She's convinced Catherine is in trouble."

Josh put his mug on the table. "Have you told the sheriff's office all this?"

"We tried to tell them, but Roo and I both got the impression they weren't convinced Catherine's disappearance was suspicious. They've suggested several times that she probably just went away and didn't tell anyone."

"I'm going to talk to Stanholt in the morning, and if he won't listen to me, well, then I'll have to go to the press. Know anyone I could talk to?" He smiled. "I'm serious about talking to him, but not the press part. Not yet."

Enid hit his arm gently with her fist. "You're such a troublemaker."

CHAPTER 52

Enid was sitting at her desk the next morning, speculating on how Josh's conversation with Sheriff Stanholt would go. She forced herself to put it out of her mind for the moment, as she had to get the article about Sylvia's death ready for tomorrow's edition. Later, she'd fill in whatever tidbits of information Stanholt provided the press. She was deep in thought about Sylvia when she heard a tap on her door. "Come on in, Ginger."

"I've got this call on hold. It's kinda weird, so I wanted to talk to you before you picked up."

"Weird? In what way?" Enid asked.

"She says she's looking for someone named E Blackwell, or she thinks that's the name. Then she said something about a patient at a nursing home."

The hairs on Enid's arm stood up. "I'll take it. Thanks." She waited for Ginger to get out of earshot. "Hello, this is Enid Blackwell. How can I help you?"

"Thanks for taking my call. I know that young woman thinks I'm a crackpot, and maybe I am."

"Why don't you just tell me why you called."

"I'm an aide at a nursing home. One of my patients asked me to call someone, and I'm wondering if that might be you. But I can't talk right now. Can we meet somewhere? I'm calling in sick today."

Enid's this-could-be-trouble antenna shot up. "Can't we just talk by phone when you're available?"

"I know this sounds crazy, and I'm sorry to have bothered you."

"No, don't hang up. Tell me where you want to meet. Can I bring someone with me?"

"Well, I guess that's alright. I'm not a dangerous person or anything. I'm just being cautious. I live near Whitmire, but we can meet at the Grille on Main in Newberry if that works for you."

Enid glanced at the clock on her wall. "I'll be there at noon."

"I saw your picture online, with one of your articles, so I'll recognize you."

After the mysterious caller hung up, Enid debated on who to take with her. It wasn't that she was afraid. After all, she had been in far more dangerous situations. But she wanted someone else to hear the conversation. This woman might be delusional, although she sounded normal, and a second person could help assess the woman's credibility. Ordinarily, she'd ask Jack, but he had his hands full right now. After all, this might be a fool's errand. Roo was still traveling out of the state, and Josh might be tied up with the governor all day. No telling what kind of mess he would be in after talking to Stanholt. She could always take another reporter. She was mentally going through the list when her cell phone rang. "Karla, I'm glad you called. What are you doing today?"

. . .

When Enid and Karla walked into The Grille on Main, it had just opened for lunch and the crowd was sparse. "That's her, near the back," Karla said.

Enid started to ask how she knew, but Karla was already headed toward the young woman. When she saw Karla and Enid coming toward her, she stood up. "Thanks for coming. Please have a seat." After they all sat down, the woman said, "I'm Susan." She looked nervous.

Enid introduced herself and Karla and then pulled a pad and pen from her tote. "May I take some notes?"

Susan glanced around the restaurant. "I guess so. I could get fired, and probably will, for talking with you."

"We just need to know more about the patient you mentioned," Karla said.

"What is your patient's name?" Enid asked.

"That's the thing, I have no idea. She's in room 121 and that's what we all call her, 121."

"Haven't you seen her medical records?" Karla asked.

"No one has been allowed to see them. It's all very strange," Susan said.

"How long has she been there?" Enid asked.

"Several months, I think. I've only been working with her a couple weeks."

"Does she have visitors?" Enid asked.

"I've never seen any. Nurse Louise says 121 has no relatives, other than her."

"You mean the nurse is related to 121?" Enid asked.

"That's what she said."

"Did the nurse admit 121 to the nursing facility?" Karla asked.

Susan's shoulders slumped. "I wish I could answer all your questions, but I can't. I just don't know."

"Tell me why you decided to contact me," Enid said. "You said you had a note or something from this patient."

Susan pulled her cell phone from her purse and tapped on a photograph. "She wrote this on my clipboard of daily rounds. I washed the note away before I turned in my sheet, but I took a photo of it first."

Enid turned the photo around several times to look at it.

"I traced the last part with my finger, and that's how I got Blackwell out of it. When she tried to write the first name, if that's even a name, her hand was shaking. She only got one letter."

Enid handed the phone to Karla to look at the photograph. "Catherine is a smart woman, far more so than people give her credit for," Karla said. "I think she realized she could only get so much written, and she knew it would be much harder to find an 'Enid B' than 'E Blackwell.' She also knew it would be easier for Susan to find you than me or anyone else she might have written down." She handed the phone back to Susan.

"I don't know about all that," Susan said. "She stays pretty drugged up."

"Can you email me that photo?" Enid asked.

Susan's eyes widened. "I don't think I should do that. If Nurse Louise found out . . ."

Enid glanced at Karla, then asked Susan, "Why do you think 121 tried to reach out to me?"

Susan was silent.

"I think you know why," Enid said. "Your patient is in danger and she knows it. That note was a cry for help." Enid paused. "She must have trusted you a lot to take that chance. Thank you for reaching out to me."

"Where is this nursing home where you work?" Karla asked.

"It's kinda out of the way, but not far from here." Susan glanced around again. "I've worked at several hospitals but never for a nursing home. Even so, this one seems really strange."

"Why is that?" Enid asked.

"For one thing, none of the patients get visitors. It's almost like a dumping ground, pardon me for using that expression, for old people. It's heartbreaking. Makes you wonder what will happen when you get old like that."

"Do you think 121 is being held against her will or abused in any way?" Enid asked.

Susan's eyes filled with tears. "One day, I found her in soiled diapers, and she had bruises after Nurse Louise attended her. Another time, 121 had a black eye. Nurse Louise said 121 had fallen." Susan got a tissue from her purse. "It's just not right what they're doing to her."

Enid glanced at Karla who was sitting stoically. Then Enid flipped the paper over on her pad to a clean sheet and handed it to Susan. "Please write down the name of the facility and any directions you can give us. If you're not working today, that might be a good time for us to go."

Susan shook her head. "Oh, no. Please don't go today. That might look suspicious if you show up when I'm not there. Besides, you have to be on an approved visitor list to see 121 or any of the patients. I was told only 121's medical power of attorney was allowed to talk to her."

"But you said she didn't have any visitors," Karla said.

"No, she doesn't. But you won't be able to get in if you're not on the list."

"Then how can we get in?" Enid asked.

"I think I know a way," Karla said.

Enid nodded to Karla, then said to Susan. "We appreciate your taking this chance. We won't give up your name, but if 121 needs help, we're going to do everything we can to help her. Even if she's not our friend, it sounds like this woman is in trouble. Elder abuse is a serious crime."

CHAPTER 53

At the sheriff's office, Stanholt sat in the same desk chair Josh had occupied not too long ago. "I'm a busy man, Josh, but I'm happy to make time for the former Bowman County Sheriff. What can I do for you?"

Josh bristled at "former" but let it go. "I've got some information about two of the murders you're investigating. Thought I should share it with you."

Stanholt sipped from his cup. "Guess I should have offered you some coffee."

Josh shook his head. "I'm fine."

"I'm not real up on all the official protocol, but aren't you supposed to go through your boss first, you know, the governor, when working with local law enforcement?"

"I'm sick and tired of going around my ass to get to my elbow. This matter is urgent, and I'll deal with my boss later. And, by the way, I'm not the former sheriff. I'm still the sheriff of Bowman County."

Stanholt gave what looked like a forced smile. "Fair enough. So tell me what's going on."

Josh paused briefly to gather his thoughts. He tapped his fingertips together while thinking. "It began with the killing near the old barn, the one we all assumed was a gang hit because of the 14 tag spray painted on it. But I was never convinced we were dealing with one of the larger, known gangs, like MS13, Crips, Dirty White Boys, or any of the

Neo-Nazi groups. All of these gangs, and at least a dozen more, operate here in South Carolina, but something about the crime scene was off. The murder was brutal, but we were not able to determine that the victim, Daniel Boodemore, had any gang connections. Typically, gangs kill to establish dominance in an area, so they kill their rivals in a brutal manner to warn others. Sometimes, innocent people do get killed in initiations or as bystanders. But the gangs typically don't make a ritual out of it like the way Boodemore was killed."

The conversation was interrupted by a deputy standing at Stanholt's door. "Sheriff, you have a meeting in five minutes. Just wanted to remind you."

"Thanks, but tell them I won't make it. They can handle it without me." He turned back to Josh. "Sure you don't want that coffee now?"

"Don't mind if I do, but I can get it."

Stanholt motioned to a small room behind him. "I got a pot going back there, the one you left behind. Help yourself."

When Josh returned with coffee in hand, he sat and began again. "All that made the task force doubtful of any gang connection, but the second killing, a couple miles away, does have all the hallmarks of a gang hit. The victim was a woman known to associate with gangs. And the coroner's report said she was pregnant—probably what got her killed."

Stanholt began scribbling some notes on his pad, which Josh took as a good sign. At least he was listening. "Go on," Stanholt said. "Anything else?"

"The third killing is especially suspicious."

"That's the one from yesterday, right?"

"Correct. Her name was Sylvia Ryce, and she lived right down the street from the old barn and across from the missing woman. Well, here's the funny thing about that . . ." Josh paused to sip his coffee. "You see, Sylvia's grandson was friends with the Boodemore boy, the first victim. Apparently, they went to high school together and hung out, and both were into the local drug scene. Sylvia lived across the street from Catherine Murray, who has been missing, or at least out of touch, for a couple of months. While she's been gone, her house was vandalized and tagged with that same 14 we saw at the barn."

"You told me earlier about the significance of 14, but refresh my memory."

"It's a gang creed that contains fourteen words. I can't remember it exactly without my notes, but it's something about securing the existence of white people and a future for white children. Pretty sick stuff."

Stanholt took more notes. "Other than all of this happening in relatively the same area, is there any other connection between Catherine Murray and the other three murders?"

Josh hesitated before responding. Most of the information he knew about Murray came from Enid and Roo's investigation, and he didn't want to pull them into the conversation. "Supposedly, Sylvia witnessed some legal documents Murray signed just before her disappearance."

Stanholt shrugged. "That's it?"

Josh decided to stop without revealing anything further. He hadn't decided yet how far he could trust the acting sheriff who was clamoring to make the position permanent. "It's my understanding Murray's great-niece reported all this to your office. You should have more details on record."

"Fair enough." Stanholt pushed back from his desk. "So what exactly are you asking me to do with all this?"

"Honestly, I'm not sure, other than to give Murray's disappearance a serious look. My gut tells me it's all connected, at least the first murder, the disappearance, and the third murder, but I have no proof. Besides, your office is in charge of the investigation."

"I'll see where we are with it." Stanholt stood up, a sign he was dismissing Josh. "If you decide you want your job back, maybe you can put in a good word for me to take your cushy spot."

"You mean you'd like to work on the gang task force?" Knowing what he knew now, Josh couldn't imagine anyone wanting the politically charged job. Or at least anyone other than Stanholt. "Will do."

As Josh was walking out the door, Stanholt called out to him. "Give Ms. Blackwell my regards."

. . .

Sheriff Stanholt smiled to himself as Josh left his office. As a sheriff in South Carolina, Stanholt reported to the governor but had little day-to-day interaction with the man himself, working instead with the governor's aides. He picked up the handset and began punching in the governor's number. About halfway through, he hung up and decided he needed to think about what he would say to Governor Larkin. *Hey, did you know Josh Hart is running his own investigation instead of letting the sheriff's office do its job?* Josh would surely be dismissed from the task force. If so, would Larkin put Josh back into his old job, forcing Stanholt out? Or would Josh be fired outright? Knowing what he did about his boss, Stanholt was betting it would be the latter. With Josh out of the picture, the governor would likely appoint Stanholt to fill the sheriff's position permanently.

He began dialing the number again. Before he tapped the last number, he saw his son's picture, in its polished wood frame on his desk, out of the corner of his eye.

Stanholt had tried to be a good dad and to teach the boy, now a father himself, right from wrong. Before Stanholt's wife died, he promised her he would raise their son to be kind, honest, and hard-working. As far as the sheriff could tell, he had scored a trifecta. His son told his father that he often asked himself, "What would Dad do?"

He hit the disconnect button and sat back in his chair. Life was not as simple as his son sometimes saw it, and Stanholt sometimes got annoyed when his son couldn't see the complexities of a situation. Stanholt would like to think he'd be in line for Josh's task force position, should the vacancy arise. But the odds were slim that he'd be appointed. In fact, he might not win the next election for sheriff. Stanholt asked himself if he'd be able to explain to his son why he called the governor to have Josh reprimanded and perhaps fired. How could he explain his motivation? Josh wasn't a bad guy, in fact, he was someone Stanholt envied for his experience and personality, not to mention his good looks.

Stanholt glanced at his son's photo again, sighed, and then dialed an inter-office extension number. "Hey, bring me the file on that missing woman." He glanced down at his notes. "Name's Catherine Murray."

CHAPTER 54

After hearing Karla's plan to get into the nursing home to see 121, Enid paced back and forth. "That's a crazy plan. If you get caught, you could go to jail."

"Which is why I want to do this alone. I owe Catherine a lot, and on the outside chance 121 *is* Catherine, I can't sit by and do nothing."

"You've never really talked about how you and Catherine met. Roo said you might be related by marriage."

"Catherine is not a spinster. She was married once when she was very young, to my brother Chitto. They immediately had a child together, a daughter named Emily, and only a year of wedded bliss before . . . before tragedy struck. Emily was diagnosed with a rare form of pancreatic cancer and died two months later."

"How awful for Catherine. She never hinted at any of this. Why hasn't Roo mentioned it?"

"Roo didn't know. She and Catherine only connected later in life. Up until then, they lived in different cities and were just distant relatives who rarely, if ever, saw each other."

"I think you should also tell Roo about Emily. I'm sure she'd like to know."

"Perhaps. Unfortunately, her story gets worse. After Emily's death, my brother was distraught, inconsolable. Less than a month later, he drove his car off a cliff in the Blue

Ridge Mountains. It was ruled accidental, and the insurance company paid off without hesitation. But Catherine and I were both convinced it was suicide."

Enid put her face in her hands and shook her head. "That's awful. Poor Catherine lost a child and her husband. And you lost a brother and a niece."

"It was hard on everyone. Catherine was twenty-five when she moved here from Virginia, and she never looked back. She buried herself in small-town living for decades, and as you know, worked with the town council to found the Madden Historical Society. I tried to stay in touch, but it was only in the last ten years that she and I became close again. I think I reminded her too much of Chitto."

"Thank you for telling me all this."

Karla nodded slightly to Enid. "Of course. You have earned the right to know."

"But how did Catherine amass millions of dollars in her bank account?"

"Chitto had a good job and left her a fairly large insurance policy. When our parents died, Chitto and I each got a sizeable amount of money, and his estate went to Catherine as well. She never wanted to use the money for herself and insisted that she would use it only for her long-term care, if she ever needed it. She didn't want to burden anyone with that responsibility. That's why picking the right power of attorney and executor was so important to her."

"Roo mentioned that most of the estate was going to charity."

"That's right. Catherine vowed never to remarry and committed to leaving the bulk of her estate to charity."

Enid paused. "I'm just trying to process all this. Right now, I'm feeling a bit foolish for not checking further into Catherine's background."

"I didn't tell you earlier, because none of it is relevant to her disappearance. And I was sworn to keep her secret. I can't explain why, other than to say that Catherine wanted to compartmentalize that part of her life. That was then, and she closed the door on it. Or at least she tried to pretend she had. She also didn't want anyone's sympathy. I've come to accept that many families harbor deep secrets. Under the circumstances, I think Catherine would agree you've earned the right to know about her past." She paused. "I told you once that you, Cade, and Josh were all connected warriors together searching for the truth. You have another piece of the truth now."

"The warriors have split up."

"What do you mean?"

"Jack has cancer and is limiting his work, and Cade has moved to London on a long-term assignment. And now Josh is hinting that he may leave his job and return to New Mexico. The warriors are no longer a team."

Karla made a fist and gently tapped her chest. "You are all connected here, in your hearts. That won't change. You are now being asked to step away from your fellow warriors and to take a leadership role. This is not a test. This is a confirmation. You are ready. This part of your journey is about realizing your own potential. And as scary as it may seem, you will blossom and step into your own greatness."

Enid smiled. "I don't mean to offend you, but that sounds like a new-age philosophy lesson."

Karla smiled. "New-age is merely the ancient ways coming back to us." She took Enid's hands in hers. "You are so much more than you think you are. Don't be afraid of your future."

"Well, I am afraid of this hair-brained scheme of yours. If you impersonate a social worker, you could get into big trouble."

"So you're suggesting I contact the real Social Services office, a government bureaucracy, and file a request for them to forget all the red tape and barge into the nursing home right away to check on a woman known as 121 who might not even be Catherine. Is that your counter-plan?"

"Something like that." Enid gently pulled her hands away. There was something about Karla's touch that made her feel transparent, as though she couldn't conceal anything. It also made her feel vulnerable.

Karla pointed toward the ceiling to emphasize the point she wanted to make. "Here's a tip for you. Write an article about the failings of Social Services in this and other states. While many are good, hard-working people trying to do what's right, they are understaffed and too often put rules ahead of human welfare. Not to mention they move slowly, if at all."

"Thanks for that tip. I'll keep it in mind."

"Seriously, by the time they decide if they will even investigate, which is unlikely given the sketchy information we have, it may be too late. You heard Susan describe 121's condition. If it is Catherine, I won't let her down. If it's not her, then we'll file an official complaint, assuming we find anything concrete to report."

Enid pulled her laptop from the other side of the table toward her and opened the cover. "I did a little checking on that facility. It's been reported a number of times for various infractions regarding patient welfare."

"And yet, they are still in business. I rest my case."

"If we do this, we're doing it together. I'm not letting you go in there alone."

"I have to go in alone. Your picture has been in all the newspapers, and with that copper hair of yours, you are easily recognized. Besides, you could lose your job. I won't let that happen."

"Then I'll wait in the car for you."

"I've always wanted my own getaway driver," Karla said.

"Now you've got one. But I still think this is dangerous and crazy."

"Don't tell anyone what we're doing—not Jack and especially not Josh. We can't put either of them in a situation where they have to compromise their ethics."

Enid laughed. "So I don't have any ethics left to compromise. Is that what you're saying?"

Karla smiled. "We are the chosen warriors this time. It's you and me now."

CHAPTER 55

The next day, Enid and Karla executed their plan. From her car in the parking lot at the nursing home, Enid watched Karla walk through the front door. Enid was surprised to see how natural Karla looked in a tailored pants suit. "Got it from a consignment store in Columbia called Roundabouts," Karla had said. "They have pretty much anything you could want, and at great prices." Bargain-hunter was a side of Karla that Enid had never seen.

It was nearly ten in the morning, so the breakfast rounds should be over. Karla had pulled the logo and other information off the state government website and had created an impressive looking ID card. She commented that it was amazing how much you could find online. To complete her new look, Karla had bought a pair of reading glasses at Walgreens, and Enid had helped her with her hair and makeup.

At one time, Enid would never have withheld information from Jack or from Josh. But Jack had enough on his mind, and she didn't want to pull Josh into her and Karla's scheme. He was in enough trouble already. Before getting out of the car, Karla had turned on the recording app on her phone in case she needed it. All Enid could do now was wait in the car.

. . .

When Karla walked through the large glass doors of the nursing facility, she momentarily had second thoughts. Enid was right: she could end up in jail. But then she recalled Susan's description of the woman in room 121 and walked up to the reception desk. "I'm Amanda Peterson with Social Services. I'm here to check on one of your patients." Karla pretended to flip through notes in a file. "I'm sorry I don't have her name handy, but she's in room 121." She pulled her ID from her borrowed briefcase. "Here's my identification."

The young girl tapped on her keyboard. "She's not allowed visitors."

"Perhaps you didn't understand me. I'm not asking your permission. I am here on an official visit."

"I'll have to check with my supervisor." The young woman called a number and waited briefly before hanging up. "My supervisor is not in her office. Stay here. I'll be right back."

Karla watched the young woman walk down the hallway. The signs on the wall showed room 121 to be down the opposite way. Karla watched the woman turn a corner and disappear, and then Karla walked briskly toward 121. She passed several rooms before she saw the small number on the closed door. She glanced back down the hallway to make sure no one was coming and turned the lever to open the door.

Inside the room, Karla's eyes had to adjust to the dim lighting. Blackout curtains were pulled closed and the lights were off. A figure was in the bed with her back to the door.

Karla walked over to the bed. What if the woman saw her and started screaming?

"Hello?" Karla whispered. "Ma'am, are you awake?"

The woman in the bed didn't stir. Karla walked around to the other side of the bed so she could see the woman's face. The woman was in a fetal position and had a lightweight thermal blanket pulled up and covering most of her face. Karla took a deep breath and reached out to touch the woman. "Catherine?"

The woman stirred and moaned softly.

"What do you think you're doing?" a woman bellowed.

Karla jumped back at the sound of the voice at the door. "I'm here to see this patient. My office has received a complaint filed on her behalf." Her heart was pounding in her chest.

"You people think you can just waltz in here. You were told to wait up front." The woman squinted over her reading glasses. "I'll need to call and verify your identity. Let me have your ID."

"And I'll need to file a report on you." Karla walked toward the door to leave before the nurse called security. "You'll be hearing from me."

As she was leaving the room, she heard a voice, faint yet distinct. "Karla, help."

Karla walked back into the room, brushing the nurse aside. "Catherine?"

Catherine Murray's face said it all. She was terrified.

Karla turned to the nurse and looked at the metal nameplate on her uniform. "Nurse Louise, who admitted this woman? Why is she here?"

Louise grabbed Karla's arm and held her tight. "Who are you?"

Karla pulled away. "Let me go or I'll file assault charges against you. Answer my question. Who admitted this woman?" Karla looked into Catherine's wide eyes and tried to reassure her.

Nurse Louise looked out into the hallway. "Susan, come here." The nurse's aide who had met with Enid and Karla in Newberry stopped in her tracks. "Call security now."

Susan glanced at Karla before replying to the nurse. "Yes, ma'am."

Karla said to Catherine. "I'll be back with help. You're okay now. Don't be scared." She nearly knocked the nurse off her feet as she pushed her aside and jogged down the hallway.

"Lock that front door," Louise called out. "Don't let her get away."

Karla ran as fast as she could. The young woman she had talked to at the front desk stood with her mouth open as Karla pushed on the heavy glass door.

"Lock it down, you stupid . . ." Nurse Louise screamed at the woman.

Karla was a few feet into the parking lot when she heard the lock engage on the front door behind her.

Enid saw Karla running and began driving toward her. She slowed the car enough for Karla to jump in.

"Go, get out of here," Karla said. Once in the car, she rested her head on the back of the seat and closed her eyes.

When they were on the highway again and satisfied no one had followed them, Enid asked, "What happened?"

"It's Catherine. I saw her."

CHAPTER 56

Ginger was standing near the front door when Enid and Karla entered the newspaper office. "You look like hell," Ginger said.

Ignoring her, Enid motioned for Karla to follow her. "Come on. I'll see if Jack is in." For a moment Enid hesitated to tell Jack what happened, but he would want to know. She was sure of that.

Enid tapped on Jack's closed door. "Jack, are you in there?" She tapped again. "Jack?"

The door opened slowly. "Sorry, I think I may have dozed off at the desk. Come on in." He glanced at Karla. "Hey, Karla, good to see you again. Please come in."

Enid and Karla sat in the two chairs across from Jack's desk. "I'm sorry to barge in on you like this," Enid said. "But I didn't want you to get caught off-guard."

Jack rubbed his neck. "What have you gotten into now?"

Enid filled him in on their visit to the nursing home, and Karla told him about her encounter with Nurse Louise. "She didn't have a last name on her badge."

"I remember Louise Fletcher playing Nurse Ratched in *One Flew Over the Cuckoo's Nest.*" When both Enid and Karla just looked at him without responding, he added. "Never mind. Just a random thought." He cleared his throat and took a sip of water from the bottle on his desk. "We'll need to report this right away, of course. Catherine may be in worse danger now."

"I agree," Enid said, and Karla nodded. "We'll contact the sheriff's office."

"Perhaps Roo should be the one who files the complaint," Jack said. "She's the closest blood relative and the person who filed the original complaint."

"He's right," Karla said to Enid, shaking her head as if to rid it of her thoughts. "I keep hearing Catherine begging for help."

Enid put her hand on Karla's arm. "We'll get her out of there. I promise."

Karla nodded.

"Is there anything I can do to help?" Jack asked.

"No, I just wanted to bring you into the loop," Enid said.

"Just—" He was interrupted by Enid.

"I know, just be careful. We will. And I'll try to keep the newspaper out of all this."

"Don't worry about that. Just help Catherine and get the story. I don't mean to sound insensitive, but this will make a great article, or perhaps a series."

Enid turned to Karla. "Let's go to my office and see if we can find Roo."

When Enid called Roo's cell phone, she got her voice mail. "Roo, this is Enid. Call me as soon as possible."

Karla held her hands in her lap. "I don't feel good about any of this. Who put Catherine in that place? And why? She doesn't have dementia and is perfectly capable of taking care of herself."

"I think we are dealing with an abduction, and if I don't hear from Roo soon, we'll go to the sheriff ourselves," Enid said.

"I can't fail Catherine. She's counting on me."

"You won't fail her, don't worry." Enid looked at the stack of messages and then at the clock. "I need to do some work while we wait on the call."

"I'm going to walk a little outside," Karla said. "I need some air. Be right back."

After Karla left, Enid called Josh and left a message for him to call her. She was past the point of worrying about keeping him out of this situation.

. . .

The image of Catherine kept playing in Karla's head as she walked down Madden's main street. She had left her purse and cell phone in Enid's office, but it didn't matter. She was just going to walk down past the historical society and then back to Enid's office. The weather was warm, so she took off her black blazer and carried it on her arm. Her usual wardrobe of flowing skirts and thin blouses was much more comfortable. And these heels. Why would anyone wear them voluntarily?

As Karla passed the historical society, she looked at the sign on the door: "Closed Until Further Notice." Roscoe had moved on. Karla made a mental note to encourage Catherine to document all the stories from her memories to preserve them for future generations. That is, if she ever saw her again. Would anyone step into Catherine's role as town historian when she was gone?

Karla pushed those thoughts from her mind and walked on further down the street. Since the historical society was at the end of the business section of Main Street, the sidewalk ended just past it. An empty lot where a house had once stood was now a small park with large trees and a couple of benches.

The solitude in the park looked enticing, so Karla walked into the grassy area for a short period of meditation. Just what she needed right now. The benches appeared to be well maintained with a fresh coat of green paint on the slats and black paint on the metal bench frame. Karla sat and closed her eyes, enjoying the cooler air in the shade and the peace of the small park.

She was trying to steer her thoughts away from the painful image of Catherine when suddenly she felt something rough around her neck. "What—" She tried to pry his fingers from her neck, but the more she struggled, the tighter his grip became.

"Did you think we wouldn't find you, bitch?" a male voice said in her ear. "You should have minded your own business."

Karla gasped for air and was unable to talk. She was beginning to get dizzy from lack of oxygen She tried to pull away, but her captor was strong, and she just kicked her legs in the air. The world was getting dark, and she had no strength left to fight.

CHAPTER 57

Pete Barnes, the Madden police chief, was returning from a meeting at Mayor Carter's house near the edge of town and was driving past the historical society to return to the police station. Madden was a pretty town, and while he missed working with Joshua Hart, he had been excited to step into the police chief's role when Josh became sheriff. Mayor Carter was pleased with Pete's work and had told him so several times, including today over lunch. She liked that Pete, barely thirty, was able to relate not just to the younger generation in Madden but also to its older citizens. The mayor also appreciated that Pete was a computer whiz who often helped her with technical issues at the office and at home.

As Pete drove past the park, he glanced out the passenger window, admiring the large oak trees. He had liked trees since he was a kid and had built his first tree house. And then, something caught his eye. A woman was sitting on one of the benches and a man was behind her. At first, Pete wondered why the man wasn't sitting with the woman. Then he realized something was wrong. Pete pulled into one of the empty parking spaces, jumped out and ran toward the park. "What's going on here?"

The man standing behind the woman looked up at Pete and appeared to be startled. He pulled out a knife and held it to the woman's neck. "I'll kill her," he said.

In the short time Pete had been in law enforcement, he had never once drawn his pistol. But he did today. "Don't make me shoot you. Throw down the knife and put your hands on your head."

In a swift motion, the man ran the knife across Karla's neck, drawing blood. With shaking hands, Pete aimed at the man who had taken off running in the opposite direction. Pete fired and the man almost fell, but he regained his footing and kept running.

Pete wanted to chase him, but the woman was bleeding, so he holstered his gun and ran to her. He took the black jacket laying on the bench beside her and pressed it against her neck. She was nearly unconscious and moaning. He radioed for one of the town deputies to send an ambulance from the nearest hospital, which was in the next town.

A few minutes later, Karla gained consciousness and the bleeding had eased a bit. Thankfully, the knife didn't hit her artery. When a deputy arrived to assist, Pete left him with Karla and called the Bowman County sheriff's office to put out an APB on the man. Pete had gotten a good look at him and was able to describe the suspect. But he couldn't describe the vehicle that had been parked on the street on the back side of the park. It was a white van. That's all Pete could provide. He also alerted the area hospitals and urgent care centers. Pete felt sure he had nicked the man in his leg or lower side.

CHAPTER 58

Enid was about to call Roo again when she heard the ambulance siren. It sounded close by. She looked out the window and then walked to the front desk. "Ginger, any idea what's going on outside?"

Ginger had earbuds in both ears. When she saw Enid, she pulled one side out. "What?"

"Never mind. I'm going to step outside."

Ginger shrugged and replaced the earbud.

When Enid saw Pete, she jogged across Main Street toward him. "Pete, what's going on?"

"A woman was attacked in the park." He pointed toward the park bench.

"Who was it?"

"The deputy's getting her information. She's in the ambulance now. Luckily the wound was superficial. It could have been fatal if the man had known how to do it. You know it's not as easy to cut someone's—"

Before he could finish, Enid had walked to the back of the ambulance, ready to flash her press credentials if needed.

The EMT and deputy were both hovered over the woman lying on the stretcher, so Enid couldn't see her face. Craning her neck to get a better look, Enid saw the black pants leg. Just hours earlier, she had admired the same fabric on the black pants suit Karla had worn.

"Deputy, can you please tell me who the victim is? I may know her."

When he moved aside, Enid saw Karla's face. "Karla, oh my God. What happened?"

"Ms. Blackwell, you need to step aside. Police Chief Barnes will give you a statement later."

Ignoring the deputy, Enid stepped up into the back of the ambulance and kneeled beside the EMT attending Karla. "Are you alright?"

"I think so," Karla said, her voice raspy.

"You don't need to be talking, ma'am," the EMT said, giving a sideways glance to Enid. "We're taking her to the county hospital for observation. You can talk with her there."

Enid took Karla's hand. "I'll see you later at the hospital."

Karla nodded and managed a slight smile.

Enid jumped out of the back of the ambulance and stalked over to where Pete was standing. "That's Karla Burke. My friend. Who did this to her?"

"Are you asking me for an official statement? Because I can't give you one yet."

"No, Pete, dammit. I'm asking who tried to kill my friend."

With a sheepish look on his face, Pete replied, "I don't know. Maybe I hit him. We've got an APB out for him."

"Be sure to talk to Sheriff Stanholt. I can't explain now, but I know why they tried to get her." Before Pete could say anything further, Enid jogged back to her office, cell phone in hand. "Josh, someone tried to kill Karla. I've got to talk to you. Please call."

Before she got back to her desk, Josh called. "I'm on my way. Stay at the office. I mean it."

While Enid wanted to get to the hospital, she knew she wouldn't get to see Karla right away. Her phone rang, and this time it was Roo's number that appeared.

"Sorry, I just got your message. What's going on?"

"We found Catherine, and someone just tried to kill Karla. When are you coming home?"

"Oh, no. That's awful. I mean, great that you found Aunt Cat, but I'm so sorry about Karla. My flight leaves in two hours. I'll come to your house instead of going to Charleston. Is Aunt Cat with you?"

"No. It's a long story. Just get home as soon as you can."

. . .

When Josh arrived, Enid ran to him, throwing her arms around his neck. "I'm so glad to see you."

Josh held her briefly and then pulled away to look at her. "Are you okay?"

"I'm fine."

"Any update on Karla?"

"It wasn't a deep cut, so she's alright."

Josh walked to the small break area and came back with a cup of Lady Grey tea for Enid. "You look like you need something stronger, but maybe this will help."

Enid took the cup, cradling its warmth in her hands. "Thanks."

"Now tell me what's going on."

Enid told Josh about going to the nursing home and finding Catherine Murray and about Karla's narrow escape. "Nurse Louise must have had someone follow us."

Josh lowered his head, shaking it from side to side. "I'm trying not to think about what could have happened. I spent the entire morning in a meeting, arguing with the committee about the first killing near the barn. They're more interested in containing the information and keeping it away from the press than anything else. I have no idea why I'm in this role. It's all politics and meetings." He sighed. "I might not have to worry about it much longer. I went to see Stanholt and filled him in on everything. He probably couldn't wait to call Larkin and complain that I was interfering in his investigation."

Their conversation was interrupted by Enid's office phone ringing. "Yes, this is Enid Blackwell." She glanced at Josh. "Yes, I can come to the hospital. I'll be there in about thirty minutes." She ended the call. "That was the sheriff's office. They want me to give them a statement. I'm afraid I ran off without saying much to Pete. I was more worried about Karla."

"He was probably scared to death. He's never had to deal with anything like this. I'll go with you."

"Are you sure? If you're right about Stanholt calling Governor Larkin, your showing up won't go over well."

"Come on, let's go."

CHAPTER 59

It took nearly an hour for Enid to finish giving her statement to the deputy. Josh sat at the other end of the waiting area so as not to interfere. "I need to know what will happen next," Enid asked the deputy.

"I can't say, ma'am. Sheriff Stanholt is overseeing this investigation. My instructions were to take your statement." He smiled slightly. "He told me you are a reporter and to be careful about what I said."

Enid couldn't help but laugh. "I'm sure he did. Well, thanks. I hope my statement helps you rescue Catherine."

"Yes, ma'am." As he turned to leave, he noticed Josh and held out his hand. "Good to see you, sir."

"Same here," Josh said. He walked over to where Enid was sitting just as Stanholt showed up.

"Well, well. If this isn't a cozy little scene. The governor's golden boy and our very own star reporter."

"Evening, Sheriff," Josh said. Enid was silent, her chin raised slightly in defiance. "I need to talk to you," Josh added. He nodded toward Enid. "And she needs to stay. Whether you like it or not, she's helping you resolve this case."

Stanholt eyed Enid head to toe before he spoke in a sarcastic tone. "Then let's all be friends, sit down, and chat." They sat at the end of the waiting area where no one else was nearby. "Before we start, I want to tell you that I reviewed the cases, at your request," he said looking at Josh, "and I agree the first killing does not appear to be gang related, as we originally thought. We've found nothing to tie the murder or the alleged gang tag to any of the known gangs in the area. Of course, there are new rag-tag groups popping up all the time, mostly neighborhood punks that have watched too many movies. They usually fizzle out or merge with other, bigger gangs. But we don't have any indication that's the case here. The second murder, the pregnant woman a few miles away, was apparently a gang hit. As for the neighbor being strangled, that's a puzzle. It would be a stretch to say it's just a coincidence, given the location and other information we've got. So, for now, we're working with the assumption that the disappearance and two of the murders *may* be connected. We've been trying to contact Sylvia Ryce's grandson, Robert, as he seems to be the next of kin, but we haven't been able to locate him. We'd also like to talk to him about the first victim, Danny Boodemore, since they were acquaintances."

"What about the attack on Karla Burke this afternoon?" Enid asked. "Do we know who did it?"

"Not yet. The Madden police chief is fairly certain he shot the perp in the hip or leg. We've alerted all the medical facilities nearby."

"What about Catherine Murray? We found her, but she needs to be taken out of that place immediately."

"I haven't read your statement, so you'll have to fill me in," Stanholt said.

Enid told him about Karla's and her trip to the nursing home and about Karla's narrow escape.

"Impersonating a social worker is illegal, you know." Stanholt glanced at Josh, perhaps hoping for confirmation.

"Can we deal with all that later?" Josh asked. "Perhaps if Enid and her friend had gotten more support and involvement from the sheriff's office, they wouldn't have taken matters into their own hands."

Stanholt held up both hands. "Now, now, let's not get testy. I'll go to the place myself and see what I can find out. It's out of my jurisdiction, but I'll let the county sheriff know what's going on. Hopefully, he won't hold us up with red tape."

"Thank you, Sheriff," Enid said. "Please let me know what you find out."

Without reply, Stanholt stood to leave. "I hope I don't have to say this, but you need to stay out of this matter." He looked at Enid and then Josh. "Both of you."

. . .

When Enid and Josh returned to her house, Roo was waiting for them. When they walked in, Roo rushed toward Enid. "What's happened? Where did you find Aunt Cat?"

Enid hugged Roo. "We found her in a nursing home but couldn't get her out."

"A nursing home? How did Aunt Cat end up there?" Roo asked.

"We're still trying to figure all that out." Enid told Roo about the attack on Karla and that Stanholt had gone to the nursing facility. "Despite what we think of him, I don't think he'll leave without answers."

Roo took Josh's hand and Enid's in hers. "I'm so sorry I had to leave town with all this going on. What would I have done without you? What if . . ." Her voice trailed off.

Enid squeezed her hand. "Everything will be fine." If only she believed her own words.

"How is Karla?" Roo asked. "I feel responsible for her getting attacked like that. It should have been me going with you to the nursing home."

"No one blames you. And it was Karla's idea to go in. She's still under observation, but I've talked with her briefly. Thank goodness the cut wasn't deep and didn't hit her artery. They will probably release her tomorrow."

Enid turned to Josh. "Isn't there something we can do? Why are we just sitting here talking?" She tried to push the thought out of her mind that they might never see Catherine alive again.

Josh put his hands on her shoulders. "You've got to let Stanholt do his job." He laughed. "I can't believe I'm defending him."

"Let's all get some rest. We're going to need it." Enid said.

CHAPTER 60

When Sheriff Stanholt arrived at the nursing home, the front door was locked. He pushed the doorbell for after-hours entrance. After waiting a minute, he rang it again. A tired-looking man of about sixty ambled to the door. "Can I help you?" He looked at Stanholt's badge. "You here to visit somebody?"

Stanholt pushed the door open. "I need to come in to check on a patient for the family."

"You'll have to talk to—"

Before he could finish, Stanholt interrupted. "I'm not asking. Now move aside, or I'll have you arrested." He couldn't, but the man didn't know that.

The man shrugged and moved aside. "Alright, then." He walked back to the vacuum cleaner where he had been working.

Stanholt followed the signs and walked straight to room 121. He tapped on the door before opening it slightly. "Hello. I'm coming in." When he walked into the room, his mind flooded with memories of his father's death. Of all things, he remembered most the stark bareness of his father's hospital room when he walked in to see him, not knowing he had died an hour earlier. Everything but the furniture had been stripped from the room. That's the way room 121 looked now: a bare stained mattress on the hospital bed frame. The bathroom door was open, and there were no towels or other typical toiletry items visible.

Stanholt walked back to where the old man was vacuuming and unplugged it from the wall. "Where is the patient from room 121?" Stanholt asked.

The man turned around to look at him with a puzzled expression and shrugged. "I'm just the janitor."

"Who's in charge?"

The man shrugged again.

"Well, you'd better find out fast."

The man walked to the unattended front desk and pointed to a piece of paper on the wall. "Here's the emergency number. Maybe they can tell you."

A nurse's aide in a blue uniform approached the two men. "What's going on here?" She looked at the janitor and then Stanholt. "Is he in trouble?"

"Nobody is in trouble yet, but somebody needs to start talking to me. Where is the patient in 121?"

The aide looked at the clipboard in her hand. "I just started my shift, and my chart shows she was dismissed to family."

"What's the family member's name?"

"I don't have that information. You'll have to talk to—"

Before she could finish, Stanholt yanked the paper with the emergency number off the wall and walked outside, leaving the janitor and the aide staring at him. Stanholt called the number on the paper. "Hello. This is Sheriff Stanholt. Somebody better come meet with me right now, or I'll shut this damn place down." Another empty threat, but hopefully they didn't know it. "Okay, fifteen minutes. You'd better be here by then."

As promised, a woman soon drove up in a gray SUV and parked next to the sheriff's car. "What's going on?" she asked as she got out.

"You had a woman in room 121 who may have been held against her will. She was supposedly released to family, but I need to talk with the patient to confirm all this and verify she's alright."

"Come on inside."

Stanholt followed the woman to her office. "Have a seat while I check her records." She pulled a file folder and skimmed it. "It says she arrived in a state of traumatic amnesia. Couldn't tell us her name or anything."

"Who admitted her?"

The woman looked at the file again. "A relative." She paused. "Wait just a minute." She flipped a few pages and read. "It appears one of our nurses is related to the patient and assumed responsibility."

"Is the nurse paying for her care?"

"I don't know. I'll have to check with accounting in the morning." She closed the file and returned it to the cabinet. "Why do you think this patient is in danger?"

Stanholt ignored the question. "Is this nurse the same one who discharged her?"

The woman sat in her chair. "I think I need to talk with our company attorney before I answer anything further."

Stanholt slammed his hand on her desk. "Either you give me the information on this nurse, or I'll do everything in my power to shut you down. It appears you've had quite a few complaints filed against this place through the Department of Social Services. Things like patient neglect, health code infractions, and even patient abuse. It wouldn't take much to close you down for good, so I suggest you start telling me what I need to know." He leaned across the desk. "A woman's life may be in danger. Got it?" Flecks of spittle filled the space between them.

The woman tapped on her keyboard, wrote information on a piece of paper, and handed it to Stanholt. "That's all I've got. Louise Smith's mobile number and address. I think she lives with her boyfriend."

Stanholt smiled and had good reason to. He had gotten the nurse's name, which was likely a fake, and her address. Even better, she lived in Bowman County, his domain. He scribbled his phone number on a piece of paper. He didn't want to hand her a business card and bring attention to the fact that he was out of his jurisdiction. "Here's my cell number. If you hear anything from Smith or this patient, you notify me immediately."

CHAPTER 61

Stanholt radioed ahead for one of his deputies to meet him at Louise Smith's address. "Not sure what we're dealing with. Proceed with caution and don't enter until I get there."

The address was at a run-down apartment complex just a few miles from the old barn where the first murder occurred. When Stanholt arrived, his deputy was inconspicuously parked up the street a little way. The sheriff flashed his lights to let the deputy know he was there, and the deputy flashed his lights in reply.

With backup now by his side, Stanholt walked toward the apartment. He wouldn't be surprised if the woman had given him a bogus address. Nonetheless, he kept his hand on his holster as he pounded on the door. No one answered. He knocked again, harder this time. "Sheriff's office. Open the door."

A voice from behind startled him. "You looking for someone?" a man in blue hospital scrubs said. "I live next door."

"You know who lives here?" Stanholt asked.

"Not really. I mean I see her sometimes, but I don't know her. She's got some asshole guy shacking with her. He's a piece of—"

"She a nurse?" Stanholt interrupted.

"Yeah, but we don't work at the same place. I work—"

"Thanks," Stanholt interrupted again.

"I hope you arrest that son-of-a—"

"Alright, man, thanks for your help. We can take it from here."

The man walked back toward his apartment, looking disappointed that he had been dismissed.

"Can we go in without a warrant?" the deputy asked.

"Only if we think there's a crime in progress or someone is in danger." Stanholt kicked in the flimsy door. "And I think there is." He called into the apartment. "Sheriff's office. Anybody here?" The apartment was dark, so he flipped the light switch in the entrance area. "You look around," he told the deputy. "Stay alert."

The deputy walked down the short hallway toward the bedrooms, while the sheriff checked the kitchen, closets, and hall bath. "Sheriff. I found something," the deputy said.

Stanholt walked toward the bedroom. "What you got?"

The deputy pointed toward a small pile of clothing on the bed. The bloody pants had been cut with scissors, not torn, and the shirt had smears of blood that looked like a handprint."

"Get the crime scene unit out here now," Stanholt said. He used the end of his pen to look through the pile of clothes. At the bottom of the pile was a lightweight cotton gown with small pink roses on it, the kind a grandmother might wear. "You stay here. I'll get you some backup. There's something I need to check on."

Stanholt radioed for another deputy to come to the address and waited until he arrived a few minutes later. Recalling his conversation with that reporter, Enid Blackwell, he drove to Sylvia's house, the scene of the latest murder. Personally, he wasn't convinced that all the pieces she had pulled together were related. Might be hogwash. Or maybe she had connected the dots they missed.

As he approached the house, it was dark. He killed his lights and stopped a half block away. He briefly considered calling for backup, but decided it wasn't necessary. The owner was dead, and no one appeared to be at the house. The only nearby car was parked across the street in another driveway. He grabbed his flashlight and checked around. No sign of anything unusual.

He knew the house across the street was where the missing woman had lived. Then why would there be a car parked there? Perhaps a relative was staying in the house, maybe that great-niece.

He got out of the car again and walked over to Murray's house. It was dark in front, but he could see a dim light in one of the side windows. He approached the front door. Before he could call out, a round of bullets pierced the door. The thought flashed through his mind that he was glad it wasn't a shotgun. Warm liquid oozed down his side and leg. He had been hit. His side was bleeding and burning with pain. With one hand, he compressed the area and held his gun in the other hand. He managed to radio for help.

A deputy patrolling the area arrived quickly, and within a few minutes, a swarm of deputies surrounded Catherine Murray's house, waiting for a green light to storm it. "Proceed," Stanholt barked into his radio.

An EMT arrived to look at Stanholt, but the bullet had only grazed his side, inflicting a flesh wound with minimal damage. While the deputies broke through the bullet-riddled door, Stanholt watched from the back of the emergency medical team's van.

Less than a minute later, he heard gunshots. He picked up his radio. "What's going on?" he asked the lead deputy.

"We got 'em sir," the deputy replied. "The male suspect pulled a gun and was shot. Looks like he'd already been shot. He's presumed dead. The female suspect tried to run, but she's in custody."

"Was anyone else with them?"

"Negative, sir."

CHAPTER 62

Louise was sitting on the edge of Catherine's sofa with her hands cuffed behind her. She was thin and looked to be in her late twenties or early thirties. Her blonde, shoulder-length hair was pulled back into a ponytail. She had the world-weary look of someone who had seen her share of hard times. Sheriff Stanholt stood over her. "Where is she?" he asked.

Louise shrugged. "Who you talking about?"

Stanholt leaned over until his face was inches from hers. "Don't play games with me. I've been shot, and I'm pissed off. Where is Catherine Murray?"

"Don't know her."

"And yet, here you are, in her house. How'd that happen?"

"It was just vacant, and we decided to check it out. Might want to buy it if the owner is willing to sell. Nice neighborhood."

Stanholt stood up. "Except for the murders, you mean. Yeah, nice place." He called over his shoulder to the deputy standing behind him. "Take her in and book her for attempted murder of a police officer. And call the canine unit to get here asap."

"Sure thing, sir," the deputy said.

When the canine unit arrived, Stanholt instructed them to get the bloodhounds to track the scent on the nightgown.

"If the dogs don't get a hit over there at the apartment, bring 'em here."

As the canine unit was leaving, another vehicle drove up and parked. "Get that car out of here," Stanholt yelled. The deputy walked to the car and leaned in to talk to the driver. "Damn fool," Stanholt muttered to himself. "That's how you get yourself killed." He marched over to the car and looked inside. "I might have known you'd show up," he said to Enid. "No press allowed."

. . .

Enid got out of the car and motioned for Roo to follow her. "This is Catherine Murray's great-niece. We heard from an anonymous source there was police activity at her aunt's house." Jack had gotten a tip from his friend at the sheriff's office. "She needs to find out what's going on and has a right to be here. I'm accompanying her."

"Evening, ma'am," Stanholt said to Roo.

"Have you found my aunt?"

"No, I'm afraid not. We have one suspect dead and another under arrest. But we'll find your aunt. Don't you worry." He winced and appeared to be in pain.

"Are you alright?" Enid asked.

"I'm fine. Just a graze. I'll let you stay, but nothing goes to press until I approve it," he said to Enid. "Got that?"

"Of course. But why did you call out the canine unit?" Enid asked.

"I'm just working a hunch. Nothing concrete to go on." He looked at Roo. "We're just being cautious, ma'am.

Would you recognize if a nightgown belonged to your aunt?"

Roo shook her head. "No, I'm afraid not. I live in Charleston and I've never seen Aunt Cat in a gown when I visited. She was particular about her clothing, always dressed nice when I saw her. But where are the dogs looking for her?"

"At the suspects' apartment. We don't know that Murray was there, but we need to rule it out. Now both of you, stay in the car. This is a crime scene. I'll let you know if anything changes."

Enid and Roo waited for nearly half an hour before the canine unit's SUV pulled up in front of Catherine's house. The deputy got out with an evidence bag in his hand. "That must be the nightgown the sheriff asked you about," Enid said to Roo.

"That's not a good sign, is it?"

Enid put her hand on Roo's. "Let's not jump to conclusions."

The deputy opened the bag and let the bloodhounds sniff the gown again. The dogs immediately began to smell the sidewalk and then they were taken inside the house. A few minutes later, the dogs and their handler came out. "They went crazy in there, so the person who wore the nightgown was definitely in that house at some point," he said to Stanholt.

"Then that confirms it was Catherine Murray's gown. If she's not in the house, then let's widen the search area," Stanholt said.

"Stay here," Enid said to Roo as she got out of the car. Enid walked over to where Stanholt was standing. "Sheriff, are you going to check the area around the old barn?"

Stanholt squinted as he focused on Enid. "Why is that?"

"I didn't want to say this in front of Roo, but we both know there's a good chance you're looking for a body."

"Agreed. And, I can't believe I'm saying this, but I also agree with you on checking around the old barn since all this now seems to be connected." He pointed toward the car where Roo was. "Keep her away from there. Understand?" He walked across the street to Sylvia's house where the dogs were sniffing. The sheriff said something to the deputy that Enid couldn't hear, and then he began walking toward the old barn.

Enid went back to the car and sat with Roo, both of them silent, until the dogs were on the move again. "You stay here," Enid said. "I'm going to see what I can find out."

Roo put her hand on the door. "She's my aunt, I'm going."

"No. That's precisely why you can't go. You're a relative, and Stanholt won't let you get anywhere near, assuming they find anything. I'll let you know what I find out. Please stay here, okay?"

Roo slammed her head back against the headrest and crossed her arms across her chest.

Enid got out of the car and gently closed the door so as not to alert the deputy standing in Catherine's front yard. She waited until he walked back into the house before heading toward the old barn. As she approached, Stanholt heard her and turned around. "I told you to stay put. The dogs will be here after they sweep the second house, and I don't want you in the way or contaminating anything."

"Come on, let's look around until they get here." Enid was already walking into the barn.

Stanholt radioed to the canine team deputy. "Hey, you got anything there?" followed by, "Well, then, come on down to the old barn. It's about a block and a half east."

Enid could hear the bloodhounds baying as they approached. "Does that mean they smell something?"

"When they find something, they'll start barking faster. Right now, they're probably just excited. They love doing this work. Besides, if the perps drove the body here in a vehicle, there wouldn't be any scent on the street. But all this is speculation." He motioned to a space near the barn. "Stay over there out of the way."

Following his instructions, Enid watched the bloodhounds' giant floppy ears skirting the ground as they worked their way toward Stanholt. When they got closer, one of the dogs sniffed her feet and legs but quickly moved on inside the barn.

Stanholt looked at her and held up his hand. "Stay there or I'll have a deputy escort you back to your car. And keep your phone in your pocket. No videos or recordings. I mean it."

She heard the dogs moving around inside the barn, but they were not barking. After a few minutes, the handler led them out the back and towards the surrounding woods. Stanholt followed them, so she waited until he was ahead of her before following at a distance. Suddenly, the dogs began barking, this time louder and shorter barks. The dogs were moving in unison, back and forth across the footpath that led to the area where the first victim, Daniel Boodemore, had been found. The handler was running now to allow the dogs to move quickly, and Stanholt was running, too. Enid was about to close in on them, but she heard a voice.

"Have they found her?"

Enid spun around. "Roo, I told you to stay in the car." She sounded just like Stanholt addressing her.

"I'm staying. Come on." Roo took off running.

By now the dogs were out of sight in the woods, but their rapid barks were an indication they had found something. Stanholt heard them running and turned around with his finger pointed at them. "Stay there."

"Have you found her?" Roo screamed at him.

"Sheriff, you need to come here," the dog handler called to Stanholt.

Enid and Roo walked a short distance behind him. When they got to the wooded area, the deputy was holding back some brush. "Got something," he said.

Behind the dead bush was something large. When Stanholt shined his flashlight on it, the intense LED beam revealed a large object covered with a quilted blanket like movers use. Stanholt ran his light across the object, and then the light stopped moving. A human hand was sticking out from the covering.

"Oh, God, no." Roo's hand flew to her mouth. She turned to Enid. "It's her, isn't it?"

Enid put her arm around Roo. "We don't know yet. Come on, let's go back to the car."

Roo pulled away. "No."

Stanholt pulled rubber gloves from his pocket and leaned down, groaning in pain from his wounded side. He pulled the quilted covering back, being careful not to disturb the crime scene. "Get the EMT here. I think she's breathing," he called to the deputy.

Within a few minutes, the emergency technicians who had treated Stanholt were running down the footpath with a stretcher.

Enid took Roo by the hand. "We've got to get out of here. Come on." She pulled on Roo until she relented. As they jogged back to their car, Enid ignored the pain in her leg. That was the least of her worries at the moment. "We'll follow the ambulance."

CHAPTER 63

Stanholt walked into the hospital's waiting area and motioned for Enid to come to him. Roo saw him and jumped up. "Is it her? Is she going to make it?"

"We'll let you know something as soon as we can. I know it's tough, but just hold on a bit longer."

As Enid walked over to the sheriff, Josh burst into the waiting area, practically running.

Josh immediately headed to Stanholt and Enid. "What's going on?"

"Cool your jets," Stanholt said to Josh. "I just need for the relative or your girlfriend to ID the person we found." He showed Enid and Roo a photo on his cell phone. "Is that Catherine Murray?"

Enid nodded. "Yes, that's her." While it was clearly Catherine, she appeared to be much older now. Her skin was gray, and her usually neat hair appeared to have been crudely chopped. "What are her chances?" Roo asked.

"The doctor will have to talk to you about that," Stanholt said.

Josh stepped in closer. "Come on, man. Tell me, at least. These two women have been looking for Catherine Murray long before you were, so don't yank them around now."

Stanholt's jaw tightened and he appeared ready to explode. Instead, he took Josh by the arm and led him away. Enid watched at the two men left the waiting area. She walked back and sat down with Roo. "They won't tell us anything. But they're pretty sure it's Catherine they found."

Roo buried her face in her hands. "Oh, thank God." She looked toward the ceiling. "Please, God, let her pull through this."

Enid put her arms around Roo and held her close. She could feel her trembling as she cried softly. "I should have been more attentive, visited her more often. Maybe none of this would have happened."

"Don't do this to yourself. You're not responsible."

Roo pulled away and looked directly at Enid. "Why did they try to kill her?"

"I don't know. Maybe that woman they arrested, the nurse, will have some answers." Enid heard Josh's footsteps as he walked toward them. Stanholt wasn't with him. "What did you find out?"

Josh looked at Roo. "This isn't an official statement, understand? I'm just a friend right now." Roo nodded and he continued. "Catherine is alive but barely. She's been drugged, and she's dehydrated and malnourished. They're doing all they can."

Enid reached into her tote and handed a tissue to Roo. "All we can do now is wait."

Josh sat on the other side of Roo, so that she was between him and Enid. He put his arm on the back of Roo's seat and his fingers touched Enid's shoulder. She leaned back slightly so that her cheek touched his arm and then closed her eyes, suddenly overcome with fatigue.

. . .

Enid heard Josh's voice but was disoriented and couldn't remember she was at the hospital. "Enid, wake up."

"Sorry, I dozed off." She looked at Roo who was curled up on the small sofa, asleep.

"I'm going to the sheriff's office to sit in on the nurse's interrogation. Will you be alright to wait here with Roo?"

Enid rubbed her eyes. "Of course. But what will your boss say?"

Josh tapped the tip of her nose with his finger. "Frankly, my dear, I don't give a damn."

Enid watched Josh walk toward the door of the hospital's waiting area. He was putting his career on the line to help Roo and Catherine Murray. That ought to count for something, and she'd tell Governor Larkin, if she ever got the chance. She walked over to check on Roo, who was still asleep. It was nearly daylight, and soon the hospital would be teeming with activity again. Enid decided to let Roo sleep.

Enid made a mental list of things she needed to do, like letting Karla know Catherine had been found. Her thoughts were interrupted by a woman in a white jacket.

"Ms. Murray?" she asked Enid.

"No, I'm just a friend. Let me wake her." Enid walked over to Roo and gently shook her awake. "The doctor needs to talk with you."

Roo sat up and looked at the doctor. "How is she?"

"May we talk alone?" the doctor asked Roo.

"No. I mean, Enid helped me find her. You can say anything in front of her."

The doctor nodded. "Alright then. Your aunt is hanging on. She was severely dehydrated and over-sedated. Her breathing is shallow, so we've got her on oxygen and drugs to counteract the overdose. She's unresponsive, but we're still hopeful. We'll let you know if anything changes."

"I want to see her," Roo said. "Maybe she will respond if she hears a familiar voice."

The doctor hesitated briefly. "Well, I guess it can't hurt anything." She looked at Enid. "But I can only let a family member in."

Enid squeezed Roo's hand. "I'll wait here."

. . .

When Roo walked into Catherine's room in the intensive care unit, she was overcome with emotion: anger, sadness, outrage, and guilt. Catherine's eyes were closed, and she had oxygen and IV fluids fortifying her limp body. Numerous machines were monitoring her heart, blood pressure, and other vitals.

"Just a few minutes," the doctor said. "I'll leave you alone, but don't force her to wake up. She will when she's ready."

Roo nodded. There was only one metal chair in the ICU room, so she pulled it up beside the bed and sat beside Catherine and gently took her hand. "Oh, Aunt Cat," she said softly. "I'm so sorry. Please be alright. Please." Roo caressed her aunt's hand, being careful to avoid the IV and monitors strapped to her. "You're safe now, so you can wake up when you're ready. Nothing is going to happen to you."

Perhaps it was Roo's imagination, but she thought she felt a slight squeeze from Catherine's hand. Probably just an involuntary muscle response. A nursery rhyme popped into Roo's head, perhaps because her aunt looked as helpless as a newborn, so Roo began softly singing. "Angels watching ever round thee, all through the night." She sang as much as she could remember, which wasn't much, so she kept repeating the only lines she knew. "I my loved ones' watch am keeping, all through the night."

Roo was still singing softly when a nurse came into the room. "You have to leave now. Doctor's orders."

Gently, Roo released Catherine's hand. "Goodbye for now, Aunt Cat. I love you." Before Roo walked out the door, an alarm went off on one of the monitors. Roo turned to the nurse. "What's that? What's happening?"

"Wait out in the hallway," the nurse said.

Roo looked at Catherine lying in the bed, now moving her head slightly from side to side. And then Catherine made a faint noise, like someone who was trying to wake up but couldn't. "Please leave," the nurse repeated.

In defiance, Roo went to the other side of the bed and put her hand on Catherine's arm. "You're safe. It's me, Ruby-Grace."

Catherine's head stopped moving and her eyes fluttered.

Roo repeated, "It's me, Aunt Cat. You're safe now. You can wake up."

The nurse hit the call button on Catherine's bed. "Send security. Stat." Then she turned to Roo. "You need to leave so I can take care of her."

Reluctantly, Roo stepped away from Catherine's bed. But when she did, Catherine began moving her head back and forth again. Roo returned to Catherine's side, and this time the nurse didn't stop her. "Her heartbeat is elevated, and her BP is up, but she's fine. Given what she's been through, she's probably having nightmares."

A hospital security guard rushed into the room. "It's fine now," the nurse told him. "Everything is under control." She looked at Roo. "Right?"

"I'm sorry," Roo said to the nurse. "I just didn't want to leave her." Roo took Catherine's hand again. "You're safe," she kept repeating. Several minutes later, Catherine's monitors quit sounding off, and she appeared to be sleeping.

"I'll go now and let her sleep," Roo said to the nurse. "Thank you for letting me stay. I didn't mean to cause trouble."

For the first time, the nurse smiled slightly. "We'll take good care of her and let you know as soon as anything changes." As Roo was leaving, the nurse called to her. "Wait."

Roo turned back toward the hospital bed. Catherine's eyes were open slightly. She then made a noise that sounded like "ruh."

"Take her hand. She needs to know you're here," the nurse said. "But if I tell you to leave again, this time, you leave."

"Yes, ma'am." But Roo's attention was on Catherine, whose eyes were now open. "Aunt Cat, it's me. Ruby-Grace."

Catherine nodded slightly. She tried to say something, but just closed her eyes again.

"Is she okay?" Roo asked.

The nurse checked her heart. "She's fine. Let's let her rest now."

CHAPTER 64

Louise sat on one side of the table, and Sheriff Stanholt sat on the other side. Josh observed from the far corner of the room. Stanholt had resisted letting Josh participate until Josh reminded him that he worked for the governor. For now, at least. Josh would probably be reprimanded, or worse, for stepping outside the boundaries of his role. None of that mattered to him now.

Stanholt confirmed with Louise that her rights had been explained to her, and a court-appointed attorney, who introduced himself as Stanley Adams, sat beside her. He had a large coffee stain on the front of his white shirt. Louise's face was blank, without expression.

"Lucky you. Looks like Catherine Murray will survive," Stanholt said to Louise. "But when she tells us what happened, you're going up for kidnapping, assault, attempted murder, elder abuse, and anything else we can think of." He looked at Adams. "I suggest you advise your client to start cooperating." Stanholt leaned back in his chair and waited.

Josh looked at the big clock on the wall, while Adams and Louise conferred in whispers. Finally, Adams said, "She doesn't want to give a statement at this time."

Then Stanholt spoke again. "Alright then." He stood up and laughed at Louise, shaking his head. "It takes a low-life piece of crap to do that to an old woman. She wouldn't have made it through the night out there in the woods. But you being a nurse, I guess you'd know that." He turned to Josh. "Come on, let's leave her to the buzzards."

The two men were nearly out the door when Adams called out. "Wait. What kind of deal are you offering if my client cooperates?" He looked at Louise who didn't protest.

Stanholt threw back his head and laughed. Looking at Josh, he said, "You hear that? They want a deal." The sheriff's face hardened as he leaned over Louise, staring at her. "The only thing I can promise you is that if you don't talk, I'll do everything in my power to make your life hell and your sentence as long as possible. Got that?"

"Let's talk," Adams said. Louise remained expressionless and Stanholt sat down across from her again, nodding for Josh to go back to his seat.

"Now that we have an understanding, tell me why you kidnapped Catherine Murray," Stanholt said. "What was your plan?"

"It was all Bobby's idea."

"For the record, Bobby is Robert Ryce, is that correct?"

Louise nodded.

The sheriff sneered at her. "Well, of course it was his idea. He's not here to say otherwise."

"Bobby told me she had money."

"Go on then," Stanholt said.

Louise glanced at Adams, who nodded his consent. "Bobby's granny asked him to help the old woman—"

Josh jumped up from his seat. "Her name is Catherine. Catherine Murray."

Stanholt shot Josh a we-agreed-you-would-stay-quiet look. "Go on," he said to Louise.

Louise frowned at Josh, "*Catherine Murray,*" she emphasized, "had a lot of money, according to Bobby. And she didn't have no family, not around here at least. Bobby was visiting his granny one day when Catherine was there. He heard her say she didn't have any close family and she wished she could find more relatives. She told him she had done one of those DNA tests and asked if he could help her locate her relatives online. He offered to help her set up an ancestry account and do some research."

"Why would she trust a low-life like Robert?" Stanholt asked.

Louise paused and for the first time teared up. "He could be real charming and sweet like, you know? Most people didn't see that side of him. Anyway, she was excited about him helping her. Later, when he found out she was loaded, I mentioned that it was a shame we weren't related to *Catherine.*" Louise glared at Josh again.

"So you could get her money, you mean," Stanholt said.

"I object," Adams said.

"We're not in court," Stanholt said.

Louise ignored Adams and shrugged. "Bobby was quizzing her about her family while he helped her, so we decided to convince her I was related. She had a cousin named Belinda, according to the family tree online, so I told her I was Belinda. I can't believe how much personal information was out there for everyone to see." She paused. "Can I have some water?"

Stanholt poured her a glass of water from a pitcher on a small tray. He pushed the glass toward her, spilling some onto the table, which Adams wiped up with the palm of his hand. "Go on," Stanholt said to Louise.

"So I wrote her, showed up, and visited with her until she trusted me. We went shopping and out to lunch several times. She's the one who first suggested I become her power of attorney," she paused. "But I might have hinted at it."

"Are you saying she willingly gave you power over her life?"

"She said her great-niece lived in another town and she only saw her a few times a year. She wanted somebody closer, you know, in case something happened to her. It was kind of like she was desperate to connect with family."

Josh squirmed in his seat. He wanted to put his hands around Louise's neck. But he managed to stay quiet.

"But the bitch . . ." Louise looked at Josh. "Sorry. *Cathe-rine* wouldn't change her will to leave me any money. She wanted to leave it to charity. Bobby was furious with her and with me because I couldn't get her to do it."

"So you, what, kidnapped her to make her do it?" Stanholt shook his head in disbelief.

"Me and Bobby looked it up and found out that if we could get her in a nursing home and declared mentally in-competent, I would be in charge of everything then, you know, her finances and her medical treatment, as her power of attorney."

"So you were planning on just keeping her under wraps, is that it? You had no intentions of hurting her, just taking everything she had."

"Don't answer that," Adams said to Louise.

Louise ignored him. "Yeah, but then we found out we couldn't change her will, so we had to keep her quiet until we could figure out what to do."

"I guess if she died in a nursing home, you figured there wouldn't be too many questions. Old people die in places like that all the time." Stanholt paused, shaking his head. "Go on. Then what happened?"

"That reporter lady and the old woman's great-niece started snooping around. They're the reason we had to dump her."

"What happened to Catherine Murray's money?" Stanholt asked. Before she could answer, he said to Adams. "Either she tells us what happened, all of it, or there's no deal."

Adams nodded, looking like he'd rather be anywhere else.

Louise looked down at the table. "Bobby sold her stocks and then cleaned out her bank accounts. I signed all the paperwork as power of attorney, but Bobby took care of all the money."

"Where's the money now?" Josh asked, ignoring Stanholt's stare.

Louise shrugged. "Dunno. I don't have any of it." She looked at Josh. "I swear."

Stanholt shook his head again. "Don't worry. We'll find it and make sure you never see it." He paused. "So let's talk about Danny and Bobby's grandmother, Sylvia. Why did you kill them?"

Adams perked up. "Whoa, she's not confessing to any of that."

Louise's eyes widened as she looked from Adams to Stanholt. "Oh, no. I had nothing to do with that. Bobby's so-called friend Danny found out what Bobby was doing and threatened to tell Sylvia."

"So you killed Danny and staged it as a gang hit." Stanholt held up his hand to Adams. "I know. Don't bother to object."

"I didn't even know about what happened. Not until afterward. Bobby did all that." Louise was now looking less like the cocky criminal and more like a cornered rabbit.

"For the record, Danny is Daniel Boodemore, right? Bobby's high school friend who was killed up by the old barn?"

Louise nodded. "Like I said, that was all Bobby's idea."

"So why did Bobby kill his grandmother, Sylvia Ryce?"

"He told me she was going to turn him in. Seems Danny talked to her, before . . . well, you know, before he died. At least that's what I heard."

Stanholt smiled. "You can save all that acting for the trial. You're up to your neck in all this."

"What about my deal?" Louise asked.

Stanholt stood up and motioned for Josh to follow him. "We're done here. The deputy will lock you back up until you're arraigned."

Louise looked at Adams. "Why do I have to go to jail? I cooperated. Can't I get out on bond?"

"I'm afraid not. You'll have to stay here for now," Adams said.

Stanholt opened the door to the interrogation room and told the deputy to take her to her cell. "Lose the key, too, why don't you. What a waste of a human being."

CHAPTER 65

When Enid awoke from napping in the hospital waiting room, someone was stroking her hair. She opened her eyes and saw Josh sitting beside her. Rubbing her eyes, she sat up. "Hi. How long have you been here?"

"Not long. I like watching you sleep." He brushed a strand of hair from her forehead. "Have you heard anything else about Catherine?"

"She opened her eyes briefly when Roo was with her. That's a good sign, but she's still not out of danger. How did the nurse's interrogation go?"

"About like I expected. She's blaming the whole scheme on her dead boyfriend."

"Why would they do that to Catherine?"

"Greed, the world's oldest motive." Josh's phone vibrated and he looked at the screen. "The boss is looking for me."

"Then you'd better answer."

Josh put his phone back in the clip on his belt. "I wanted to talk to you first."

Enid smiled. "I guess I should be honored that you put me ahead of the governor. What do you want to talk about?" Enid felt her shoulders tense.

"I'm going to leave this position."

"But—"

"Wait, let me finish. This is not a rash decision. I guess I knew immediately I was a bad fit. I knew the job would be political but not to this extent." He paused. "And I'm not saying this to make you feel bad, but one of the main reasons I took it was to ease the situation between us." He laughed. "Little did I know, I just made things worse."

"Josh, I feel awful."

He put his hand on her cheek. "Please don't. Everything will be fine."

"But what will you do? Will you go back to your old job as sheriff?"

"The governor will make that decision, but I doubt he'll do me any favors. I just hope I can quit before he fires me." He exhaled deeply. "Remember me telling you about my sister Kimi?"

"Of course. She left home when she was a teenager and you only recently heard from her. Didn't she change her name or something?"

He nodded. "She goes by Heather now."

"That's right, I recall your saying how much she loves purple heather."

Josh smiled. "She does." He lowered his head. "I need to see her. It's time we talked."

Enid sat upright. "Has something happened to her?"

Josh took Enid's hand. "No, at least not that I'm aware of. She's just been on my mind a lot."

Enid knew where this conversation was going. "She's still in New Mexico, I assume."

Josh nodded.

"How long will you be gone?"

Josh was silent.

"Are you coming back?"

He looked into Enid's eyes. "All I know is I want you with me." He held up his hand to keep her from speaking. "And I also know you won't go."

Enid fought the tears welling in her eyes. "Josh, I . . . I honestly didn't have aspirations of being a small-town newspaper reporter. I always assumed I'd eventually join a bigger paper, or . . ."

"Or go back with Cade and work at the Associated Press."

She nodded slightly. "At one time, maybe that was in the back of my mind. But Cade and I are different people now. I'll always share a history with him, but that's all." She cleared her throat and blinked away tears. "I like it here in Madden. It's home."

"Jack is a big part of your staying, and I understand that. Especially now that he's undergoing cancer treatment." He paused. "I don't blame you. He's a great guy, and he loves you almost as much as I do." He held up two fingers indicating a measurement. "Maybe I'm still a little ahead."

Enid just wanted to lie down again and sleep to avoid this conversation. "I'm not staying solely because of Jack. He knows I'll help as much as I can, but I won't stay here forever. I don't want to run a paper. I'm a reporter." She paused. "Will you come back to me after you visit your sister?"

"There's nothing for me here. Other than you, that is. But I have to make a living. What will I do here? Look, I don't mean to sound bitter. I'm not. You've given up so much for the people you love. First leaving journalism years ago to care for your mother. And then staying in your bank job to bankroll her medical bills and Cade's lifestyle. You've found happiness, and I won't let you walk away from what you love doing. I won't. Even if it means leaving you behind."

"I love you for saying that, but can we just take this one step at a time? Go visit your sister and then we'll see what we can do to make it work." She leaned over and kissed him. "I want this to work. I love you, far more than I've let myself admit. Please promise you won't just drift away for good. If it's space you need, we can just put us on hold for a while."

"That's the sappiest but sweetest love story I've ever heard," Roo said.

Enid spun around to look at her. "How long have you been eavesdropping?"

Roo grinned. "I'm going to get some coffee. Can I bring anything back for you two lovebirds?"

"We're good. Thanks," Enid said.

As Roo walked down the hallway toward the elevator, Josh said, "You asked me when I was leaving. I've given that a lot of thought. Assuming Governor Larkin releases me immediately, which I'm sure he will, I'll leave right away. I don't like long goodbyes."

Enid struggled to keep her voice steady. "So this is the last time I might see you, for a while at least?"

Josh embraced Enid and held her so tightly, she was having trouble breathing.

"Jeez, would you two get a room already?" Roo said as she walked toward them. "The nurse told me there's coffee over in the corner. Who knew?" Roo walked toward a small semi-enclosed area at the back of the waiting area.

"Goodbye, Josh. Call me. I'll be waiting for you." Enid watched as he walked out of the waiting room.

CHAPTER 66

Roo had barely gotten back to her seat in the hospital waiting area when the doctor came through the swinging double doors and walked toward her. "Miss Murray, your aunt is awake."

Roo jumped up, spilling coffee all over herself and the floor. "Uh oh."

"Go on in and see her," Enid said. "I'll clean this up."

Roo followed the doctor to Catherine's room. "Don't overdo it," the doctor said. "She's weak and a bit disoriented." She smiled at Roo. "But I think she can make a full recovery."

Roo rushed past the doctor to Catherine's bedside. "Oh, Aunt Cat. I'm so happy to see you awake." She leaned over and gently kissed Catherine's forehead. "How are you feeling? Wait. Stupid question. Don't answer that."

Catherine produced a weak smile. She pointed one finger toward the chair beside her bed. "Stay," she said in a voice barely louder than a whisper.

Roo pulled the chair to the side of Catherine's bed and took her hand. It was cold and leathery, like a pair of old shoes that hadn't been worn in a while and had lost all the moisture from its skin. "I love you," Roo said.

Catherine raised her other hand slightly and pointed to the water glass on the table. Roo poured water from the

Styrofoam pitcher and put a straw in the glass. She bent the straw and put it to Catherine's lips.

Catherine took a few small sips and laid her head back against the pillow. "I love you, too." Her voice was a bit stronger but still barely above a whisper. "I am so sorry."

"What are you sorry for? None of this was your fault."

Catherine coughed to clear her throat. "Yes. My fault."

"Please just rest now. We can talk later. I'm not going anywhere." Roo gently stroked Catherine's cheek with the back of her hand. "Just rest."

Before Roo could put the chair back against the wall, Catherine was asleep, snoring slightly.

. . .

When Roo returned to the waiting area, Enid was sitting alone. "Where's the handsome prince?" Roo asked. When Enid looked up at her, Roo asked, "What's wrong?"

Enid shook her head, not trusting herself to explain. "We can talk later. How's Catherine?"

"Tired, but otherwise, I think she'll recover, at least physically. I'm sure she'll have a hard time forgetting all that's happened to her."

"What's next? Where will she go?" Enid asked.

"I've been thinking about that, and I've decided to move up here and stay with her for as long as she needs me. I don't want to disrupt her life further by dragging her back to Charleston with me. I'll rent out my condo for the time being. I need to get repairs done on her house before we can move back in, though. I don't want her to see any reminders of what's happened there. She may want to sell it and move somewhere else, away from the memories."

"Why don't the two of you move in with me while repairs are being done?"

"Thanks, but that's too much to ask of you. We'll find somewhere to stay."

"Don't be ridiculous. Besides, I'll need some company since . . ."

"You mean that thing we're not talking about. I get it. Are you sure we won't be in the way? I'll have to work from your place until I decide what to do. I can't just walk away from my work."

"I'm not there during the day. Besides, if we start to get on each other's nerves, I can always move into Jack's spare room temporarily."

"Well, I don't know how to thank you enough. I'll start getting the repairers in right away. Hopefully, it won't take more than a week or two." Roo leaned over and hugged Enid. "You're the best sister I never had."

CHAPTER 67

The mid-afternoon traffic was light, so she made it to the newspaper office in less than an hour. Praying she had left a small zippered bag of cosmetics, her emergency stash, in her desk, she also hoped Ginger would not grill her when she walked in. Enid just wasn't in the mood.

She parked beside the empty space where Ginger usually parked and felt guilty at her enormous relief. Jack's pickup was in his usual spot under the big oak tree at the back of the lot.

Going straight to her office, Enid fumbled around in the bottom right drawer until she found the worn makeup bag. "Thank you," she whispered to herself. There was a hand wipe in the bag, so she used it to wipe away the mascara smear on her face. She didn't have a mirror, so she would have to go to the ladies' room to repair the rest of the damage. She tiptoed down the hallway, past Jack's office. His door was closed. The bathroom was at the end of the long hallway, and when she was nearly there, one of the old wooden floorboards announced her presence. She heard Jack's door opening.

"Is that you, Enid?" he asked.

Without turning around, she called over her shoulder. "I'll come see you in a few minutes." She nearly ran to the bathroom and slammed the door more forcefully than she had intended. Looking in the mirror, she said aloud, "Oh,

God. What a mess." Her eyes were slightly swollen, and there was no trace of makeup left. She looked so bad, she laughed at her image.

The mascara had been almost empty when she put it in her emergency stash, and now it was nearly dried up. She hadn't used it in a while, so it was mostly clumps. The liquid foundation, ordered online, turned out to be a darker shade than she needed, but instead of returning it or throwing it out, she had put it in the bag along with the used-up mascara. She tried to blend it into her skin as much as possible, but she looked like she had orange tanning cream on her face. "Well, that'll have to do for now." She made one more attempt at blending the off-color makeup and then pitched the mascara and foundation into the trash.

When she opened the bathroom door, she jumped back, startled. "Jack, you scared me. Why are you standing there like that?"

"Because I'm worried about you. No offense, but you look like crap. What's happened?" He grabbed her arm. "Come on. I think I heard Ginger come in, so you and I are going to have a drink. Leave your car. We'll get it later."

"Jack, as you noted, I'm a mess. I can't go anywhere."

"I've got the perfect place."

. . .

On the way to Glitter Lake Inn, Jack called Theo and asked him to prepare a picnic basket of wine, cheese, and a few snacks.

When they arrived, the housekeeper handed them the basket. "Here's a picnic blanket, too. In case you need it."

Jack and Enid walked down the path to the lake where Cassie's memorial bench sat at the edge of the water. The afternoon sun was setting behind the tall trees surrounding them. Jack spread the blanket on the ground in the thick grass. "Madam, your table is ready," he said, motioning for her to sit.

She sat on the blanket, cushioned by the grass, and slipped off her shoes. Jack poured a glass of wine for each of them and proposed a toast. "To the most beautiful, wonderful woman and friend I know."

After they tipped glasses, Enid took a sip before speaking. "Jack, I . . . I've had a rough day, and while all of this is impressive, I'm not sure I'm going to be very good company."

"Nonsense. You'd be good company even if you just sat and stared at me. When was the last time you ate?"

Enid couldn't remember, so she reached for a piece of cheese and a slice of French bread. After a few bites, she realized how hungry she was. She reached for one of the linen napkins, embroidered with the inn's GLI logo on the corner, and wiped her mouth. "You're right. I feel better already."

Jack smiled. "I'm usually right."

Enid swatted him with her napkin. "Stop it. That's not true." She paused. "Did you talk to Josh?" She didn't want Jack to have to pretend he didn't know what was going on. Even though Josh and Jack had not known each other very long, they shared a male-bond thing she envied and sometimes resented.

"Yes. We talked briefly. He didn't want to leave you. I hope you know that. But he has to get away and figure out his life."

"I know. And it wasn't a total surprise. He was unhappy with the new job, and he's been trying to get me to go to New Mexico for the past year. It'll be good for him and his sister to reconnect. They have a lot of catching up to do."

"I appreciate your help at the paper, but I don't want your pity or for you to stay when you're ready to go." Jack said. "Got it?"

After taking another sip of wine to buy some time, Enid replied, "I worry about you, but I do *not* feel sorry for you. I'm staying here because I need to make my own life for a change. This is where I want to be, and this is what I want to do, for now at least. I've stopped trying to plan too far ahead. Life has a way of changing even the best-laid plans."

"I'll drink to that." Jack tipped his wine glass to hers. "I'm very happy you're staying, for a while a least. I know things could change. You may decide later to join Josh, but for now, you've got a newspaper to manage."

It took a few seconds for Enid to realize what Jack had said. "I'm not sure I . . ."

Jack pulled a business card from his shirt pocket and handed it to her. "Here. There're 499 more of those on your desk."

Enid read the card: "Enid Blackwell, Managing Editor, *Tri-County Gazette*." She looked up at Jack. "I don't understand." Then, "Where are you going to be?"

"I'm going to be right by your side, driving you crazy, but also giving you all the support and encouragement I can."

Enid looked down at the card again. "Jack, I'm flattered, but I'm not a manager or an editor. I'm just a reporter."

"Oh, please." Jack made a face at her. "You've got a nose for news. You know how to find the great stories. You're a natural. And the other reporters can learn a lot from you." He took the card from her and pointed to "Managing Editor." "You won't be the only editor. I'll be a reporter and a senior editor. And, I'll even handle all those pesky HR issues you hate so much. For now at least. Then we'll see how it goes." He handed the card back to her. "Besides, I've got $24.99, plus tax and shipping, invested in this decision. What would I do with all those business cards if you turned me down?"

Enid waved the card in the air. "You couldn't have been too confident or you would have ordered at least a thousand. They're much cheaper that way."

Jack shrugged. "Alright, so I had a small doubt you'd stay. Josh can be pretty persuasive." His smile faded. "There are some conditions that go with this offer."

Enid suddenly felt a sense of dread. "Go on."

"As I said to you the first time I asked you to collaborate on a story with me years ago, this is not a come-on. I genuinely like working with you, and I do admit to loving you, but as a treasured friend. I respect you too much to put you in a situation that wouldn't be good for either of us, or for the paper. Got that?"

"Yes, sir." She wanted to cry again, but this time from gratitude for Jack's friendship.

"Second, as I told you before, I would not turn this paper over to just anyone. I trust you with my newspaper and with my life, should it ever come to that. And if you need to leave, then together, we'll find another solution. You are not tied here."

"I'm not sure how to respond. I'm humble, grateful, a bit scared, if you must know, and also a little overwhelmed. I love you, too, and I can only do this if you're beside me every step of the way. So, you've got to get well."

Jack held out his little finger. "Pinky promise."

CHAPTER 68

After the conversation with Jack, Enid decided to move into his spare bedroom to give Roo and Catherine more space and privacy while Catherine's house was being repaired. Roo and her aunt had a lot to talk about.

Catherine's insurance was taking care of the vandalism to her house, but other than social security, the rest of her funds, stolen by Robert with Louise's help, were still being tracked down. Stanholt told her she would likely get some of the money back at some point, other than what Robert and Louise had spent before he was killed.

When Jack learned of Catherine's situation, he immediately offered to give or loan her money, but she was too proud to accept it. Jack mentioned it to Theo, who had an idea. He invited Catherine to speak about Madden's history at an invitation-only event at the inn. Guests would pay one hundred dollars each for dinner prepared by a prior Michelin-rated chef and the chance to learn more about their town. Word had already gotten out, and advance tickets had already sold out.

But Catherine was a nervous wreck. "I'm not a public speaker," she protested. When Enid agreed to interview her as a way of doing the presentation, Catherine agreed and was overwhelmed with the town's generosity.

Late one afternoon, as Catherine and Enid were sitting on the back porch at Enid's house putting the final touches on the interview questions, Catherine turned to Enid. "I have no right to ask, but would you do something for me?"

"Of course. What do you need?"

Catherine's eyes focused on the edge of the woods. "She's beautiful."

Enid followed Catherine's gaze to see what she was talking about. When Enid saw the doe, she smiled. "That's a good sign. Everything is going to work out." Josh's face flooded her memory. "For all of us."

"I'm a foolish old woman. I've made so many mistakes and hurt so many people."

Enid put her hand on Catherine's. "What are you talking about? You're one of the kindest people I know."

"I need to tell you what happened, and then I want you to write about it. To warn others not to do what I did."

"Are you sure that's what you want?" Enid couldn't imagine in a small town like Madden having one's life so exposed.

Catherine nodded. "It's the least I can do for all these people who are helping me."

"After your dinner presentation, we'll work on it."

The doe bounded back into the woods and Catherine looked at Enid. "I'd like to tell you now, if you have time."

Jack was cooking for Enid tonight, and she had promised not to be late. But if anyone would understand, he would. The story always came first, he would say.

After Enid excused herself to call Jack, she came back to the porch with her iPhone and a fresh writing pad. "I'm going to record this if that's alright with you."

"Of course," Catherine said.

"Why don't you just tell me what you want to, and then I'll ask questions if needed. If you get tired and want to stop, just let me know."

Catherine nodded and closed her eyes briefly before speaking. "The person I've hurt the most is Ruby-Grace. She blames herself for what happened, and that makes me even sadder. We had never been really close. I mean I'm her only living aunt, actually her great-aunt. Her mother was a mean person, although I hate to speak ill of the dead. When Ruby-Grace was a teenager, she ran away to escape her mother's mental abuse. I didn't blame Ruby-Grace then for leaving, and I don't now. She did what she had to. She moved in with a friend, worked part-time, and finished high school. Later she put herself through college while working full-time. She's had a hard life, but it hasn't hardened her. She's a good person with a kind heart."

Enid nodded in agreement.

"We've gotten to know each other better these past couple of weeks. I didn't realize how fearful she had become of trusting people. Her mother had crippled her emotionally, causing Ruby-Grace to keep a safe distance from everyone. As two of only a few known survivors of our family, we kept in touch with the appropriate holiday cards, a few phone calls and visits during the years, and promises to do better. At the time, I felt like I had kept up my end of the bargain. I invited her to visit with me, and sometimes she did. But more often than not, she stayed away. I was hurt and had no idea why she seemed to avoid me." Catherine shook her head. "I had no idea how much she wanted to get closer to me but was afraid of being hurt, like her mother hurt her." Catherine closed her eyes again.

"We can do this later if you're tired." Enid thought Catherine had gone to sleep, but in a moment, she continued.

"I didn't take the time to figure Ruby-Grace out. I was a lonely old woman, feeling left out of her life and fearful of my own advancing years. So when Belinda, or I should say Louise pretending to be Belinda, contacted me, I jumped for joy. I thought I had found another relative, one who would be more attentive than Ruby-Grace." Catherine paused. "Do you know how awful that makes me feel to say that? I turned my back on Ruby-Grace for a stranger with a phony story. How could I have been so stupid?"

Enid put her pen down. "Catherine, I can't imagine how you must feel, but you're being too harsh on yourself. Roo doesn't blame you for anything. You know that. And we all make mistakes judging people. Louise and Robert lied to you, took advantage of you, locked you away in that awful place, stole your money, and then tried to kill you by dumping you in the woods. Your mistake was trusting them, that's all. You were not foolish. You were just lonely."

"You're a good person, Enid. And I thank you for your kindness, but it's going to take me a while to forgive myself. If I ever do." She took a deep breath. "Anyway, my old attorney wouldn't hear of my changing my power of attorney and executor for my will. He insisted I was being too impulsive. I got mad at him and went to another attorney. Someone that Louise recommended, of course. The only thing I did that was smart in this whole mess was not leaving all my money to her. I'd have been dead by now if I had. But I did give her power of attorney and total control over my life if I became incapacitated. I have learned from the detective handling my case that Louise drugged me and admitted me to the nursing facility, convincing them that I had dementia. It was a shady facility anyway, so they didn't ask too many questions. The place has been shut down while the authorities investigate how all of this could have happened." She shook her head. "It's so sad how many unwanted people were dumped there."

"Thank goodness you didn't change the beneficiary on your will."

"When Louise found out, she tried to change it anyway. But they found out a power of attorney can't do that, so they just sold most of my stocks and took all my money out of the bank, which accomplished the same thing." Catherine shook her head. "I had no idea a power of attorney could do all that. I've rehired my former attorney, the first one. He says I'll probably get some of the money back. They've just got to go through the legal process of proving what happened." Catherine dabbed at her eyes with a tissue. "I don't know what happened to my car. They took that, too. And poor Sylvia, killed by her own grandson. I'm also responsible for that."

"No, Catherine. He killed his grandmother to protect himself. You didn't cause it."

"He was so sweet to me at first, a very charming young man." Catherine continued to look out into space, with what soldiers call the thousand-yard stare. "When Louise took me to that old family cemetery, I knew she intended to kill me."

"Why is that?"

"Louise had nursed a member of the Byrne family, so she knew about the legend of the empty grave with the blank headstone."

"I remember the stonemason telling me that the family believed it was a place for wandering spirits to rest. But why take you to the cemetery?" Enid was scribbling notes as she talked.

"Remember that by the time we went there, she had my complete trust. She told me there were other members of our family buried there. It was another way she was trying to build family ties with me, but it backfired."

"Why is that?"

"She didn't know it, but I had done some research years back on that cemetery, the Byrne family, and their tale about the empty grave. The article, "The Fifth Stone," was in the newspaper back when it was the *Madden Gazette* and before your time. You can check the archives."

"So you knew that Louise was lying about your family being buried there."

Catherine nodded. "When I told Louise I was familiar with that cemetery, she knew the jig was up. That's when she pulled a syringe from her purse and put it against my neck. She said it was poison and would kill me instantly, and that I needed to get back in the car with her. There were people at that little produce stand out front. Why didn't I scream?"

"Because you were afraid, just like any of us would be."

"I think I need to sleep now. Ruby-Grace will be home soon, and I want to see her before I go to bed. Do you have enough for a story?"

Enid smiled. "More than enough. And I thank you for sharing all of this with me. I'll make sure we don't jeopardize the county's case against Louise before I publish this. Now you go rest."

Enid put her phone and notes in her tote and left her own house to go back to Jack's. She thought she would miss being in her own place, but in a way, she was relieved to be gone for a while. Memories of sitting on the porch with Josh, holding hands, and making love there were still too much to deal with. She had not heard from him since he left. Maybe she never would.

CHAPTER 69

Nearly a month after Catherine had left the hospital, Theo hosted the fundraiser for Catherine. For nearly an hour after dinner, Enid sat at the front of the room and interviewed Catherine about various events that had shaped the small town of Madden. Catherine was much stronger now and actually seemed to enjoy sharing her experiences and knowledge about the area. After answering a dozen or so questions following the interview, Catherine asked if she could say a few words on her own.

The crowd was quiet as they waited for Catherine to begin. "There are no words to thank all of you for what you've done to help me. If I can get my money back, or at least some of it, I'll repay each and every one of you. And I will hold each of you in my heart for as long as I live." She wiped her eyes with a lace-edged handkerchief. "I invited Susan Everhart, the nurse's aide who saved my life, to join us tonight." She smiled at Susan who was sitting near the front. "Thank you for all you've done. I will never forget you." The audience clapped along with Catherine, and eventually all of them stood to pay tribute to Susan, who risked so much to do the right thing.

When the applause ended, Catherine turned to Enid and Karla, who were seated in the front row of folding chairs. "And Enid and Karla, thank you for being relentless and brave. I wouldn't be here without you." The audience clapped and stood again for Enid and Karla.

Catherine continued. "Some of you have asked me when I will return to the Madden Historical Society. Sadly, I will not be doing so. I need to look for any real members of my family who are left, and more importantly, I need time to spend with Ruby-Grace and get to know her better." She smiled at Roo sitting a few feet away. "And I need to have some fun. I've almost forgotten what that means. I might even get a tattoo." The crowd laughed, happy to escape the seriousness of the moment. "I've talked with Mayor Carter and told her my decision."

One of the guests called out, "But who will document our town's history now? With that new distribution center and all the newcomers in town, things are changing fast. Our grandchildren need to know what it used to be like in Madden."

"I understand your concern," Catherine said, "but there's no one to continue the society's work."

"You're wrong," a voice called out from the back of the room.

Catherine squinted, trying to see who was talking. "Excuse me? Please stand so I can see you."

As the young man walked to the front, Catherine's hand flew to her mouth. "Roscoe, is that you?"

"Yes, ma'am. It's me." He walked to the front of the room and took Catherine's hand before turning to face the group. "The mayor was able to get a grant that will pay me a small salary for two years. I'll also explore some online teaching opportunities to make up the difference. During those two years, I'll make sure all the information we have is documented and cataloged. Also, the distribution center recognizes their presence has created changes in Madden and has made a large contribution to the historical society's work. Their management has assured Mayor Carter they want to help preserve the local culture as much as you do. Excuse me, I meant as much as *we* do." Roscoe looked at Catherine. "I'll need your help and guidance, but I promise to make you proud of me." He straightened his bow tie and grinned.

Catherine hugged Roscoe with tears streaming down her face. "I've always been proud of you. Thank you, thank you."

Everyone in the room stood and gave Roscoe and Catherine a standing ovation. After a few moments, Theo called out. "The bar's open. Let's all celebrate Catherine's retirement and our new town historian."

CHAPTER 70

After reviewing Susan's statement and the other evidence against Louise, her attorney encouraged her to take a plea deal. She pleaded guilty to fraud, extortion, and elder abuse, all of which had lesser sentences than kidnapping and attempted murder. The county prosecutor agreed not to pursue accessory to murder charges for Danny's and Sylvia's deaths. Without Sylvia's grandson Robert, they had little to dispute Louise's assertions that she had not been involved in the killings.

Enid agreed to hold her article until after Louise's case was finalized and she was sentenced. The story was picked up by the *State* newspaper in Columbia, the *Post and Courier* in Charleston, the *Herald-Journal* in upstate South Carolina, and several other dailies. Catherine's cautionary tale was also picked up by the Associated Press, thanks to Cade's connections, so Enid wasn't surprised when a bottle of champagne and a dozen roses were delivered to her office. The note read, "Proud of my girl. Wish you were with me in London to celebrate. Love, Cade."

Jack invited Enid to a celebration dinner at Al's Upstairs Italian in West Columbia, which had become her favorite restaurant. The view overlooking the Congaree River and the lights of Columbia from the second level of the building were beautiful at night. They had more to celebrate than just Catherine's story: Jack's cancer was responding to treatment, and he was beginning to look more like his former self.

Enid heard a vehicle pull up in front of her house, and she looked out the window to confirm it was Jack. His pickup looked freshly washed and polished. She got her purse and met him as he was coming up the steps.

"Looks like you're ready to go," he said.

"I'm actually pretty hungry. And looking forward to Al's shrimp fettuccine."

"Good. I'm hungry too."

Jack held the door for Enid as she climbed into the pickup. As Jack was walking to the driver's side to get in, Enid's cell phone pinged to notify her of an incoming text. She glanced down to see if it was anything that couldn't wait until after dinner.

Jack got in and locked his seatbelt in place. "We're off." He saw her staring at her phone screen. "Everything okay?"

Enid nodded as she read the message from Josh: "Missing you."

PLEASE . . . a request from the author

Thank you for taking time from your busy schedule to read this (or any other) book. We need more readers like you.

I hope you enjoyed The Fifth Stone. If so, please do me a giant favor and leave a review on Amazon and/or Goodreads. Reviews encourage other readers to explore authors they may not be familiar with.

Thank you in advance for your review!

www.Amazon.com

www.Goodreads.com

. . .

If you'd like to contact me directly, please visit my website: www.RaeganTeller.com/contact. I'd love to hear from you.

A NOTE FROM THE AUTHOR

Writing a book does not get any easier for me, even after this fourth volume. And I find that writing a series is particularly challenging, although it is also rewarding. While I know Enid, Jack, Josh, and the other characters intimately and don't have to start from scratch imagining them, I find it difficult to balance an individual book's story with the overall arc of the series. Each book tells a story, but the series tells an even bigger story. Thus far, Enid's journey has spanned more than 1,300 pages.

Another challenge for me is that, like Stephen King, I write about what scares me the most, and some stories are particularly disturbing to me— like this one. I try not to be salacious just for the sake of shocking readers, but instead to say, "Pay attention—this could happen to you or someone you love."

If you have read other books in the Enid Blackwell series, you know that deception, betrayal, and broken trust, as well as love and family, are often themes in my stories. My characters are usually people just like us. Like one of my favorite authors, Harlan Coben, I'm fascinated by ordinary people who find themselves in extraordinary circumstances.

While my books are fiction, each was inspired by an actual event that inspired my murderous tale.

A final note: While the general information about gangs in South Carolina is factual, as far as I know there is no WS14 gang in existence here or anywhere else.

ACKNOWLEDGEMENTS

The more I write, the more I appreciate the people who support and encourage me. Without them, none of this would be possible

I particularly want to thank my husband, William Earl Craig—my rock, my foundation. He makes it possible for me to spend endless hours locked away from reality in my imaginary world. As I am writing this, he is downstairs vacuuming the dust bunnies and cat hair I've been ignoring in order to finish this book. He also provides valuable input to my work, as he is a masterful storyteller.

A special thanks also to my beta readers: Jane Cook, Martha Anderson, and Irene Stern. Jane writes poetry as Jane Marie and gives me sisterly love when I need it most. Martha provided valuable assistance in my ancestry research. And Irene, "The Novel Mechanic," is my proofreader, pet sitter, and dear friend who supports me in more ways than I can list here.

My developmental editor for this book, as well as the others in the series, is Ramona DeFelice Long. She has helped me become a better writer—and an award-winning author. I'm honored that two of the books in the Enid Blackwell series received Honorable Mention in the Writer's Digest Self-Published Book Awards.

I also want to thank our personal estate attorney, Mike Howell, who, over the years, has given my husband and I more information about wills and trusts than I could ever use in twenty books. However, if there are any legal inaccuracies herein, don't blame him; blame the writer.

I especially want to thank my readers. Without you, I couldn't exist. I appreciate your loyalty, your comments and

emails, your support, and your feedback that helps me grow
as a writer.

Raegan

ABOUT THE AUTHOR

Raegan Teller is the award-winning mystery author of the Enid Blackwell Series. She lives in Columbia, South Carolina, with her husband and two feline companions.

She graduated summa cum laude from Queens University, Charlotte, North Carolina. Before writing fiction, Raegan was a business writer and copy editor, communications consultant, executive coach, and insurance manager—among other things. While working her way through school, she even sold burial vaults at a cemetery. How apropos is that for a mystery writer!

For more information about Raegan or to contact her, visit http://RaeganTeller.com

www.ingramcontent.com/pod-product-compliance
Lightning Source LLC
Chambersburg PA
CBHW031938110726
47902CB00001B/219